D0354432

BABYLONNE

CATHERINE JINKS

CANDLEWICK PRESS
CAMBRIDGE, MASSACHUSETTS

Copyright © 2008 by Catherine Jinks
Map illustration copyright © 2008 by Zoë Sadokierski

First Candlewick Press edition 2008

Library of Congress Cataloging-in-Publication Data
Jinks, Catherine.
Babylonne / Catherine Jinks. — 1st U.S. ed.
p.   cm.
Summary: In the violent and predatory world of
thirteenth-century Languedoc, Pagan's sixteen-year-old
daughter disguises herself as a boy and runs away with a priest
who claims to be a friend of her dead father and mother,
not knowing whether or not she can trust him, or anyone.
ISBN 978-0-7636-3650-0
[1. War—Fiction. 2. Orphans—Fiction. 3. Middle Ages—
Fiction. 4. France—History—Philip II Augustus,
1180–1223—Fiction.]   I. Title.
PZ7.J5754Pah 2008
[Fic]—dc22   2007021958

2 4 6 8 10 9 7 5 3 1

Printed in the United States of America

This book was typeset in Weiss.

Candlewick Press
2067 Massachusetts Avenue
Cambridge, Massachusetts 02140

visit us at www.candlewick.com

To Emma and Molly Jinks,
the new girls

SUMMER 1227

‡CHAPTER ONE‡

Oh, no.

I've killed the chicken.

How could I have killed it? How could this have happened? I wasn't trying to kill it—I was trying to shut it up, the stupid thing! What was I supposed to do? Let it squawk away until they found me?

It's all floppy now, like a bolster that's lost most of its stuffing. Did I squeeze it too hard? Did I smother it by putting my hand around its beak? This is bad. I'm in so much trouble. If Gran ever finds out about this, I'll be eating wool grease and nutshells for a month.

But she won't find out. She won't. I'm going to hold my breath and keep quite still, and with any luck . . . with any luck . . .

They're nowhere near this fowl house. I can hear their footsteps; they're poking around behind the broad beans. *Rustle, rustle.* Mumbling to each other in some strange language that must be Latin. I've heard people praying in Latin, and it's all *um* and *us*, like the stuff I'm hearing now. They say that monks speak Latin to each other, and these men are probably monks. Or priests. I wouldn't know. I didn't stand still long enough to get a good look at them.

Let your breath out slowly, Babylonne. That's it. Very slowly. Very quietly. There are feathers everywhere, stuck to my skirt and my sleeves and my hair. Please, God, don't let me sneeze. Please, God, keep the feathers away from my nose.

Please, God, keep those priests away from this fowl house.

I'm very sorry that I killed the chicken. I honestly didn't mean to. I was only looking for eggs, because eggs aren't animals. I mean, you can't really kill an egg, can you? Eating an egg isn't like eating a chicken. Not as far as I'm concerned. There might be a chicken inside the egg *somewhere*, but if this world is truly the Devil's realm—as Gran says— then you're doing that chicken a great service, aren't you? Making sure that it never hatches?

2

Wait a moment. Those footsteps—are they coming closer or moving away? I think . . . I think . . .

They're moving away.

Listen hard, Babylonne. Is that a door creaking? It is. I know it is. There's a door almost directly opposite the fowl house I'm sitting in. It must be the door to the cloister. Those priests must have gone back into their cloister.

To fetch some more priests, do you think? Or have they decided that the chickens were making a fuss about nothing?

It's lucky that I'm so small. They probably weren't expecting someone my size. If they had been, they would have had a good look inside this fowl house instead of just glancing through the door. Whoever did that couldn't have seen much. He couldn't have seen me crushed into this corner. Oh, please, *please* don't be suspicious. Please don't come back. Just go away and eat up your pork and your cheese and your honey, and forget about the eggs. Would you really miss a few eggs? You'd hardly have room for an egg in those great, swollen guts of yours— not after all the roasted peacocks and spiced pigeons and sugar cakes and whatever else it is that you pack into your paunches day after day, while the rest of us live on bones and millet.

3

Swinish, bloated, *greasy* idolaters that you are. It'd be a wonder if you saw me at all over the swell of your own enormous bellies.

I think they've gone. There isn't a sound. And I should make a move now, in case they do come back. Take it slowly, Babylonne. Carefully . . . quietly . . . don't disturb the chickens. The *other* chickens. The ones who can still enjoy a nice dust bath before bedtime.

Not like poor old Floppy here.

The fowl-house door is only slightly bigger than my head. Beyond it, the sun blazes down onto rows and rows of peas and beans, leeks, marrows, strawberries, all laid out like a feast on a table. I tell you, these priests of Rome eat like kings. How dare they make a fuss over one poor egg?

Anyway, it's their own fault. If one of those evil priests hadn't dug himself a secret hole under the garden wall (probably in search of women, because all gluttons have hot blood), then I would never have come in here, would I? I would never have been tempted. They can thank their own unbridled lusts if they lose a few eggs. It's not stealing when you take from priests of Rome. Men who call themselves holy should be fasting, not feasting.

Hmmm. No one to the right. No one to the left. There's the door to the cloister, straight in front of me across the feathery vines, and it's standing open. That means the priests might be coming back.

I'd better run the other way. Off you go, Babylonne. One, two, three, go!

I'd better head for the—

"Haab!"

Oh, no.

"Thieving whore!" (Where did he—? How did he—? It's as if he sprang out of the ground!) "Give me that chicken!"

You want this chicken?

Fine.

"Yowch!" It hits him full in the face. But he's blocking my way; I can't reach the hole that I got in through.

The door behind me is my only chance.

"Get her! Stop her!"

"Come here, you whore!"

Fat, fat, fat. They lumber like cows. I'm trampling all the green shoots, but I can't help it—I have to reach the door—hurry, hurry!

Through the door! Whirl around! Pull it shut, and there's a latch! A *latch!* It's as good as a lock! The

5

door shudders beneath the weight of a hurtling priest. But it's sturdy. It's oak. It won't give way.

"Open this door!" Pounding fists. "*Open this door!*"

I'm sorry, are you talking to me? You and what armored warrior, my fat friend?

Quick glance around. There's no movement. I'm in a cloister—it's very big—with a well in the center of the square courtyard and a row of columns on each of its four sides. The columns are carved with snarling, painted beasts coiled around their tops. There are doors, too, behind the columns. Lots of doors. Most of them shut.

How am I going to escape?

The church. I can see it straight ahead on the other side of the cloister courtyard, rearing up to block the sky. If I can get into the church, I can certainly get out of it. The church of Saint Etienne is open to all the people of Toulouse, all the time. I just have to work out which door I should use.

"*Open up! Do you hear me?*" Thump, thump. "*OPEN UP!*"

I can't stay. Someone will hear that noise and come running. Where are the other priests? Not in church, I hope.

Now. Take a right turn. *Go!*

"*Ooof!*"

6

Ouch! Ah! What happened? Where am I? I must have hit something and . . . I'm on the floor. The floor is dark stone, worn shiny. There's a soft leather boot under a trailing black hem.

And a face, too. Staring down at me. A thin face, as white as milk. (White with shock?) A long nose. Pale, stricken eyes. Blood on his scalp.

No, not blood. Red hair.

"Who—who are you?" he croaks. He's holding his stomach; I must have hurt him when I bumped into him.

I have to get away.

"No! Wait!" He catches my arm. Let go! Get off!

But he's strong. He's so strong. I can't shake him loose. Can't bite those long, white fingers, either, because he shifts his grip. He grabs my collar.

Bang! Bang! "Open the door! There's a thief! *A thief!*"

Curse those fat priests! Smite them with the pox on their piddlers. Oh, God, please *help* me! When I lash out with my foot, the thin priest sidesteps. He's still clutching my collar.

"*Shh!*" he hisses. "Calm down! Get in there! Hide in there!"

Who—? What—? Is he talking to *me?* One quick shove, and suddenly I'm in a room off the cloister walk. A round room full of benches and hung with fine tapestries.

"Get behind that hanging!" he whispers. "Go on! Quick!"

I can't believe it. Tapestries! Great, glittering things covered in gold stars and flying beasts. Beautiful things, like windows into Heaven. But they're too long for the walls, so I can burrow into the bunched folds piled up behind one of the benches.

It's dark and damp and stuffy. The silk smells almost like singed hair. I can hear his voice in the distance—the redhead's voice.

"A girl?" he's saying. "Yes, I think I saw someone, but I didn't know it was a girl."

Curse him!

"She went that way. Through that door."

My pepper. If all else fails, I still have my pepper. Fiddling with the strings of my purse, I strain my ears, trying to make out what's happening. Why did he hide me, that redheaded priest? Why hide me, if he was just going to turn around and betray me? But perhaps he won't betray me. I can't hear any footsteps. There are voices, but the voices are fading.

Unless I'm wrong, that redhead has sent his friends off in the wrong direction.

I can guess why, too. I'm not stupid. I know what priests are like. (I ought to, after what happened to my own mother.) Who hasn't heard all the stories about priests lifting skirts? Besides which, I just crawled through a hole that must have been dug by a sinful priest. By a sinful priest in search of women.

By the redheaded priest, perhaps?

But I'm not a whore. If he tries to force *me*, I'll scratch his eyes out. I just have to keep my wits about me. I have to be quick and clever. *Once upon a time, there was a brave and beautiful princess who escaped from a locked tower guarded by a hundred venomous serpents. . . .*

"*Psst!*"

The tapestry is twitched from my hand. There's light again—light and air. How did he come so close? Why didn't I hear him?

"It's all right," he says softly, stepping back as I scramble to my feet. He's still pushing the stiff, heavy cloth to one side. (He's so tall! He's like a tower!) "You're safe for the moment. I've sent them off to the kitchens," he continues. "But we don't

9

have much time. Nones is nearly over; they'll all be leaving the church. You must come to the guest-house, and we can talk there."

Talk. Right. You must think I've got bowels where my brains should be.

"Please." His voice cracks. He sounds desperate—almost frightened. I don't like the look on his face. You'd think he was going to faint or something. "Please," he says, "you must come—we have to talk. You don't understand—"

Whoosh! I hit him square in the eye with my handful of pepper and dodge his swinging arm. He shouts, but I'm out of the room already. Running for the door into the garden—and it's ajar! It's standing ajar!

Through the door. Over the cabbages. Past the fowl house. Threading between the bean stakes and . . .

Into the hole.

I'm safe now. I'm safe.

They'll never find me, if I keep my head down.

‡CHAPTER TWO‡

Grandmother Blanche is asleep downstairs.

She's sitting in the big, carved chair that she brought from Laurac, her head thrown back and her mouth wide open. She'd look dead if it weren't for the snoring.

She has a snore like an armored corpse being dragged across dry cobblestones.

"Babylonne? Is that you?"

Curse it. Those are Aunt Navarre's feet up there at the top of the ladder. She's coming down from the loft—and I'll never make it to my bed in time.

I'll have to slip the egg into Gran's bed. There. Like that.

Not a moment too soon.

"Babylonne! Where have you been?" Aunt Navarre is in a foul mood. (As usual.) Her back must be bothering her again. "You're late!" she spits. "What have you been doing? Idling? Gawking?"

"No—"

"Don't lie to me!"

"I'm not." Quick, Babylonne. Think. *Think.* "I'm late because a friar was preaching near the Croix Baragnon, and the crowd was so great that it blocked the street, and I had to go around."

"Around? Around what? It wouldn't have taken you *that* long to come through Rouaix Square."

"No, no, I went further than that. I took the Street of Joutx Aigues and went past La Daurade. I had to, because the friar was talking in such a loud voice that I thought I might hear some pestiferous lies of the Roman Church if I went through Rouaix Square."

"Hmmph." She's suspicious, but she can't catch me out. So she raises her voice above Gran's snores and asks about the money.

"Here. It's here." When I pull the money out of the purse at my waist, she snatches it from me.

"There wasn't any trouble?" she asks.

"No."

"And he gave you no more wool?"

"He says he'll have some on Friday. He says he'll pay the same price if we can have it spun by this time next week."

Aunt Navarre sniffs. She goes to the big metal-bound chest in the corner and opens it with the key that she always carries on her belt. She's so jealous of that key. So jealous of that chest. If you even sit on it, she'll lay into you with an iron pot.

I suppose it's her last link with the old life. The only thing that she saved from the ancestral home at Laurac, apart from Gran's chair. Personally, I was glad to turn my back on Laurac. I didn't want to spend my life moldering away in that little cow stall of a town. I'm glad we had to leave—even though the French did force us out. I can't believe I survived seven long years in Laurac.

Toulouse is my spiritual home. I might not have been born here, but I belong here. Every time I walk out the door, I feel my heart lift—because Toulouse is full of glowing colors and gilded statues and snatches of sweet music that you can hear sometimes when you pass inns or great houses. There's always something fine and beautiful in every quarter, because the city is so big. Just think: Toulouse has twenty thousand people in it. *Twenty thousand people!* It's busy and it's bright and it's also very brave. It won't bend its knee to the French King. Not now. Not ever. Toulouse will *never* belong to France.

"Where is everyone?" This place seems so empty. "Where's Sybille?"

"Sybille and Berthe have gone to fetch water," Navarre replies. "Dulcie's upstairs. And it's almost time to eat, so you'd better start soaking your grandmother's bread."

"What are we having?"

"What do you think?" A sharp retort, like a trap springing shut. "It's a fast day, remember?"

Ugh. Fast days. How I hate them. But it could be worse. It could be Dulcie's turn to cook. Dulcie's idea of cooking is to assault the nearest turnip with a big stick and a jug of boiling water. I suppose, since she spends so much time mortifying her own flesh, she believes that we should all be mortifying ours as well.

I'm beginning to wonder if she really *did* leave her husband. If you ask me, it's more likely that her husband left her—because he couldn't bear to eat another glutinous lump of mysterious gray stuff.

Oops! And here she is in person. Dulcie Faure. Climbing down from the loft with a smug expression on her long ferret's face. Sure enough, she's moving stiffly. Like someone who's just given herself a brisk beating with a willow switch.

I'd punch her in the nose, except that she'd probably enjoy it. She'd raise her pop-eyes to Heaven and offer up her suffering to the Lord. I always thought that Aunt Navarre was pious, but since Dulcie arrived I've been forced to reconsider. I don't think even Navarre ever slept with her head on a river rock.

"Wake up, Mother." Navarre gently prods Gran's chest. "It's time to eat."

"I'll join you at the table," Dulcie announces, as if she's bestowing on us all a gift without price, "though I won't eat. Not today."

"You must eat something." Navarre frowns. "If you don't, you'll make yourself ill."

"It is in Christ's hands," Dulcie simpers. I know what she's thinking. She's thinking about the *endura*. If you're a really pious Good Christian, and you starve yourself to death, you won't return to this vale of tears in another form. You'll be whisked straight up to Heaven.

I've always wondered if Dulcie might starve herself to death one day. Why not, after all? She has a head start on the rest of us because she obviously doesn't like food. You can tell by her cooking.

15

"*There* you are at last!" Navarre isn't speaking to Dulcie. She's speaking to Sybille and Berthe, who just stumbled through the front door. "What took you so long?"

Berthe is crying. She's always crying. (You tend to cry a lot when you're eight years old.) Her face is wet and so are her skirts. Sybille's looking pretty damp, too. They seem to have brought most of the water back on their clothes. Sure enough, their bucket's half empty.

"What happened to all the water?" Navarre snaps, and the words tumble from Sybille's rosebud mouth.

"A man came near!" she stammers. "He—he jostled us! He pinched my bottom!" (What? I don't believe it. How could you pinch Sybille's bottom? She doesn't *have* any bottom. You don't when you're twelve.) "He asked me to come and share his cheese," Sybille continues. "When—when I said no—when I said that eating cheese would be wrong—"

"He called us heretics!" Berthe wails. "He threw a stone at us!" Sighs and grunts. Navarre purses her lips and shakes her head. Dulcie says, "God forgive the wicked."

Gran farts.

"This would never have happened in Laurac or Castelnaudary," Navarre growls. (Here we go again. *In Laurac, the people had proper respect for us. . . .*) "In Laurac, the people had proper respect for us. They were all believers—they revered Good Christians like us. There are too many Roman priests in Toulouse. Too many followers of the Devil. This place is a sink of corruption."

"Why did you say that eating cheese is wrong?" You brainless beanpole! I can't believe that even *Sybille* could be so stupid. "You shouldn't go around saying that. Not in public."

Sybille scowls at me. Even when she's scowling, she takes care not to screw up her pretty face too much. Just in case she gets wrinkles.

"Why shouldn't I say it?" she demands. "Eating cheese *is* wrong. Because it's a product of fornication."

God give me patience. But Dulcie beams at Sybille in that patronizing way she has.

"You are right, Sybille," says Dulcie. "You are a good witness to the true faith."

"You can be a good witness to the true faith without being stupid!" (I mean, where have you

17

people *been* for the last year?) "Toulouse isn't like Laurac. There are Dominican friars living down the road. We have to be more careful."

"I am *not* stupid!" Sybille's face has gone red. "What else should I have said? That cheese is my favorite food?"

"Well, yes." That would have been a good start. "Why not?"

"Because it would have been a lie," Dulcie points out. "And we don't tell lies. You should know that by now, Babylonne."

"Well, fine." I have to steady Gran's arm as she shuffles over to the table, or she'll fall—corns over crown—and end up with her nose spread across her face like a rotten pear. "Then what about saying, 'I don't want to share a cheese with someone who smells worse than his cheese does'? *That* would have been the truth, wouldn't it?"

"Why should I say any such thing?" Sybille is looking to Dulcie for support. "*I'm* not ashamed of being a Good Christian. Maybe you are, Babylonne! Maybe you would have gone with him because he had a cheese!"

Maybe I would have, at that. But I'm not going to tell her so. "Listen." Pea-brain. "The point I'm making is that we shouldn't go looking for trouble.

18

Lady Navarre is right. There are too many worshippers of Rome in this city. As long as we keep our heads down, they won't pay us any mind, but you *know* what can happen. We all know what can happen. It happened to my mother, remember?"

Dulcie opens her mouth. Before she can comment, however, Arnaude bustles through the front door. She's squat and broad and purple-faced, like a turnip with legs.

"You're late," says Navarre. "How's Lombarda?"

"Not good," Arnaude replies. "Very ill."

Ah! So *that's* where Arnaude has been—comforting Lombarda de Rouaix. Now that we're in exile again, and living on the charity of Alamain de Rouaix, we have to be extra nice to his poor, sick wife. If we're not, he might throw our little convent out of this miserable house. And stick someone in it who can actually pay him rent.

Arnaude fusses around, putting things away. "They've summoned two of the Good Men in case she dies. . . ."

All at once, Gran thumps the tabletop. She wants to eat. *Now.*

"We can discuss the Good Men later," Navarre declares, and fixes me with an eye like a spearhead.

Oh. Right. Is it my turn again?

19

"Uh—um—" Where's the bread? There it is. I nearly drop it as I present it to Navarre with a bow. "Tell me if this is acceptable to you."

"May God inform you if it is acceptable to Him," Navarre intones.

"Bless us." Another bow.

"May the Lord bless you," Navarre replies without really meaning it. (If God ever blessed *me*, Navarre would give Him what for.)

"Bless and have mercy upon us." I know this by heart. "The meal is ready. You may go to the table when it is acceptable to God and to yourself."

"May God reward you well," Navarre chants, and turns to the others. They're all standing in their places by now—except for Gran, who's sitting, because Grandmother Blanche stands for no one. "Bless and have mercy upon us, my sisters."

"May the Father, the Son, and the Holy Spirit indulge us and have mercy on all our sins," everyone replies (except Gran, who's peering around for her bowl of mushy bread).

"Let us adore the Father, the Son, and the Holy Spirit," Navarre goes on, absentmindedly reaching for the jug of water.

"He is worthy and just."

"Let us adore the Father, the Son, and the Holy Spirit."

"He is worthy and just. Our Father, who art in Heaven, hallowed be Thy Name. . . ."

And so on, and so on. Yawn. Just another fourteen paternosters to go. You could drop dead of starvation with the bread sitting right in front of you. Gran's beginning to drool. Arnaude's desperate to tell us about the Good Men; you can tell by the way she keeps rocking from foot to foot, like someone whose bladder's about to burst. Dulcie's clasping her hands together, her pale face raised to the ceiling, her eyes firmly closed.

Navarre's serving out the portions. She always does. And I always end up with the smallest piece of bread.

"...and-lead-us-not-into-temptation-but-deliver-us-from-evil-amen," she babbles. "Let us adore the Father, the Son, and the Holy Spirit."

"He is worthy and just."

"The grace of our Lord Jesus Christ be always with us all."

"Amen."

"Bless us; have mercy upon us. Be seated, my sisters. Babylonne, you can feed the Lady Blanche today."

Sybille smirks. Everyone's had to wait and wait, and now I won't be able to eat until Gran's finished her meal. No wonder Sybille's looking pleased.

I wish her mother would die. Then maybe her father might change his mind about dumping her here with us and summon her back to his castle to look after him, and we wouldn't have to put up with her forked tongue anymore.

"So tell us about the Good Men," Navarre says to Arnaude, munching on a mouthful of dry bread. "When did they arrive?"

"This morning," answers Arnaude. "They stopped at Laurac on their way up from Montségur, but Bernard Oth threw them out."

"Ah!" Dulcie presses a pale hand to her breast. "How could Lord Bernard imperil his immortal soul like that?"

What a stupid question. Why else would you imperil your immortal soul, unless it's to save your mortal skin? Cousin Bernard is a coward. No more and no less. He was afraid of the French King's army when it came down into Languedoc last year, so he made his submission. And now he's persecuting the Good Christians because that's what the King of France wants him to do.

Why else would he have told his own grandmother to get out of Laurac?

"If I were my sister," says Aunt Navarre, "I would be ashamed of having a son like Bernard."

Suddenly Gran stirs. The hairs on her chin tremble, her toothless mouth opens, and bits of soggy bread spray across the tabletop.

"Bernard is his father all over again," she croaks. "Guillaume was a Roman, so Bernard is a Roman at heart."

"That's true." Navarre wouldn't disagree with her mother if Gran said that the King of France was a giant toenail. "Not wishing to speak ill of the dead, but Guillaume probably came back to earth as a dung worm in a cesspit."

There she goes again. Navarre never has a good word to say about anyone. Personally, I always admired my uncle Guillaume. He might have believed all those Roman lies, but *he* never betrayed the Count of Toulouse. Not like his son Bernard.

Uncle Guillaume set his face against the French and fought them until the day he died.

"I blame Bernard's wife," Navarre continues. "She's a Roman. She's poisoned his mind."

"I thought you said that they loathed each

other." (Have I missed something here?) "Last week you said that they weren't speaking to each other. How can she have poisoned his mind if they haven't been speaking to each other?"

Aunt Navarre frowns and colors. She hates to be caught out. Berthe goggles, and Dulcie pretends not to hear.

Gran coughs. "Bastards should always keep their mouths shut at the table," she creaks.

Dead silence. I'm not going to blush. I am *not* going to blush. I'm going to quietly, calmly, and very, very gently push this battered metal spoon *right down the old bitch's throat if she talks to me like that again*!

No, I'm not. I'm going to swallow the insult, as usual. What else can I do?

Sybille is smiling. Arnaude has her head down. Navarre says, "Yes, hold your tongue, Babylonne. You let it wag too much. Now, what other news from the Good Men, Arnaude? Tell us more."

Everyone leans forward (except Gran). Arnaude raises her head. She seems embarrassed to be the subject of such intense scrutiny.

"They had a hard time crossing from Montségur, because Lord Humbert de Beaujeu is laying waste to the lands south of here," she replies. "He's pulling up vines and burning houses. . . . They had to hide in a cave near Pamiers for three days. No one would take them in, for fear of Lord Humbert."

"Who is Lord Humbert?" asks Sybille, puckering her seamless brow.

"You know." Arnaude speaks patiently. "Remember, we talked about this? Lord Humbert is a vassal of the King of France. He was left here with five hundred knights to make trouble after the King went back to France last year. He's been pestering all our lords who are still faithful to the Count of Toulouse."

"Did the Good Men have no protectors on their journey?" Dulcie inquires as Gran slowly rises. She doesn't want any more bread. After dishing out all those vigorous insults, she needs another nap.

At last I can eat my own dinner.

"Two knights were with them for part of the way, in case they ran into the French, but left them near Castelnaudary," says Arnaude, and Dulcie clicks her tongue.

"They should not have left the Good Men." Dulcie's tone is very solemn. "God will punish them for that."

And suddenly there's a squawk. A squawk from behind us.

Oh, no.

Catastrophe.

Grandmother Blanche has sat on my egg.

‡CHAPTER THREE‡

It's so good to get away from Saint Pierre des Cuisines. It's so good to get away from the *smell* of that parish.

I'm sure that we're all very grateful to Alamain de Rouaix for lending us one of his houses, but did he really have to stick us in the middle of the leather-workers' district?

"Sybille?" It's Berthe speaking. I wish she'd shut up. I wish she and Sybille would *both* shut up and let me enjoy the smell of the spice shops in peace.

"Yes, Berthe?" Sybille replies.

"Yesterday, Lady Blanche said that Babylonne was a bastard." Berthe skips over a pile of horse manure. "Why is she a bastard?"

"Because her parents were not married to each other," Sybille responds gravely. I'm trying to ignore them. It's easy to ignore them with so much to look at. The Saracen wall, for example—that's very interesting. You can see where those wicked French knocked the tops off all the towers the last time they got in here.

"Sybille?"

"Yes, Berthe?"

"Isn't it a *good* thing that they weren't married? I thought it was bad to marry."

"It *is* bad to marry, Berthe." Sybille's so glad that Berthe was placed in my grandmother's care. Now she can finally lord it over somebody else. "It's also bad to have children, because it's bad to fornicate." A pause. "Especially when you're a Perfect," she adds, "and you fornicate with a Roman priest."

That's aimed directly at me. I know it is, even though I can't see Sybille's face. She's walking behind me, but I can feel her sly gaze boring into my back.

Not that I'm going to pay any attention. Here's the Portaria, its twin towers looming above us. I wish I could climb a tower one day. It would be good to see Toulouse from the top of a tower. You would feel like God, looking down. Up there, you wouldn't be so close to the dung and the slops and

28

the vermin. It would be all sun and air, and birds, and bells, and empty roofs. The chatter of voices would fade away.

Sometimes I wish that I were a bird.

"Oh!" says Berthe. "Did a Perfect fornicate with a Roman priest?"

"Yes," Sybille sighs. "I'm afraid so."

"Who?" asks Berthe. "Who was it?"

"It was Babylonne's mother. Lady Mabelia."

I'm not going to listen. I *refuse* to listen. There's the house of Bernard de Miramonte, the richest man in Toulouse. He's a knight, but I heard that he married an armorer's daughter.

No wonder Navarre keeps saying that the nobles in this town are poisoning their own wells.

"Oh, no!" Berthe sucks in her breath. "Did your mother fornicate with a priest, Babylonne?"

"Don't talk to Babylonne." Sybille's practically preening herself; I can hear it in her voice. "She's not allowed to talk for three days, remember? Because she lied about the egg, and her tongue is cursed with the venom of deceit."

"Oh, yes," says Berthe. "I forgot."

Pause. Look at that man over there—I've never seen a hat like that. He must be a foreigner. Oh! And smell that bakery!

29

My stomach's growling.

"Sybille?"

"Yes, Berthe?"

"Why did Lady Mabelia fornicate with a Roman priest if she was a Good Woman? Perfects like her aren't allowed to fornicate."

God give me patience. I can't stand this anymore. Here we are, on Pujol Street. One of the town consuls lives down there somewhere. . . .

"I don't know why she did it, but I do know that she was punished for it." There's relish in Sybille's voice. "Her throat was cut by the evil French knights when they captured Lavaur."

"Because she fornicated with a priest?"

"Because she was a Perfect, you moron!" Swinging around to confront them both. I don't care who's listening. I don't care what happens. "Because she was a Good Woman! Because the French killed *all* the Perfects in Lavaur!"

Berthe gasps. "You talked! Babylonne, you talked!"

"I'm going to tell Lady Blanche that you talked," Sybille hisses like a snake.

"Go ahead." You steaming heap of ripe pig's offal. "And I'll tell her that you drank water last night without saying the Lord's Prayer first!"

30

Berthe stares at Sybille, wide-eyed. "Did you do that, Sybille?"

"No! I did not!"

"Yes, she did. And as for you, Berthe . . ." This'll shut your big, flapping mouth. "You ate the product of fornication yesterday."

"No!" Berthe jumps as if she's been slapped. "No, I didn't!"

"Yes, you did. You ate wool. I saw the fluff on your bread and you ate it."

Berthe's bottom lip begins to tremble. Tears fill her eyes. "I didn't mean to!" she whimpers.

"Anyway, it's not a sin to eat wool." Sybille's desperately trying to fight back. But she hasn't a hope. She doesn't know the meaning of the word *fight*.

Not like me.

"Of course it's a sin to eat wool." I'd better lower my voice, because there are people all around. Strangers. Monks. "Wool comes off sheep, doesn't it? Sheep are animals."

"But there's wool fluff everywhere in that house because of the spinning!" Sybille protests feebly. "It's hard *not* to eat wool!"

"It's hard not to eat eggs, either. But we're still punished if we do." As I lean into her face, she

31

flinches. I can see a pimple on her chin. "We're *all* sinners, Sybille. Haven't you heard Dulcie say that a thousand times? We're all sinners." She swallows, so I drive the point home, drilling my finger into her breastbone. "I think you'd better remember that."

There. I've shut her up, at long last. Now I can enjoy the bright morning and all its many gifts: the gleaming red silk on that lady over there; the flock of pretty black goats scurrying past; the bunches of smooth, white cylinders hanging from the yawning doorway of a candlemaker's shop. Strewing herbs sweeten the air like an angel's breath. A song drifts down from an upstairs window. If I concentrate on these good things, I can forget much of the cruelty and ugliness around me (at least for a short time). It seems odd that, in a world forsaken by God, there should be so many bright flowers and dancing flags. Surely they cannot have been put here on earth to make me feel better?

But over the rooftops rises the square spire of Saint Etienne's—and it makes my heart turn over, thinking about what happened yesterday. In the cloister of that very church.

The market is awfully close to Saint Etienne. I hope I don't bump into any priests who recognize me. Any *redheaded* priests who recognize me.

"Listen." (I can talk freely to Sybille now. She won't dare tell Aunt Navarre about it.) "I don't want you coming with me to buy the fish. Berthe looks too hungry, and you shouldn't buy fish when you're looking hungry. It'll drive the price up."

"But—"

"I want you to wait here. Right here." We're at the entrance to the church of Saint George. All around us are surging crowds: men with sacks on their backs, women with legs of pork under their arms, and children scanning the ground for fallen nuts or rotten fruit. Above these people, serene stone faces stare blindly down, their painted skin flaking and faded. (I wish I could shield them from the weather somehow. They look so pitiful. So abandoned.) "Stay here, and I'll come back for you."

"But—"

"I know what I'm doing. I've done it before." (When I was allowed to take care of things by myself, without having the pair of you sent along to spy on me.) "Just stay here, all right? Don't move."

It's all a lie, of course; Berthe doesn't look any hungrier than I do. But I don't want the pair of them hanging off my skirts while I talk to Master Vital. It would be like swimming in the river with chains on my feet.

"Master Vital!" There he is—big and round and bristling with curly hair. He's always smiling, because his teeth are so good. The man beside him must be another fishmonger, judging from the silver scales all over his hands and the nasty stains on his tunic. "Master Vital, I've come to buy some fish."

"Aha." Master Vital has very small, sharp eyes, like chips of black marble. "Been in the wars again, Little Hornet?"

"What? Oh." That's right. My bruises. Navarre gave them to me for stealing the egg. "Oh, no. I fell over."

"A likely story." Master Vital turns to his fishmonger friend. "Eleven years ago, when Simon de Montfort was burning the city, I saw this little one throwing a stone at an armed knight after he split open some poor fellow's head with an ax. She hasn't changed since then."

"Yes, I have. I'm taller."

"You think so? Well—maybe." Master Vital grins. "I remember your mother running after you, telling you to stop."

"It wasn't my mother." I don't want to get into this. "Simon de Montfort killed my mother."

"Ah?" His grin fades, but his eyes remain bright and piercing. "Well, it was the women of Toulouse

34

who killed that stinking spawn of Satan with a big, fat stone from their catapult, so your mother got her revenge. Now—you want fish? I have a very special fish for you today. I set it aside with you in mind."

"This one? This is my fish?"

"This one, yes."

"Yes, I think I recognize it. It's the same fish you gave me last week."

Master Vital's friend laughs. Master Vital raises a shocked eyebrow. But I'm not going to yield.

"Little Hornet, this fish is fresh," Master Vital insists. "It was pulled out of the Garonne this morning."

"It is not fresh. Look how milky its eye is!"

"You won't be eating the eye, Little Hornet."

"I won't be eating the *fish*, Master Vital." How I love this kind of haggling! You can laugh, and joke, and play silly games, and no one will tell you to shut your brazen mouth or else. If I could haggle in the marketplace every day of the week, from sunup to sundown, I would be as happy as an angel in Heaven. "Show me another, if you please, or I will go elsewhere!"

I will, too. I don't mind. The longer I spend in this market, the better. I love it here.

"Very well." Master Vital heaves an elaborate sigh and reaches across the eels for something that gleams as bright as silver in the sun. I like the look of that fish. I like its clear eye and its clean smell. It feels good, too. Meaning that it will taste even better.

I'm so glad that we're allowed to eat fish. It's lucky that fish spring miraculously from the water and don't hatch out of eggs the way chickens do. "Yes, I'll take this one." Even Navarre couldn't complain about a fish like this. "And those ten others over there, as well. For one *pourgeoise.*"

Master Vital reels back. "One copper *pourgeoise!*" he exclaims. "For all that good fish? Little Hornet, are you trying to sting me again?" (He's enjoying himself.) "I had a customer here this morning—for ten of those fish he gave me one *livre tournois!*"

What? Oh, please. "One *livre tournois!*" What do you think I am, a fool? "That must have been after you told him they were the fish Christ our Lord used when He fed the five thousand."

Master Vital's friend laughs again. Even Master Vital's lips twitch. But he recovers himself quickly.

"Little Hornet," he says in a grave tone, "I would not be ashamed to feed these fish to our Lord. Only look how fat they are."

And I'm opening my mouth when I see him. The priest.

The redheaded priest.

He's over there, staring straight at me. White-faced. Long-nosed.

I think I'm going to be sick.

"I'll—I'll have five, then." Quick! *Quick!* I have to get out of here! "Five fish for one *pourgeoise*."

Master Vital looks surprised. He was expecting more of an argument.

"Five?" he rumbles. "Well, now . . ."

"That's reasonable. You *know* that's reasonable." Come on, will you? Come *on!* "Just give them to me!"

Master Vital regards me for a moment, his expression blank. (Perhaps he's a little offended?) But at last he shrugs and begins to lay the fish in my bag. Where's Sybille? There. Over there. I can glimpse her through the moving crowds, gaping at a man with a brace of dead hares.

Time to go.

Grab your bag, Babylonne. Keep your head low. Slap down the money. Duck behind the trestle. Scramble under it, past a barrel of pickled herring, a forest of shuffling legs, a puddle of fish guts. Scurrying along, bent double, weaving through clusters of gossiping women and bleating livestock. At last—a portico. The pillars are nice and thick.

Thick enough to hide behind.

God, I can hardly breathe. And here I am, pressed to the back of a pillar before the astonished stare of a snot-nosed, bare-bottomed afterthought of a child. What are *you* staring at, pig swill?

When I gnash my teeth, he toddles away.

But I'll have to risk a look. I must find out if the priest saw me. What if he did? What if he learns who I am? Would they flog me for stealing an egg?

Carefully . . . carefully . . . one peek around the smooth stone shaft . . .

And there he is. Redhead. He's so tall that he stands out like a torch in a crypt. I can see him craning over the milling heads, peering around, searching for me. He walks forward. Stops. Scans the square again. In the hard sunlight, he looks paler than ever; his hair has drained all the color and warmth from his skin. He has the coldest, longest, most immovable face I've ever seen. A face like the ones on the stone saints that are carved over the south door of Saint Etienne.

I have to get out of here.

Now.

‡CHAPTER FOUR‡

The beautiful princess draped the magic cloak about her and was suddenly invisible. Though the evil sorcerer searched every corner of his lair, she slipped by him like the scent of lavender on an evening breeze. . . .

I'll be safe now. I know I will. I'm out of the market. I'm almost out of the city quarter. Just a few more steps, past the town hall and the church of Saint Quentin, and I'll be through the Portaria, into the Bourg.

Surely he won't come looking for me in the Bourg.

It must have been a coincidence. What terrible luck! I hardly ever set foot outside the house. I hardly ever have a chance to see the sky, or hear people laughing, or smell the aroma of fresh fruit piled up on tables. And when I'm finally set free, to enjoy these modest blessings—boom! The priest is there, buying a nice trout for his dinner.

Except that priests don't buy trout. Not if they're living together in a cloister. Their servants buy the food. Their servants cook it.

So what was that priest doing at the market? Was he passing through on his way back from one of the hospitals?

He can't have been looking for me. He *can't* have been. *Ouch!*

Get out of my way, piss-brain!

Well—at least I can protect myself now. At least I have more pepper. That was smart, to stop at the pepperer's on Cervun Street. Smart girl, Babylonne. The trouble is, pepper costs so much. Two whole fish for three pinches of pepper! Aunt Navarre will be suspicious. Very, very suspicious.

She might not let me buy fish ever again.

Here's the Street of the Taur, and there's the friars' monastery. (Stay well clear of *that*.) I wonder if Sybille will find her way back. She doesn't know Toulouse the way I do. She's so feeble and whiny and useless—what if she gets lost?

If she does, I'll be blamed for it. No matter what I say. Because I'm always blamed for everything.

Who gets her ears boxed when the oats are moldy? Babylonne. Who gets her backside kicked when someone steals the lamp oil? Babylonne.

If I had a weak skull, I would have turned into an idiot long ago. Navarre would have pounded my brain into soup. I wish that I had a *livre* for every time she's cracked a broom across my face.

God curse her.

I can smell the river at last. (Not far now.) I can smell the tanneries. Around this corner, across the street, and past the tavern—the Golden Crow. I might just slow down to see if there's a fight going on in the tavern's downstairs room. Or maybe a knot of strangely dressed, bleached-looking northerners on their way to Compostela. Or perhaps even a *jongleur*, singing or dancing or juggling cups. I've been praying for another *jongleur*. The last one I saw here had the voice of an angel. He sang about a beautiful princess and a brave knight. When he sang, I could see everything as clearly as if it had been happening in front of me: the snow-white castle, and the silver chain-mail, and the golden bird that carried the love letter. And when the knight met his death, I cried, because it seemed real to me then—though I know it wasn't. That *jongleur* made it real. He made you believe that the earth was Heaven and that love was a common blessing that could be found in every leaf and stream and flower.

Pity I never found out what happened to the princess. When Aunt Navarre caught me dawdling in the street, listening to a sinful *jongleur*, she practically knocked my head off my shoulders. For Aunt Navarre, it's the Devil that lurks in every leaf and stream and flower. Not love.

Maybe she's right, at that.

No. There's nothing to see in the Golden Crow. And now that I'm almost home, I don't want to be here. I'm sweating like a coward. My mouth is dry. The front door looks like a great, toothless, yawning mouth, waiting to eat me up.

She's going to give me such hell about these fish.

"Babylonne?"

There she is. Navarre. Leaning out the downstairs window, flanked by flapping wooden shutters. "Where's Sybille?" She's scowling. "Where's Berthe?" All I can do is spread my hands. (Look—no tongue!) "Come in here!" she scolds, and pulls back into the house. The shutters slam.

My feet don't want to move.

They have to be dragged, step by step, over the

threshold. Inside, I can see Gran, Arnaude, and Dulcie, but no Sybille. No Berthe. Arnaude's tending something on the fire. Dulcie's spinning. Gran's belching to herself thoughtfully.

"Well? Where are the others?" Navarre demands, snatching my bag of fish from me. I put my finger to my lips (I've been muted, remember?) and—

Whoomp!

Ouch! God save us!

Give Navarre her due—she's fast with her fists.

"Don't be clever with me, you little sow!" she roars. "I give you *permission* to speak! Now speak! Where are the others?"

"I don't know." My ears are ringing. My teeth are humming. "They wandered off while I was buying the fish. They left me there."

"You mean *you* left *them.*" Oh, no. She's opened the bag. She's gaping into the bag, her face a mask of astonishment. "What do you call this?"

"I—"

"Three fish for one *pourgeoise?* Is this all you could get?"

I can't talk. I can only swallow and nod.

"You're lying!" Her spit is flying through the air. "Last week you got four! Four big fish!"

What can I say? That the catches are smaller this week? If only she hadn't clouted me over the ear, I could think more clearly.

But as I open my mouth, someone bursts through the door behind me.

"Babylonne!" It's Sybille. She looks as if she's been dragged by her feet through a thicket of thorns, then hung upside down in a cow byre and milked. "You ran away! You *left* us! Where did you go?"

"Where did *you* go?" This is going to require some quick thinking. "I looked around and you'd disappeared."

"We did not!" Sybille throws herself on Navarre's mercy. She practically throws herself on her knees, in fact. "Babylonne told us to wait near the church of Saint George!" she cries. "We waited and waited, but she didn't come! We asked for her at the fish-monger's stall, but he said that she'd gone already!"

"Babylonne *told* you to wait by the church?" Dulcie echoes.

Oh, no.

Now I'm in trouble.

"You were *talking*?" says Navarre, narrowing her eyes at me.

Sybille claps a hand over her mouth. I don't know what to say. Should I—? What if I—?

44

"You were *talking?*" Navarre repeats. "Without permission?"

She's advancing toward me. One step. Two steps. When I try to retreat, there's a wall in the way.

"What would you expect from a Roman priest's bastard?" mutters Gran.

Navarre raises a hand and—*whump!*

It's just a slap, but it stings.

"Ow!"

"Have you no shame?" *Whump!* "Have you no respect?" *Whump!* "Where would you be, if it wasn't for our mercy?" *Whump!* "Do you think you're welcome here? A mark of shame like you?"

"Lady Navarre!"

It's Berthe. Berthe's home. Thank God—she'll be a distraction.

As Navarre turns, I manage to shield my face.

"What?" Navarre snaps.

"There's a priest!" Berthe is panting like a dog. She's wild-eyed and shrill-voiced. "There's a priest outside! A Roman priest!"

Oh, God. No.

Not the priest.

"A what?" says Navarre, frowning.

"A priest! There's a priest!" Berthe begins to cry. "He followed us! He came after us!"

He must have heard Sybille ask about me. He must have trailed her all the way from the market.

Mercy. Oh, mercy in the Lord.

Navarre strides to the door, pushing Berthe aside. Sybille and Dulcie are cowering. Arnaude rises and stumps after Navarre. The two of them peer cautiously through the door into the street beyond. Navarre advances a few more steps, until the sun is beating down on her uncovered head. She puts her hands on her hips. She looks to her left and to her right.

She glances back over her shoulder.

"Where is he, Berthe?" she says. "Show me."

Berthe whimpers. She's gnawing at her thumb and doesn't want to go out again. But Sybille gives her a shove, and she stumbles over the threshold.

I can hear a horse's hooves. The priest wouldn't be riding, though.

No. The *clop-clop-clop* is fading away.

There's blood on my lip.

"Is he gone?" Sybille squeaks. Dulcie seems to be mumbling a prayer. Navarre hustles Berthe and Arnaude back inside; she bolts the door behind them. "He's gone," she says, and swings around to face me. "Do you know anything about this priest?"

46

"No."

"You're lying! You've been consorting with *Roman priests!*"

"I have not!"

"Like mother, like daughter," Gran rasps, and Arnaude puts out a timid hand.

"Maybe he was a Dominican," she suggests nervously. "Maybe he saw that she was wearing sandals and realized she must be a Good Christian. Maybe he's one of those wandering preachers, and he wants to convert her."

Navarre, however, isn't listening. Her face is blotched with red. She grabs me by the collar. "Is that where you got the egg?" she spits. "Did a *priest* give it to you?"

"No! I told you! I found it!" Christ save us. Has she gone mad? Her eyes are popping out of her head. "A—a man tried to take the wool from me, and I pushed him, and I ran, and I hid behind a cart, and the egg was there on some straw! A stray hen must have laid it!"

"You're a liar." She shakes me. Ow! The back of my head hits the stone wall, again and again. "You're a liar and a thief and a glutton and a whore!"

"Let go!"

"You've been trading"—*thump!*—"your favors"—*thump!*—"with Roman priests!"

That's enough. Get *off* me!

"I have not!" A mighty push makes her stagger. (Take that, you cow!) But she doesn't fall. She doesn't even stop shouting.

"Again and again we have forgiven you!" she cries.

"For doing all the work around here?" Duck, Babylonne! "For tending the fire and chopping the wood and fetching the water—"

"You have a black soul, like the soul of your father before you! You poison our wells and fill our house with strife!"

What? *What* did you say?

"*I'm* filling our house with strife?" I've had enough of this. "*You're* the one with the temper! *I* never broke a sack of beans over anyone's head! *I* never punched a horse or kicked a hole in a barrel!"

"*Have you no shame?*" She's screaming like a slaughtered pig, and she asks me if I have no shame? What about the neighbors? "*When I think of your martyred mother, I weep tears of blood!*"

Oh, no. Not my martyred mother. When Navarre starts talking about my martyred mother, I'm in serious trouble.

48

Tears of blood aren't a good sign, either.

My retreat's blocked off. Arnaude's in the way. But if I can just—

"*Ow! Aah!*"

Let go! Let go of my hair!

"Something must be done about you." Navarre jerks, tugs, drags—*yeowch!* "The Good Men will decide."

What's she—? Oh, no. No!

"No!" Not the chest! "Wait! Stop!"

"In you get."

"*No!*"

Get off! Let go! You can't! Scratch—kick—bite—STOP!

Thump.

The lid comes down. She must be sitting on it, because I can't push it open. She's locking it! No!

"NO! HELP!"

"There's air enough in there, Babylonne. Air enough for a sinner like you."

"*Let me out!*"

"Not until you repent. You're a wicked girl, and you belong in an abode of darkness until you mend your ways."

She wants me to beg. But I'm not going to beg; I'm going to calm down. Calm down, Babylonne.

Breathe slowly. That's it. There's a crack up there. A crack with light coming through it. The money's digging into my back, but there's fur next to it . . . soft fur . . .

I'm not going to cry. There's nothing to cry about. This isn't so bad. I could have been thrown down a well and stoned to death by the French, like my aunt Guiraude. I could have been hanged, like my uncle Aimery. I could have had my throat cut, like my mother.

I wish my mother were here.

There once was a beautiful princess who was imprisoned at the bottom of a deep, dark well. The well was so deep and dark that all she could see above her was a pinprick of light like a shining star. Every day, the wicked witch who had imprisoned her would winch down a loaf of bread and an apple. And some cheese. And a roast chicken. And perhaps a few dried grapes.

Then one day, as she was waiting for her food, something else tumbled into the well. It was a ladder made of golden rope, held by a noble knight in silver armor. . . .

‡CHAPTER FIVE‡

"She's sixteen years old, Holy Father. Sixteen years old! And for all those years, I have striven to make her a Good Christian, according to her mother's wishes. But she is a crooked stick. She will not obey God's law. It's the priest's blood, I am certain—her mother was never like this."

Aunt Navarre is doing what she likes best: abusing me in front of other people. Namely, in front of Benedict de Termes, the Good Man. The Perfect. I remember him quite well from his visit to our house in Laurac. It must have been early last year, before the King's army drove us into Toulouse, because Dulcie had joined our little convent.

She kept trying to kiss Benedict's disgusting, horny feet.

He's a little older, a little grayer, but essentially the same. His neck is like a chicken's leg, his ears are like slabs of lichen, and his teeth—yecch!—are like flecks of rotten meat, all black and green.

I can't believe that he's wearing dark blue. Dark blue *and* sandals. He might as well be wearing a sign saying I AM A HERETIC. Does he *want* the Roman idolaters hereabouts to start pelting him with rotten eggs?

What a fool.

"Has she been punished?" he asks Navarre in his hollow, tired voice.

"Oh, many times. Many, many times." Navarre begins to count on her fingers, which are bandaged where I scratched them. "With fasting, with prayers, with the rod. We've forbidden her to speak. We've stuffed her mouth with tow. We've shaved off her hair once or twice. We've even locked her in that chest over there. And she remains incorrigible. She's eaten up with sin, Holy Father. I don't know what to do with her anymore. She'll never be a Perfect. She gets worse and worse as she gets older."

"She's a Roman priest's bastard," Gran suddenly

rumbles from her ancestral chair. "What do you expect?"

I wonder if the others can hear this. They've all been sent upstairs, but I know what it's like upstairs. You can hear practically everything if you put your ear to the floor. I bet Sybille has her ear to the floor. And Dulcie. And Arnaude. I bet Sybille's really enjoying the fact that Aunt Navarre can't say a single nice thing about me. Not a word about how hard I work or how helpful I am. According to her, I'm just a bottomless pit of vice.

Well, I might be a sinner, but Navarre is worse. What kind of Good Woman goes after one of her novices with an ax? Navarre has the heart of a rampant wolf. As for Gran, she doesn't fool me. I know that she can do more than she pretends. I know that she just wants us waiting on her hand and foot.

"Babylonne." With an obvious effort, Benedict turns to look at me. He seems exhausted, as if he can barely summon up the energy to raise an eyebrow. "Tell me," he sighs, "do you wish to be saved, Babylonne?"

What sort of a question is that? What does he expect me to say—no?

"Yes, Holy Father."

"Then why do you torment your friends and family?"

"I don't torment them." It might be worth pointing this out. He might actually listen. "They torment me."

A gasp from Aunt Navarre. "Wicked girl!" she exclaims. "Holy Father—"

"I never beat *you*! I never threw scalding water on *you* and burned *your* leg!" Is everyone blind in this house? Look at my face! Look at my feet! "I never pushed *you* down the ladder!"

"Don't listen, Father. She has a serpent's tongue."

"Please." Benedict lifts one languid hand, which doesn't look much better than his feet. "You both scold like peasants. You offend my ears."

Navarre mumbles something that could be an apology. I don't even bother. It can't get much worse for me now—an apology won't make any difference.

"Babylonne," says Benedict, peering at me with his muddy green eyes, "would you rather live in darkness among those damned for eternity than follow the difficult path of righteousness?"

Beg your pardon?

"Because that's what you'll be doing if you fail in your life here." He sighs again. "If you do not wish to become a Perfect, in pious communion with other women dedicated to the way of Christ, then you will have to get married. There is no other choice."

What? "Oh, but—"

"We can't do that, Holy Father!" Navarre jumps in. She sounds worried. "We can't marry her off! Her mother would never have allowed it!"

And suddenly Gran interjects. "She might be a bastard," Gran creaks, "but she is Mabelia's bastard. We can't endanger her immortal soul."

Benedict frowns. I don't think he's used to having women argue with him.

"Then you must look to your own strength," he says irritably. "It seems to me that you must either suppress the demon in her or condemn her to marriage."

You can't be serious. Condemn me to marriage? Who on earth would want to marry *me?*

"My sister died a martyr," Navarre frets. "We owe it to her memory that her child be kept from sin. Babylonne might deserve perpetual torment, but her mother is in Heaven now. Should we keep her child from her by condemning Babylonne to eternal damnation on earth?"

"Babylonne can always repent on her deathbed,"

Benedict points out as if I'm not even here. "The *consolamentum* will save her then."

"But suppose that when she dies, there are no Perfects around to give her the *consolamentum*," says Navarre. "If that were to happen, I would have failed her mother. We all would have. And I swore that I would never fail Mabelia."

"You *swore*?" Benedict draws himself up in his seat. "With an *oath*?"

"Oh, no!" It's wonderful to see Navarre looking so cowed. "I mean, I made a promise. To God. I didn't take any oath."

"Babylonne!" It's Gran. She's come to life again. "Out," she says, and jerks her chin at the back door.

What? You're not serious.

"Yes, Babylonne. Out you go. You shouldn't be here." Navarre doesn't want me to see her being scolded by a Good Man any more than Gran does. "Go and chop the wood."

"But—"

"Do it! *Now*!" Navarre turns to Benedict. "You see, Father? She's so disobedient."

I should have known it. They're going to marry me off without even waiting to hear what *I* might say on the subject. Not that my opinion counts for

56

anything. But they could at least let me stay and listen.

Chop the wood. Ha! I don't need to chop the wood; it's in splinters already. But if they don't hear the sound of chopping, they'll probably throw me on the fire. For disobeying orders in front of Benedict de Termes.

Out into the little yard, where Navarre's beans are failing. (Not enough sun for those beans, because the walls are too high.) Mud and dung and old straw and—yuck! Rats in the woodpile again. I honestly can't understand why those rats stay around, since there's never a scrap of food to eat. Perhaps they know about Perfects. Perhaps they know that Perfects can't kill any living creature— not even a rat.

If you ask me, we should get ourselves a dog. A really good rat-killer. If our dog killed the rats, we couldn't be blamed for it, could we?

Yes, it would be good to have a dog. Maybe, if we had a dog, it would sleep at my side and follow in my footsteps and protect me from angry people. Maybe it would be my friend—a faithful friend. A cuddly friend. Like that beautiful gray alaunt hound I saw pass this house the other day, with its bright eyes and long, smooth, intelligent face. That dog looked as if it could talk. As if it had the soul of an enchanted prince trapped in its little wiry frame.

No. On second thought, I wouldn't want a dog like that. How could I condemn a dog like that to a house like this? The poor creature would die of starvation, because we couldn't feed him any meat. He would have to live on fish and barley, and that's not much of a life for a dog.

Probably better than *my* life, mind you. I don't know. Maybe I should get married. Except that— well, what if it endangers my immortal soul? I don't want to do that. I don't want to come back as an earwig when I die. I want to go to Heaven.

There once was a beautiful princess condemned to live the life of a peasant girl. One morning, when she was chopping wood, a tiny creature sprang out. It was a little silver demon with glowing red eyes, and it said to her, "Beautiful maiden, if you marry me, I will give you three wishes. . . ."

Tah! This ax is getting blunt. I can't sharpen it, though, because the water is inside. And I can't go back inside because I might overhear Navarre talking about the kind of husband she wants for me: a husband who'll beat me thoroughly every night before we go to bed. *Oof!* There. You see? This ax *is* too blunt. It's going to keep getting stuck in the wood. I hate it when the ax gets stuck in the wood.

I can never pull it out; I haven't enough strength in my arms. Where's the maul? That might help. I could knock out the blade with the maul.

"*Psst!* Babylonne!"

What—?

Oh. It's Sybille. Hanging out of the loft window. Just ignore her, Babylonne.

"So you're going to be married?" she titters. (I *knew* she was eavesdropping.) "I don't envy you your husband. Ugh!"

"What do you mean?" They can't have made a decision! Not yet! "What husband?"

Titter, titter.

"*What husband?*" You smirking slab of pig's tripe! "Tell me!"

She does, because she wants to. She's dying to. I can see it in her face.

"He's a relative of Pons Saquet," she says. "He lives out near Lanta, and he's so old that he won't imperil your immortal soul." Titter. "You know." She lowers her voice until it's a hiss. "With *fornication.*"

"You mean—he's impotent?"

"He's ancient." She snickers behind her hand. "He keeps seeing giant olives bouncing around his bed."

Oh, no. Not the giant olive man. I've heard Lombarda de Rouaix talking about him.

"You'll have to feed him and wipe his bottom and save him from the giant olives," Sybille continues maliciously. "And then when he dies, you'll become his son's servant—because what use will you be otherwise?"

Lanta. That's a little hamlet east of here. It would be worse than Laurac. *Much* worse than Laurac.

Do they seriously expect me to spend the next ten years cleaning up after an incontinent old man in the middle of nowhere?

If so, they're going to be sadly disappointed.

‡CHAPTER SIX‡

Once there was a beautiful princess whose wicked stepmother wanted her to marry an evil sorcerer. But if she did marry him, the sorcerer would cast a spell on the princess. During the day, she would turn into a donkey. Only at night would she return to her true shape.

The princess didn't want this to happen. So she had no choice but to open her dead mother's magic chest and take out her dead mother's magic boots, which would take her halfway across the world in the blink of an eye. . . .

Will this night never end? I seem to have been lying in bed forever.

It's so uncomfortable, too, with all this stuff hidden underneath me. I can feel the money digging into my back: two *livres tournois* and a handful of

Caorsins. That's a fair share, I think. It's much less than my dowry would be. Navarre would be losing more than two *livres tournois* if I were stupid enough to stay around. And the scissors—well, I *must* have the scissors. As well as Gran's winter hose and fur-lined boots. I mean, I can't wear sandals, can I? And boots don't really work without hose.

Scissors, boots, hose, money. Altogether, they'd be worth less than the dowry I'd have to pay that crazy old man and his son. It's not as if I'm stealing. I'm just solving Navarre's problem in another way. In a *better* way.

I can hear her snoring over there near Gran. They're both snoring. Gran has to sleep downstairs because of the fire, and Navarre has to sleep downstairs because of Gran. As for me, I'm the one who gets clouted if the fire goes out, so I get to sleep downstairs as well.

Speaking of clouts, my nose is a mess. Throb, throb, throb. (Navarre can't seem to look at me without hitting me anymore.) But it's just as well, I suppose, or I might have fallen asleep by accident. I don't want to miss the first cockcrow. This is my only chance. Unless I make it to the city gates before Dulcie wakes up at sunrise, I'm finished. Navarre will find out that I've taken the money and the scissors and the clothes from her chest, and she'll kill me. She really will. She'll chop me up with an ax before she can stop herself.

I have to get out of here.

A strangled sound. But the snoring resumes, and all is well. Somewhere, a cricket chirps. Somewhere in the distance, a baby's crying. I can't believe that I've come to this point. I can't believe that it's really happening. To have actually laid hands on Navarre's keys—well, that's a feat in itself, because she's a notoriously light sleeper. But I did it. I snuck the keys off her belt. I opened the chest. I took out the money and the scissors and the clothes. And then I slid the keys back under her blankets.

If I can do all that, I can certainly do the rest. I can certainly reach the kingdom of Aragon.

That's the best place for me. Over in Aragon, with all the exiled *faidit* lords—the ones who lost their ancestral lands to the King of France. Like the Viscount of Carcassonne, for example. Or Olivier de Termes. These are great men, and staunch. They must be as tall and strong as oak trees; they must have a fire burning in their eyes that can never be extinguished. When I first saw the carving of Saint Michael, at the church of Saint Etienne, I knew that the *faidit* lords must look like that—straight and stern and handsome, with fine surcoats flowing down their hips like water. Men like that walk with long strides and ride as easily as they walk. They are kind to the weak and merciless to the cruel. Men like that would not turn me away.

I could cook for them and clean for them. I could mend clothes and throw rocks. I could help them win back Carcassonne and Termes from the King, and I would do it proudly. Because I would be serving those valiant knights who have never bent their knees to France. Who are *honorable* and *brave.* Unlike Bernard Oth, my cousin.

I would rather die with the noble *faidit* lords than live locked up with a useless old madman who thinks I'm a giant olive.

The princess knew what she had to do. One night, when all in the castle were sleeping, she disguised herself as a squire and escaped from her wicked stepmother. She went off to join a band of noble knights in shining armor who had sworn to slay the venomous serpent laying waste to her country.

There! The cockcrow!

Off you go, Babylonne. Quickly, now. Quietly. Don't make a sound. And don't forget your bundle — you can't go without that.

The back door creaks a bit, but it's all right. Nobody's moved. (Close the door behind you,

remember. And watch out for that chopping block!)
Already the sky is lightening, over in the east.
Where are my scissors? There. Right.

Hair first.

Ouch! Yeowch! It's harder than I thought; these
scissors must need sharpening. They're worse than
the ax. And without a mirror, I can't be cutting
straight. I hope I don't look too odd. I don't want
to attract attention. And what am I going to do
with all this discarded hair? Stick it in my bundle,
maybe. Get rid of it afterward.

If Navarre sees it lying around on the ground,
she'll know what I've done. She'll know that I've
cut my hair short.

Now for the skirt. Knee-level, I think. It's going
to fray, but I can't help that. Save the leftover
cloth; it might be useful. Stuff it into the bundle,
too. In fact, wrap the money in it, so that the coins
won't chink. Now for the hose. They're not too
big. I was afraid that they might be, but they could
be a lot worse.

The boots smell like very, very old cheese—the
kind that frightens little children. I hope they last.
I have to cross the Pyrenees in these boots, and
they already look as if they're about to lie down
and die.

Oh, well. I have money. If I must, I'll buy more boots.

Another cockcrow. I have to hurry, or I'm going to get caught. I won't throw the bundle over the wall because someone might pick it up before I get to it. I'll bring it up the woodpile with me.

Careful, now. Here's the tricky bit. I'm not at all sure about this woodpile. I don't think it's very stable. And everything's so dark, I can hardly see where I'm—

Whoops!

That was close. God save us, that log almost rolled out from under me! And the wood's so noisy, too. It's rattling. It's crunching. It's going to wake somebody up.

One step. Two steps. That's it. Nicely done. Watch your bundle. Just a bit farther.

There.

How high this garden wall is! I never expected . . . God's angels, I'm going to break my leg jumping down from here!

No, I'm not. Come on, Babylonne, you've made it this far. Just one little drop and the worst part's over. Come on, you coward, *jump*!

Ow!

Curse it! Damnation! Damn the day! Ouch—
my ankle! But it's nothing. A little bruise. A slight
limp. I can still walk.

Down the alley, into the street.

Can't see anyone. Wouldn't expect to. The
light's very murky between the tall houses; if you
stayed in the shadows, lurking in alleys and doorways, you'd be invisible. Someone's coughing his
lungs out upstairs in the Golden Crow.

Pick up the pace, Babylonne.

It's so quiet, and the air's so still. My own footsteps echo off the brick walls on either side of
me—*slap, slap, slap.* There's a rumble of cart wheels
from somewhere far away. Another cockcrow.

And here's the first corner. Look right; look left.
Someone's shuffling along, heading west with a
sack on his back. There's a dog nosing around in
the gutter. Not another sign of life.

So far, so good.

Which gate should I take, once I'm through the
Portaria? The Saint Etienne Gate, and then skirt
the walls until I reach the Château Narbonnais?
Or should I head straight through the city and out
the Château Gate? That would certainly be faster.
And safer, too. You don't know who you're going

to run into outside the city walls. Riffraff. Prostitutes. Drunken bargemen. People on the lookout for a lone traveler . . .

I hope I'm doing the right thing. I hope no one bothers me or takes advantage. It's going to be hard, all by myself; people are going to notice me. They're going to wonder what I'm doing on my own. Even as a boy, I'm going to be noticed. It would be so much easier if I were *with* someone.

Maybe I should attach myself to a party of pilgrims. Or merchants. Or farmers returning from the markets.

But if I do, they'll start to ask questions. And then what will I say?

Maybe I should have thought about this more.

"Wait."

Ah!

Help! Who are you? Let go of my *arm!*

"It's all right." A voice. A man. (He won't loosen his grip!) "I'm not going to hurt you," he whispers.

Oh, God.

It's him.

It's the priest.

"Stop—wait—*stop it!*" He grabs my other wrist. He's got both of them now. He must have snuck up behind me. "*Ow!*" He dodges my kick, skipping backward. But he doesn't let go. "Calm down, will you?"

My scissors. If I could just—

Wait. My bundle. Where is it?

I dropped it!

"Listen. I have to talk to you." Bare feet. He has bare feet, glowing white in the dimness. That's why I didn't hear him. "Oh, no, you don't. No biting," he grunts. Help! I can't—he's so strong! "Listen," he begs. "Please listen to me."

Help!

I knew your father!

What?

It's hard to see his face because the light's so bad, and because he's wearing a hood. A brown hooded cloak, over something drab and green. Where are his priest's clothes? Where are his boots?

Why is he here?

"I knew your father," he repeats in a soft voice. He leans forward, his fingers still clamped around my wrists. "Your father was Pagan Kidrouk, was he not?"

God have mercy.

It's true. Pagan Kidrouk. That was his name: Pagan Kidrouk, Archdeacon of Carcassonne. That was my father.

69

"I knew at once," the priest continues. His voice is breathless. Unsteady. "If Pagan had looked in a mirror, he would have seen your face. It's a miracle. It's as if he's been resurrected."

Ah! "So he's dead, then?"

The priest flinches. I can feel it through his hands. He has to wait a moment before replying.

"Yes," he says, even more quietly. "Yes, he's dead."

"Good." Will you let *go* of me? "He was an evil man, and I hope his soul is trapped in the body of a maggot! Let *go!*"

"Shh!" He won't let go. And I can't raise my voice—I can't summon help—because I don't want to attract attention. Maybe he knows that. He keeps talking, looming over me like a great, dark tree. "I must speak with you. Now. Where are you going? Are you going to meet your lover?"

"My *lover?*" How *dare* you! I can't spit; my mouth's too dry.

So I stamp on his soft, white foot instead.

It must hurt. He winces and sucks air through his teeth. But he still doesn't release his grip.

"Don't do that," he gasps. "Please."

"Filthy priest! I have no lover!"

"All right. I'm sorry."

"Whoreson, lecherous stinking—"

70

"Shh! We're wasting time!" He gives me a little shake. "Why are you running away, then? Because they beat you?"

"That's not your concern!"

"Yes, it is." His tone suddenly changes. It becomes dry and strong and cold. "Listen to me. Your father was my father in all but blood. Everything that I have, I owe to God and your father. Therefore, having found you, how can I let you pass out of my sight?"

What is he talking about? This means nothing to me. And the sun is rising! It's getting brighter!

"Please! Let me go!" They'll catch me if I stay here. "I don't want your help!"

"You're going to need it, though." Still the same dry, hard voice. "How far do you think you'll get in this disguise? How far are you going?"

Oh, God, oh, God, I'll be caught. There's a man opening shutters.

"For a whole day, I roamed the streets in search of you," the priest goes on, oblivious to the splash of night soil hitting cobblestones. "Then I tried the markets. When I discovered where you lived, I took a room in the inn across the way. I've been watching your house from the window, day and night. Waiting for a chance to speak to you." I

71

can't tell what he's thinking. His eyes are shadowed. "Do you think I'm going to walk away now?" he says.

"Please." I won't cry. I won't give him the satisfaction. "Please, you must . . . I have to get out. I have to leave the city, *please.*"

"Then we'll both go."

And he drops my wrists, fastening his hand on my shoulder instead.

I can't seem to move. Too dazed.

"Come," he says. "We will walk out of Toulouse together, side by side. We will go to Lespinasse."

"L—Lespinasse?"

"The convent. Don't you know it? Lespinasse is about a quarter day's walk north of here. It's where I'm staying." He stoops and picks up my bundle. "Come," he says.

This can't be happening. I have to think. He has my bundle. I can't leave without my bundle. And his fingers are anchored firmly in the folds of my tunic.

"I am not a canon of Saint Etienne," he continues as we walk along. "Do you realize that? I *am* a canon—I've taken orders—but I was in the cathedral to visit an acquaintance. And then I saw you, and stayed longer here than I intended. But most

of my possessions are with the nuns of Lespinasse."
He speaks very gently and precisely. Everything
that he says sounds like a prayer. "So we'll go back
to Lespinasse," he explains, "and I will say that you
are my new servant, and we'll discuss our plans in
peace. In my room."

In your *room?*

Oh, no.

Wait just a moment.

"What is it?" He stops alongside me. "What's
wrong?"

"Are you mad?" (What do you think I am, an
idiot? Do you think I have bees in my brain?) "I'm
not going with you. Especially not to your *room.*"

"Why not?" He looks down his long, pale,
freckled nose. "Can you think of a better place to
talk?"

"To *talk?*" Is that what you call it? "I know what
you're after, and you can think again!"

He blinks. When he draws himself erect, it's
frightening to watch because he gets even taller.
His tone is as dry as my mouth.

"My dear girl—"

"I'm not your *dear girl!* I'm not anybody's girl—
no, nor anybody's whore, either! You priests are all

the same! You and my father are spun from the same bale!"

"Listen—"

"I don't want your help! My father is *nothing* to me! If he was here, I'd spit in his face! Just leave me alone; I can take care of myself!"

"You have the tolls, then?"

What?

He's watching me closely. I can sense that, though I can't see his eyes yet. They're still shaded by his hood. Someone nearby is shouting at someone else about eating all the meat. I can smell chicken manure.

What tolls?

"You know there are tolls to be paid on most of the roads that lead out of this city," the priest remarks in his calm, gentle fashion. "Which route are you taking?"

"I—I—"

"North? South? East?"

"South."

"Ah." He nods. "South by way of Foix, perhaps?"

"Yes." If it's any of your business.

"Then you'll have to pay a toll at Pamiers. And another at Ax-les-Thermes. And at Marens . . ."

"How much?"

He tilts his head. "Does it matter?" he asks.

Of course it matters. He knows it does, too. Though his face is set like stone, I can feel a growing confidence in the way he holds himself. In the timbre of his speech.

But I'll not be defeated.

"I don't have to keep to the roads. I can go through the fields and the forests."

"And get lost? And be eaten by wolves? If the tolls were easy to avoid, do you think they would ever be paid? Listen." He squeezes my shoulder and bends low to speak in my ear. "I swear on the Holy Sepulchre that I'll not harm you. I swear on the blood of Christ—and I am a priest, so I hold to my oaths. I want to *keep* you from harm, if only for your father's sake. And if you're traveling south— well, then, God is good. Because I, too, will be traveling south, once I leave Lespinasse. I'm on a pilgrimage to Saint James of Compostela. Perhaps, if we travel in each other's company, you will be safe. And I will be happier, knowing that you are safe."

He's lying. He must be, though he does sound as if he means it. And when he sees me peering and peering, he suddenly pushes back his hood, exposing his face to the strengthening light. It picks out the puffiness under his eyes and the hollows where his cheeks should be. He's all skin and bones.

"Do you realize what would happen to me if I were discovered fornicating in the guesthouse of Lespinasse?" he adds with a lift of his eyebrow. "I would be extremely lucky to escape with all my organs intact."

Ha! I certainly don't believe *that*! Everyone knows that priests are lechers. Everyone knows that they don't wear drawers under their long skirts.

"Besides, you have your pepper, do you not?" he says, and a smile flicks across his mouth. It's a crooked smile, but for some reason it's reassuring. For a fleeting instant, it makes him look kind. "Your pepper and many other weapons, too, I feel sure," he murmurs. "You should know, for example, that I have a weak left knee. The slightest knock can reduce me to agony. One kick would disable me for days." He releases my shoulder and steps back. "Come," he finishes. "Kick me and you'll see. I'm telling the truth. Everything I tell you is the truth."

Hmmm.

He's still clutching my bundle. Would he give that back? His expression is grave. Almost melancholy. He just stands there, waiting.

What shall I do?

He knows about the tolls. He probably knows about a lot of things. If he's telling the truth—if he really is traveling south—then perhaps he might be useful. At least for a while. He could pay the tolls and ask directions. He could provide a shield. He could certainly get me through the city gate, no questions asked.

And once I have my bundle, I can duck away whenever I want. I don't have to stay with him. I have my scissors and my pepper, and he can't keep a grip on me all the time. It's true, what he says. I'll be safer with him than I would be on my own. Even if I am disguised as a boy.

Who would dare ask questions of a boy traveling with a priest? Who would dare rob or murder him, and risk bringing down the wrath of Rome?

"You promise not to touch me?"

"I promise not to lay a hand on you," he replies, watching me intently.

"You swear that you're telling the truth?"

"I swear on the life of the Holy Virgin."

"Mmmph." It doesn't mean much, but I suppose it will have to do. And I can't linger. I have to go. Now. "What's your name, anyway?"

"My name is Isidore. Father Isidore Orbus." He holds out my bundle. "And your name?" he inquires. "I still don't know what to call you."

I could give him a false name, I suppose, but—oh, curse it, I'll just forget who I'm supposed to be.

"Babylonne." Give me that bundle. "My name is Babylonne."

✢CHAPTER SEVEN✢

So here I am. In a nunnery. I never thought I'd see the inside of one of these places. It's different from what I thought it would be. Not as luxurious. I mean, the stonework's very grand, and the ceilings are very high, but there are no golden lamps or silken tapestries or colored tiles on the floor. Everything's hard and gray and terribly clean.

Do you know, I think they must actually scrub the floors in here?

Not that I've seen much outside the guesthouse. Perhaps, in their own quarters, the nuns sleep on bolsters stuffed with goose down. Perhaps they eat roasted swans off snow-white trenchers with golden knives—or even golden forks! (I've heard about forks, though I've never seen one.)

Perhaps it's just in the guesthouse that the palliasses are stuffed with straw and the walls are bare even of painted stars and the cups are made of earthenware rather than silver.

I tell you what, though—this skinny priest isn't lacking for money. Just look at what's piled up on his bed! A fur-lined cloak. A spare pair of boots. A leather water bag. And books. Real books! *Three of them!*

They must be worth a king's ransom.

Do you think he'd mind if I touched one? I've never been so close to a book before. I wouldn't hurt it; I wouldn't even open it. I'd just touch it.

He'd never know, would he? After all, he's not in the room.

The binding feels odd. As smooth as metal, only it's not metal. It's not even leather, I don't think. It's something very thin and hard, like dry fat.

There's hardly any weight to it, either; it's easy to lift. Inside, there's a blank page. No writing at all. But it flips back by itself, and—God's glory!

Just *look* at that!

It's all red and blue and gold. There are dragons and birds and towers and tiles. There's an angel stooping down from the clouds. A little old man sits at a desk, writing. He has a long beard and a wise, gentle face. At his feet is a great tawny beast. (A lion?) The lion is panting like a dog. Why is it there? Who is the old man? Has he tamed the lion? Is he really an angel?

If I could read, I would know. All the answers must be in these letters underneath. If I had the key to unlock these letters, I could step into the painting and meet the old man and find out about the lion. Without a key, the painting will never move or talk or welcome me in.

How I wish I could read.

Whoops!

I didn't hear him coming. He moves so quietly for such a big man. (Who, me? Touch your books? Never.)

"How fortunate it is that you're dressed as a boy," the priest says, shutting the door behind him. "It's made everything so much simpler." Turning, he catches my eye. "I've just said good-bye to the Abbess, so we can leave whenever we want. Before we do, however, we need to talk." He sits down on the bed, taking care to leave some distance between us. "Tell me who your mother is."

I wish he was still wearing that disguise he had on at the inn. Those heavy black robes he's wearing now — they're like the walls of a fortress. They make him look taller and stronger and grimmer, and as white as salt.

I can see why he put them back on before he went to meet the Abbess. Even an archbishop would think twice about lording it over someone carved out of alabaster who's as tall as a church spire and wearing a mantle trimmed with black velvet.

I don't know if I should talk about my mother.

"Is she one of the women living with you in that house?" he asks carefully.

"No." God forbid he should ever think that. "My mother is dead."

"Ah." A pause. "I'm sorry."

Well, so am I. But that's not going to solve anything.

He's smoothing his black robe over his knees.

"I, too, was orphaned at an early age," he finally says. "As was your father. We were both alone in the world."

"Oh, *I'm* not alone." (I come from a big family! A noble family!) "I have many aunts and uncles and cousins."

"Is that where you're going? To one of your aunts or uncles or cousins?"

"No." I can't decide. Should I tell him the truth? Would there be any harm in it? Probably not.

Besides, I've already said that I'm heading south. "I'm going to serve one of the *faidit* lords — maybe the Viscount of Carcassonne. He's with the King of Aragon now, and I'm going to offer him my loyal service."

The priest's hands stop moving. He might be startled, but I'm not sure; his face is hard to read. He looks up and studies me with pale, expressionless eyes.

"What kind of service do you intend to offer?" he inquires at last.

"I'll cook and clean and sew. I can spin and chop wood. I'll even fight if I have to."

He turns his attention back to his knees, and once more his hands start to move. Stroke, stroke, stroke. He's going to wear out the nap on that cloth if he's not careful.

"Who was your mother, Babylonne?" he says. "Who gave you that name of yours?"

What do you mean? "What's wrong with my name?"

"'Babylon the Great is fallen, is fallen, and is become the habitation of devils, and the hold of every foul spirit, and a cage of every unclean and hateful bird.'"

Huh?

"'O daughter of Babylon, who art to be destroyed: happy

83

shall he be that rewardeth thee as thou hast served us.'" The priest stops chanting and resumes speaking in his normal voice. "Have you never heard these words? They are the words of King David and John the Divine. They are words from the Holy Scriptures." He flashes me a quick glance. "Can you read, Babylonne?"

"Of course not!" What do you think I am, a monk? "And if you want to know about my name, well . . ." A habitation of devils? A hold of every foul spirit? It's worse than I thought. (How they must have hated me!) "Well, I . . . I should never have been born, in case you don't realize. My body *is* an unclean cage, entrapping a fragment of the angelic spirit, which is exiled here in the abode of the Devil until death and the mercy of God should release it."

Briefly, he closes his eyes. I should have realized that he was very learned. He probably knows the Holy Scriptures by heart.

Even the bad bits of the Holy Scriptures, which aren't really holy at all.

"Is there something about a Babylonian exile in the Holy Scriptures?" It seems an odd question, but I have to find out. "My grandmother used to talk about a Babylonian exile before she lost most of her teeth, and . . . well . . ." I'm afraid that it can't be denied, unfortunately. "I don't really know what she was talking about."

The priest sighs. He doesn't seem to want to answer. Instead he says, "Who is your grandmother, Babylonne?"

My grandmother? For your information, Master Redhead, my grandmother is one of Languedoc's great ladies.

"My grandmother is Blanche de Laurac, widow of Lord Sicard."

Of course, I'm expecting some kind of reaction. You don't often find the granddaughter of a noble lord skulking around the Bourg in boy's clothes.

Even so, the priest's response is quite a surprise. His face loses so much color, it's hardly even white anymore. The shadows under his eyes look almost green.

"You're—you're not Mabelia's daughter?" he gasps.

What?

We stare at each other. I can't believe my ears. But I recover my breath before he does and manage to speak—though I have to clear my throat first.

"Did you know my mother?"

He rises abruptly, goes to the window, and puts one hand on the wall, as if to steady himself.

When he murmurs something, I can't quite make out what it is. Except that it's probably Latin.

"What do you know about my mother?" Well? *Well?* "You have to tell me!"

He turns and retraces his steps. Though his expression is blank, he lowers himself back onto the bed as if his knees are troubling him.

"How old are you, Babylonne?" he asks hoarsely.

"Me? I was born on the same day that a hundred and forty Good Christians were burned by Simon de Montfort in Minerve." Not that this means anything to him. He simply looks dazed. (What would a Roman priest know about our sufferings?) So I have to explain further. "I'm sixteen. Nearly seventeen."

He stares at me, but I don't think he sees me. He's working something out in his head.

When he's finished, he remarks, "I thought you must be older. I thought—I thought it must have happened before I met him—"

"Did you know my mother?"

"Yes." It's almost a groan. He drops his gaze to the floor. "I knew your mother."

"How?"

"We traveled with her from Laurac to Lavaur, your father and I. About eighteen years ago, after escaping the siege of Carcassonne."

86

After what?

"You were at the siege of Carcassonne?" I don't believe it. "But you are a foreigner! You *look* like a foreigner!"

He shakes his head. "No," he says. "I grew up not far from here. Near Pamiers."

"But—"

"I was your father's scribe. We fought with the Viscount of Carcassonne—the *former* Viscount—and then we escaped when Carcassonne fell to the French, and made our way to Laurac. To your grandmother's household." He seems to be having trouble getting air into his lungs. "Then the French came to Laurac, so we had to flee again," he continues. "We were making for Montpellier, your father and I, and we couldn't take the direct route because the French were in our way. We had to go around their line of battle, via Lavaur. We were delayed at Lavaur. . . . Has no one ever told you this?"

It's like an accusation.

"No one ever had to tell me." (So go eat dogs and die, why don't you?) "I know all that I need to know."

"Which is what, exactly?"

"Which is that my father raped my mother!"

He recoils, and his eyes widen.

87

"Oh, no," he chokes. "No, you must believe me—Pagan never did that!"

"He did!"

"He did not, Babylonne. I knew him. He would never have harmed any woman, in any way."

Ha! "You mean he *didn't* hurt my mother by abandoning her while she was carrying his child?" (You venomous servant of the Lord of Lies!) "Maybe you'd better tell *her* that! Oh, but you can't. Sorry. Because she's *dead!*"

He covers his face with one hand. Is it all an act? Surely he must be well aware that his wonderful friend and master was a suppurating wound on the stinking right buttock of sinful humanity?

Perhaps not.

He knew my mother, though. He can tell me . . . more. Apart from how good she was. And how cruelly used. And how holy.

The way Navarre talks about her, you wouldn't think she was flesh and blood at all.

"You have to understand," he suddenly says, uncovering his face, "that your father was not himself. He—he had lost a very dear friend at Carcassonne. He was full of grief. I think he would not have done what he did, had he not . . ."

The priest trails off, as if he can't find the strength

to finish his sentence. It's necessary to give him a kind of verbal nudge.

"Had he not what?" Pressing hard. "Tell me."

"Had he not been in very great need of comfort," says the priest, forcing it out.

Hmmph. "So because he needed comfort, he raped my mother."

"*No!*" The retort is so sharp, it makes me jump. He brings his hand down, hard, onto the bed. "Your mother was in love with him."

What?

You devil.

"That's a lie!"

"Shh."

"You're a *liar!*" You—you— "My mother was *good!*"

"I know. I know she was. Babylonne, I knew her." Each word falls from his mouth like a feather or a snowflake. He casts the net of his speech as if he's scattering rose petals. "She was lovely and sweet and kind. Humble. Obedient. In need of love and support. Your grandmother . . ." A pause, as his gaze fastens on my nose. "Is Blanche the one who beats you, Babylonne?"

I can't help touching my bruise. Ouch!

"No. She's not."

89

"Well, she used to beat your mother. She was very strong and . . . shall we say, certain in her mind? She knew what she wanted. She wanted your mother to be a . . ." Again he hesitates, searching for the right word. Go on, say it. Say *heretic*. And watch me stick my scissors into your guts.

"She wanted your mother to become as she was," he proceeds delicately, glancing away. "A ministrant of your beliefs."

Hmmph.

"Your mother tried to please her, Babylonne. Always, in everything. But her heart betrayed her."

Her heart betrayed her. What a beautiful phrase.

I wish I could speak like this priest. I wish I could use my voice like a *vielle* and play music upon it. He's as good as a *jongleur*. "When the French drove us from Laurac, we went first to Castelnaudary," the priest narrates. "Your grandmother remained there, but she sent us on to Lavaur, to be with your aunt Guiraude. To seek her protection. While we were in Lavaur . . ."

He stops, looking tired and drawn.

Well? Continue!

"I was mistaken in my beliefs," he admits. "I knew that they—that your father and mother shared a deep affection. But I thought it was chaste. I'm sure it would have been, had Pagan not been . . . that is to say, had he been more himself." The priest rubs his high forehead in a distracted manner. "I do know that he wanted your mother to come with us. He didn't want her to stay in Lavaur; he told me this several times. I believe it was his intention that she should accompany us to Montpellier and enter a nunnery there. Something of the sort. I had no idea . . ."

"That my mother was raped?"

These are all lies. This can't be true.

"No," he says quietly. "She was not raped. I saw them together. There was no fear. No anger or shame. There was only sorrow, and respect, and tenderness."

"She *said* she was raped!"

"Well, of course she did." For the first time he sounds impatient. "Have some sense, Babylonne. What else could she have said, once the evidence was in her belly? Think about it. She only confessed to her transgression after we were gone. After there was no concealing it. Why? Why not bring down all the curses of Heaven on Pagan's head *before* we were out of reach? Why was Pagan never accused of raping her to his face? While we were still at Lavaur?"

Because . . . because . . . um . . .

"I swear to you, Babylonne, they had nothing but devotion, each for the other. He was wrong to do what he did, but he offered her no violence. There was no violence in him. And he would have taken her away, had she agreed to come. Had she not been so afraid of her mother and her sister and the world." The priest shakes his head, in grief and pity. He's so desperately gaunt, you can practically see his skull beneath his skin. "She was a timid soul," he observes. "As fine and frail as a spider's web. Pagan took her under his wing, much as he did me; we were both lost souls. He gave her strength, I think, but not enough. She couldn't act. She felt too guilty. She couldn't save herself." The priest looks up. "Not like you, Babylonne."

What do you mean? What are you saying? I can't—I'm not—

I won't cry. I *won't* cry. Not in front of a Roman priest.

"What happened to her?" he inquires, so gently that it makes the tears burn behind my eyes. "Did she die when you were born?"

I can't speak. I want to, but I can't.

"I'm sorry," he says. "This is a hard thing for you."

"It's not hard." I'm strong. I'm *toulousainne.* I can talk, even if my voice *is* squeaky. "My mother died a glorious martyr's death." (So there!) "She was killed with all the other Perfects after the siege of Lavaur. Simon de Montfort cut her throat." Seeing the priest swallow, I drive the point home. "That was after he hanged my uncle Aimery and threw my aunt Guiraude down a well and stoned her to death."

The priest says something else in Latin—something abrupt and urgent, like steam hissing from a covered pot. He takes a deep breath.

"I didn't know this," he says. "We didn't know this, Babylonne. We heard that the French had taken Lavaur, but we hoped—we thought . . ." He crosses himself, sending a shiver down my back.

When he starts to recite a prayer, I can't be polite any longer.

"My mother wouldn't want your prayers!"

"Are you sure?" He doesn't seem offended. He speaks calmly. "You didn't know her, Babylonne."

"And whose fault is that? It's the fault of the Roman church, which sent French knights here to kill all the Good Christians, and trample the land, and conquer the true lords of Languedoc, all in the name of a false god!" Suddenly it occurs to me that I'm in a convent, thanks to the priest's quick glance at the door. I suppose I'd better lower my voice. "But we will never submit." (Whispering now.) "The

93

Count of Toulouse will never submit—no, nor the Viscount of Carcassonne, nor Olivier de Termes, nor any of the *faidit* lords! They will fight, and I will fight alongside them. The French will never be our masters, even if we have to kill every Frenchman who comes here and send their heads back to the King, their master, on the pikes of our armies!"

I might as well be throwing pebbles at a fortress wall. My words just seem to bounce off the priest's pale, motionless features.

He's watching me like an owl, without blinking.

"We'd better go," he says after a while. "If we leave now, we should reach Braqueville by nightfall. Perhaps even Muret."

"*Muret?*" If we had wings, perhaps. I'm trying to think. Muret? That's past Portet. "It was daybreak when we left Toulouse, and the bells were ringing for terce when we got here. We have to get back to Toulouse, then go around it, and then from Toulouse to Muret it has to be half a day's walk at *least*—"

"We'll be riding, not walking," he interrupts, and climbs to his feet. Gazing down at me, he adds, "I bought you a horse. From the Abbess."

Huh?

"Come." He jerks his chin. "You can help me pack."

✝CHAPTER EIGHT✝

What a day it's been.

First the escape. Then the shock of the priest. Then the nunnery. And now the horse.

I can't believe that I'm actually sitting on a horse. A living, breathing brown palfrey with a leather saddle on its back.

Not that you could really call it *sitting*. Slipping and sliding, maybe. Bumping and swaying. Holding on for dear life, because I've never ridden a horse before. No one's ever considered me good enough for a horse.

Yet the priest bought me one to ride on. This is what I can't understand. Why would he do such a thing? It must have cost him at least three *livres tournois.* Perhaps more. And how much will it cost to feed? And shelter? And—

Whoops!

Almost slipped off sideways.

You see, this is why I haven't been able to talk. This is why I've hardly even noticed where we are. The moment I stop concentrating and start looking around at the scenery—bang!

I find myself dangling off the stirrup like a loose strap.

Perhaps it's just as well, though. If I'd had my wits about me while we were skirting Toulouse, I would have had a very sweaty time of it. I would have been terrified that someone might start pointing and shouting: *There she is! The thief! The heretic thief! She stole money and scissors and a good pair of fur-lined boots!* Luckily, though, I was so worried about keeping more or less upright that I hardly spared a thought for what might be happening inside the city walls.

And now here we are, past Braqueville already.

I remember this stretch of road. We came this way from Laurac last year. I remember all the vineyards (so many vineyards!), and the river flats, and the distant, gentle hills, and the river—so *clean* here, upstream from Toulouse, with its ducks and its reeds and a fallen tree that's damming its flow. (Someone really should clear that away.) But when we came this way from Laurac, the day wasn't bright and clear. And there weren't any white butterflies or starry flowers or perfumed breezes. The trees weren't basking in the sun like lizards, and the river wasn't chuckling away as if it were guarding a happy secret. At least, I don't think it was.

Perhaps I'm wrong. Perhaps the land *was* smiling, but I just didn't notice, because I was with Gran and Navarre. When you're with them, nothing ever seems joyous or beautiful. Nothing in *this* world, anyway.

Whoops!

"You must grip with your knees, Babylonne," the priest advises, reaching across to steady me. He keeps saying that, but it's all right for him; he has long legs. My legs are sticking out like roof beams, because they're so short and this horse is so wide. How am I supposed to grip with my knees when they're on top of the horse's back, instead of hanging down against its flanks?

"Use your stirrups to help you," the priest adds. "Remember what I said?" He speaks kindly, and his expression is calm, but I know that he must be laughing inside. He's such a good rider; he must scorn anyone who can't even sit on a horse. Look at the way he moves, as if his bottom half is separate from his top half. Well, he shouldn't be riding anyway. True pilgrims shouldn't ride; they should walk. He says that he's riding because it's too dangerous to walk across this country at present, but that's just an excuse. He's riding because he's a Roman priest, and Roman priests are greedy and luxurious and always attentive to their own comfort. What true pilgrim, for example, would burden himself with three books on his journey?

If he's worried about the trip being dangerous, he should have left those books behind. You might as well be wearing an archery target on your back. Even one of those books would buy any passing brigand a perfectly good fortified farm with attached vineyard and fruit trees.

But the priest would never part with his books. Oh, no, he says—they were a gift from Father Pagan. Another lame excuse. He claims that he loved the books' owner, but I'll wager it's the books themselves that he really loves. Why not? How could anyone bear to part from that glorious picture of the old man and the lion? It would be like abandoning your own stained-glass window into Heaven.

For all I know, those books never did belong to my father. For all I know, the priest is lying. All priests are liars. And fornicators. And murderers. That's why I have to be so careful with this one. Though he might *seem* kind, he's almost certainly pretending.

I can't afford to relax my guard for an instant. He's always watching me, too. I've noticed that. I'll glance at him and he'll be gazing off at a distant flock of sheep or a toiling serf, but I can tell that he's only just looked away from me. Perhaps he's worried that I'm going to fall off my horse. On the other hand, there might be another reason. A more sinister reason.

He's sitting there now as if he got lost on his way to Heaven—as if he wouldn't know a sin if it came up and introduced itself in a loud voice. He was right when he said that I should be the one in disguise. No one could mistake him for anything but a priest, even in artisan's clothes. It's something about his somber face. And his quiet voice. And the way he keeps his arms against his sides. It's something about his hands, which are long and smooth and graceful: a priest's hands. Only his hair looks out of place. Too boisterous and noisy. Though it's hidden by his hood, at the moment.

I should have brought a hat with me. It's awfully hot in this sun.

"We must buy you a hat," says the priest, and my heart almost drops through my belly, I get such a shock. Can he see into my head? Can he read my thoughts? "I know what pain the sun can inflict," he adds. "Even on Moorish skin like yours."

What's that? Moorish skin? "What do you mean?"

He raises his eyebrows. "Your father was an Arab," he explains. "Didn't you know? He came from the Holy Land."

I don't understand. "You—you mean he went there? To fight the Infidels?"

"No, no. He was born there. He was a Christian Arab. He fought Saladin before he traveled to Languedoc—oops!" His hand shoots out, and he grabs my arm. "Don't lose your balance, now."

"He fought Saladin?" I don't believe it. "How?"

"He was squire to a Templar knight. He was born in Bethlehem. Don't you know this?"

Of course I don't! How could I, if I never knew my father? I'm waiting, now—waiting for more—but the priest stops speaking. What shall I do? I want to hear more. I want to hear more without asking for more. I don't want to seem too inter-ested in my fornicating father, who really isn't worthy of my attention. Even if he *didn't* rape my mother, he certainly went off and left her. Alone.

Besides, I don't know what to call this priest. I can't call him "Father." He's not my father, and I don't believe in calling Roman priests "Father," anyway; they don't deserve that much respect. He says that he's a doctor of canon law—a teacher from the University of Bologna, north of Rome. So maybe I should call him "Doctor," as his students do.

"Um . . ." What should I say? I want to ask about my father without seeming to ask about him. What kind of a priest was he? One of those fighting priests? "Um . . . When Simon de Montfort killed my mother, many priests helped him." (Priests like my father, perhaps?) "There are many Roman priests who would rather fight than pray."

"I fear so," says the priest with a sigh. Mmmm. How odd. I didn't expect him to agree with me.

That's all he's going to do, though. Agree with me. He isn't going to comment, not without a prod.

"When Simon de Montfort besieged Lavaur, the Bishop of Paris was with him." Hint, hint. "And the Archdeacon of Paris, who built Simon's siege machine."

The priest frowns. "How do you know this?" he asks.

101

"I was there."

"You were *there*?"

"I was only a baby. I don't remember. But I was told about it. The garrison was murdered, and all the Perfects as well, but they let the rest of us go. Riscende de Castanet brought me back to Toulouse and passed me on to my grandmother." (Sometimes I wonder why she bothered.) "It was a great battle, you know. The siege at Lavaur lasted a month. Once the French pushed an armored tower up to the castle moat and tried to fill the moat with wood and branches. But my uncle Aimery dug a tunnel that reached almost to the tower, and one night he came and took all the wood and branches back into the castle." You have to laugh, when you think about it. "He also threw burning flax and fat and other things at the tower, to make it catch fire. But the French put the fire out. They smoked the tunnel. They won, in the end. They cut a hole in the castle wall." God curse them and all their offspring for eternity.

"I am very sorry, Babylonne," says the priest.

Ha! If you were really sorry, you would have stayed and fought. Like the rest of us. "We had our revenge, though. Don't think that they weren't punished, those French." Toulouse would never bow to

102

anyone for long—not even Simon de Montfort. "Those murderers came into Toulouse, and they took everything of value, and they tore down the walls and knocked the tops off the towers, and they put many citizens in chains. But when I was six, and again when I was seven, the French were massacred in the streets of the city. I remember it well. All the people came out of their houses with mauls and axes and mattocks and sickles. They built barricades out of coffers and planks and rafters from their roofs. They chopped up the French like cabbage and skewered them like pigs. They dragged them behind horses to the gallows and strung them up at every street corner." I remember the blood. So much blood that you were stepping in pools of it. Falling over in it. "There was a man—he had his chest cut open. I could see everything in there. He stank. They all stank. Their bowels emptied when they died . . ."

He's staring at me. A fixed, frozen stare. He looks like a ghost.

"What is it?" Stop gawping! "What have I done?"

"Nothing, I . . . nothing." His gaze drops, and he wipes his hand across his face. "Forgive me. Yours has been a hard and bloody life. I am sorry for it; indeed I am."

"Salve! Pater!"

Who's that? Who's calling? Ah—I see. Over there, on that bank. Sitting under that tree.

Two monks. Two friars, in fact. Tonsured Dominicans, in grubby white and black, eating bread and cheese and drinking from a wineskin. One has a bandage around his head and a bruised cheek.

Someone must have attacked him. (With any luck.)

"Salvete," the redheaded priest replies, and launches into a tangle of Latin. The injured friar doesn't speak; he's too busy stuffing his gullet. The other one has gray hair and a brown, cheerful, dusty face. I think his name must be Durand. That's what the redhead keeps calling him, anyway.

I can't understand what else he's saying, though. Except "Compostela." And "Muret." Muret is mentioned several times. There's also a lot of hand waving: to the south, to the north, to the west.

"And where did you come from, boy?" Durand suddenly asks me, in pure *langue d'oc.* "You have the look of a Moor about you."

"I found him in Toulouse," the priest says quickly, before I have a chance to reply. (Not that I could ever bring myself to speak to a Dominican.) "He is a good servant, this one. Very good."

"Is he? I'm surprised," says Durand in a jesting tone. "There are so few good servants in Toulouse. A very proud city, full of proud people. They are always defying the church. When Father Dominic founded his priory there, the brothers were much troubled by demons."

Very proud people! That's good, coming from a Dominican. Dominicans think that they lead God around on a rope.

"Indeed," says the priest, flicking a glance in my direction. "Well, that is much to be regretted. But I myself met Father Dominic once, when I was very young. A great and holy man."

The friars are thrilled. They jump to their feet and approach the priest's horse. They start talking about Prouille and nuns and preaching and "heretics," while I sit here biting my tongue and blinking back tears. How can I go on with this priest? How can I share food with a man who reveres Dominic Guzman?

I, too, met Dominic once, Master Skinny-Priest. When I was very young.

And he wasn't so hospitable to me.

"What troubles you, boy?" Durand suddenly inquires. (Curse it! He's noticed my wet eyes!) "Are you sorry to leave your home? Be of good cheer, for you are going to a far better place. Compostela is a city blessed by God. Not like Toulouse. Toulouse is a place of pits and snares, of sin and desolation."

A nudge from the priest's foot. But I can't stop myself. I just can't.

"Only because there are so many friars in it."

Oh, dear. I shouldn't have said that. Two jaws drop. Two pairs of eyes nearly spring from their sockets and bounce off my horse's fetlocks.

"Benoît!" the priest says to me sharply. The torrent of Latin that follows is directed at the friars, who are pushing their jaws shut and blinking their eyes back into their skulls. Having offered his excuses (for that's what they probably are, all those long and elaborate arrangements of words), the priest turns to me. "Beg the Holy Fathers' pardon," he orders.

What?

"Do it. Now." His voice is hard and cold. His face is like chiseled granite. "Or you'll be walking the rest of the way."

Is he serious? I can't tell. But maybe he's right. I'm behaving like Sybille. No point baiting a trap with your own leg.

"Forgive me, Holy Fathers." Whoops! That was a little too squeaky. A little too girlish.

But the priest puts a hand to his ear.

"What was that?" he says, each word chipped from a block of flint. "I didn't hear you."

"Forgive me, Holy Fathers, and have mercy on a humble sinner, that I might walk in the way of the Lord."

It almost sticks in my throat, but I manage to push it out. Hoarse and low. Durand doesn't look the least bit mollified. He sniffs, and there's another endless exchange of Latin.

Come on, you stupid priest! Let's go!

As we finally move away, the friars remain standing on the road, looking after us. They put their heads together and pass a few comments. The priest twists in his saddle; he smiles, nods, lifts a hand. He doesn't lose his balance or speak to me or even glance in my direction. I think he must be waiting until we round the next corner and are lost from sight.

Yes, I thought so. Here it comes. I can *feel* it coming.

"Are you insane?" It bursts out of him like juice out of a grape. Nevertheless, he sounds more astonished than angry. "What's the matter with you? Do you want to be discovered?"

Oh, go and boil up your books with basil.

"If they had found out that you were a heretic,

107

they would have followed us to Muret, preaching every step of the way," he continues, glancing over his shoulder. "I had to tell them that your mother once begged from a friar in the street and was rebuffed—because the friar, of course, had no money of his own, being a firm believer in holy poverty. I had to tell them that you are as faithful to the true Church as I am. Let's hope that they believed me."

I'm already beginning to feel ashamed. He's right; it was stupid. Stupid. I could get myself killed doing something like that. What's the matter with me?

"The friars are good men, Babylonne. They eat the poorest foods; they walk everywhere; they preach; they own nothing—they are like the men you call Perfects." He's holding my reins, steadying my horse. "They are worthy of your respect."

"Them!" Don't insult me! "They're not worthy of my spit!"

"Babylonne—"

"Your precious Dominic—do you know what he did? He stood by while Simon de Montfort cut my mother's throat!" That's news to you, isn't it? Yes. I can tell from your face. "He stood by while my aunt was stoned to death!"

"Oh, no." He speaks slowly. Carefully. "I can't believe that."

"Believe it! He was there! He was there at the siege of Lavaur, with Bishop Fulk of Toulouse, whose soul will breed maggots for all eternity! Riscende de Castanet saw them both!"

"But Dominic Guzman was a man of peace. . . ."

"Oh, yes, very peaceful! He was at Muret, too, you know! The battle of Muret? When Simon de Montfort slaughtered the militia of Toulouse? When he killed the last King of Aragon? Dominic was there! I know, because Alamain de Rouaix lost a cousin—or was it a nephew? Anyway, Simon de Montfort chased them all into the river to drown, and Dominic stood by and watched as they died. Dominic and that Devil's bastard, Fulk, may his bowels be blown out like water."

The priest is silent. He releases my reins and attends to his own, his features set into lines of strain and fatigue. At last he says, "You have a great memory for battles and sieges. Were you taught anything but these stories of bloodshed?"

"Yes." I might as well make this clear right now. "I was taught never to trust a priest. Or a monk. Or a northerner."

To my surprise, he doesn't get angry. He doesn't wince or even look my way. Instead a wry smile tugs at one corner of his mouth.

"Well," he says softly, scanning the horizon, "you can trust me when I tell you this: If you continue to insult passing friars, you will never reach your destination. Horse or no horse."

And he offers me a drink of wine.

‡CHAPTER NINE‡

Yeeeooooow!

Oh! Oh, *God*, this is bad! My knees! My backside!

"Take it slowly," says the priest. "That's it. . . ."

"Ow!"

"Hold on to me."

I can't believe how stiff I am. I can't even move properly. And someone's laughing, over there by the gate. Laughing at me. When he's the one with a face like a fresh cowpat!

"Hold *on*, I said." The priest is reaching out to help. "You'll fall. . . ."

Get off! Don't touch me! I can—

Whoops!

Down off the horse, and he catches me just in time. Ow! My knees!

"Are you all right?" he wants to know. If he wasn't holding me up, I'd be flat on my face. "Don't fret—you'll find that it gets easier. Your muscles will adapt."

Well, I certainly hope so. Help! Every step is *agony*.

"Can you walk on your own?" he asks. "I have to take the horses."

"I'm fine." Gruffly, so that I sound like a boy. (There are too many people listening. We ought to get out of here.) "Where are we going, anyway?"

The priest glances around. He seems hesitant, and I don't blame him: so far, Muret doesn't strike me as a very desirable destination. I remember passing it last year and thinking how impressive it looked from a distance, with its walls rearing up out of the marshy plains. At close quarters, however, you can see that it hasn't worn well. Though it's been fifteen years since the battle of Muret, a lot of scars remain: lopped towers, patched woodwork, gaps in the battlements. Everything has a dirty, run-down appearance—at least compared to Toulouse. The region around the East Gate is all soggy straw and lounging militia and discarded nutshells. You can hardly see the cobbles for the manure.

Wouldn't you think that they'd pick up their dead dogs occasionally?

"Those friars suggested the priory of Saint Gemer," the priest says in a low voice. "They mentioned that it's near the Toulouse Gate somewhere."

The priory of Saint Gemer! "We're not going there." Thank you very much. "Bishop Fulk stayed there during the siege."

"Bab—I mean, Benoît—"

"It was pounded by the Toulousian mangonel. *Pounded.* With huge boulders."

"Oh." The priest frowns, and I know exactly what he's thinking. He's thinking about leaky roofs and crumbling walls. "Saint Sernin, then. It's supposed to be near the citadel."

"Wait." By tugging at his sleeve, I can make him stoop until his eyes are nearly level with mine. "Must we stay in a cloister?" (Quietly.) "Can't we go to an inn?"

He shakes his head. "There would be more questions about me at an inn than there would be about you in a cloister," he murmurs. "There is also more privacy in a canons' guesthouse than in the loft of an inn. Only look—we're attracting attention already."

It's true. We are. (I blame the horses, which will

113

always attract a crowd in an out-of-the-way place like this. If you have a horse in Muret, you *must* be important.)

I can see the beggars converging.

"We'll go to Saint Sernin," the priest decides. "It's more likely to have decent stables."

Very well, then. If you say so. When we start to move, we're only just in time—because someone empties a bucket of slops from the parapet of the city wall. If we'd lingered, it would have hit us.

Someone else (that man in the green cloak, who looks like an interesting collection of unwashed root vegetables) laughs noisily. He scowls at my response.

"Benoît!" gasps the priest. "Where did you learn that gesture?"

"You mean the sign of the pike up the—"

"Shh! Behave yourself."

He sets a course through the Chatelet, weaving between heaps of flyblown dung, turning right and right again until we reach the next gate. And here we are in the marketplace, which is long and narrow and set directly under the eastern wall of the city. At this time of day, there's nothing much in it. Except for the squashed grapes and pig mess and urchins with sticks.

The urchins all stop what they're doing to gawk at us.

"This is such a one-church town." Look at them all. No one in Toulouse stares at strangers like that; we might as well be in Laurac. "You'd think we had udders growing out of our ears."

"Shh!" says the priest.

Ahead lies an inner wall with a gate—rather like the Portaria in Toulouse, only smaller. Even the garrison militia on the battlements are staring down at us. You can tell that they aren't real soldiers. They must be bakers and cutlers and wool carders and rope makers, doing their garrison duty in borrowed leather and horn. Real soldiers wouldn't take their eyes off the city approaches for an instant.

One of them spits, and his spittle lands suspiciously close as we plod past house after house with big cracks in their walls.

"Saint Sernin might not be a wealthy foundation," the priest remarks softly, and it's obvious that he's looking at the cracks too. "I'll ask for cells to sleep in, but there may only be dormitories." He glances down at me and in a dry voice adds, "I'll say that I must have my own quarters, because I spend all night in prayer and self-mortification and will keep you awake if we share a room."

115

Prayer and self-mortification? Oh, no. Not another Dulcie.

"What is it?" he says. "What are you looking at me like that for?"

"You . . ." Let's see. How shall I put it? "You don't go around beating yourself with a willow switch, do you?"

"I don't make a habit of it, no."

"Or wearing prickly undergarments?"

The priest regards me for a moment. "You disapprove?" he finally asks.

"Oh, well . . . not really." It's good and pious behavior, I suppose. "I just don't like washing clothes that have blood all over them."

"Ah."

"I mean, I'll have to wash *your* clothes, won't I? If I'm your servant?"

He blinks and raises his eyebrows. "I don't know," he says slowly. "I hadn't thought."

"Well . . . I wouldn't worry about it. Not yet. They look pretty clean to me." That hem, for instance, can be brushed. "You probably won't need anything washed for another two weeks, if it doesn't rain."

"I see."

"Black's a good color, too. Not even blood shows up on black."

116

"Oh, there won't be any blood." He clears his throat. "You must understand that any reference to self-mortification would be purely a means of gaining for you your own private room. Personally, I find that flesh is torment enough without seeping scars. Or scratchy drawers."

Hear, hear. My own flesh is *killing* me. But I have to keep walking; I have to hobble through the inner gate and turn right—because there's no street leading straight up to Saint Sernin. Though I can see the church tower over the roofs in front of us, getting to it will be a matter of following the line of the outer defenses. Otherwise we're going to get lost.

There's a woman (a wet nurse?) sitting on an upturned bucket, suckling a baby in a small patch of late-afternoon sun. She glares at the priest as we go by, and I wonder: Is she a believer? Just in case she is, I'd better keep my head down. If she's a believer, she might have been to Laurac or Castelnaudary. She might know someone who knows someone who knows me.

The priest, for his part, doesn't notice the woman. Or doesn't *seem* to notice her, anyway— perhaps because her big, white breast is exposed to the air. Priests might be lecherous, but they know how to hide it. Mostly they behave as if women don't exist.

Ah! And here's a well. I was wondering when we'd reach one. You always find people sitting around a well, and in Muret it's no different; about ten people watch us trudge past, their chatter dying on their tongues. One or two of them bow slightly to the priest. A bareheaded girl whispers to her friend, who giggles.

Up ahead looms the citadel, throwing long, deep shadows across the square. It's not a big square. And the church isn't a big church. You could fit it inside Saint Etienne, only you wouldn't want to, because Saint Sernin is dull, dull, dull. Small windows. Lots of blank walls. Hardly a carving to be seen. The cloisters and chapels attached to it look like after-thoughts—like a collection of pigpens and fowl houses tacked onto the back of a shepherd's hut.

The priest stops.

"I can't see any canons around, can you?" he says. "They may be at worship, though I didn't hear any bells."

"You go in." Those people by the well are prob-ably listening, so I can't raise my voice above a murmur. "I'll stay here with the horses while you find someone."

He hesitates. He's frowning. I feel so much like snapping at him, but remember the eavesdroppers just in time. "I won't make off with the horses, if that's what you're worrying about." (Hissing through my teeth.) "I'm much too sore."

To my surprise, he actually smiles. "I'm not worried about the horses," he says quietly. "I'm worried about you. I'm worried about leaving you on your own."

Ha! A nice little lie, my friend, but you can't fool me. "In a town like this, I'll be safer on my own than with a priest." Or haven't you noticed? "Some of the people here don't like priests. I can tell. And the rest probably think that you're an easy target. Ripe for the plucking, I mean." He's gazing down at me with an arrested expression on his face— and I *wish* he'd stop doing that! "What? What is it?"

Another crooked smile. A little shake of the head.

"You can be so much like your father," he says.

He goes before I can recover my breath, shoving the reins into my hands and hurrying off across the square. Lying priest. I am *not* like my father! I might look like him (I must, if the priest recognized me), but I don't resemble him in any other way. I do *not*.

I'm like my mother. At least, I think I am. I must

be. Except that I'm not beautiful or virtuous or sweet-tempered. Navarre says that my mother would be ashamed of me, but I don't think that's true. I've dreamed about her sometimes, and she always speaks to me kindly—though I can never remember what she says. I can never remember what she looks like, either. No matter how hard I try, I can't see her face. There's always too much light, or too much shadow.

And what's this? An audience. Now that the priest's gone—now that he's vanished inside the church, like a wolf into its den—all the little scurrying animals can emerge again from their hidey-holes. Here's one. And there's another. Rat-faced gutter-creepers. Shaggy-headed street boys, dressed in rag girdles and scraps of old blanket and bits of discarded sacking.

They're both quite young. They don't have beards yet.

"Can I hold your horse?" says the smaller one, who's still a lot bigger than I am. I'll just ignore him. (Hold my horse? He must think that my brains are boiled!)

"Where are you from?" asks the larger one, who's got a wart on his cheek the size of a fortified farm. If I let drop a mouthful of nonsense, they might believe that I'm a foreigner speaking a foreign tongue, and shut the hell up.

"*Oodle-pargabarranturnis.*"

Sure enough, it works. They start talking to each other loudly, as if I'm not even here.

"I told you," says Wart-Face. "I told you he was foreign. See how dark he is."

"There are saddlebags," his friend replies. "On the gray palfrey."

Wart-Face nods and sidles away in a suspicious manner. His gap-toothed friend flashes me a big grin and strokes my horse's nose. "You—Catalan?" he asks, pointing at me. "You—Lombard?"

What's Wart-Face doing back there? Stay away from those books, you leprous little horsefly!

Gap-Tooth is still in my face. Trying to distract my attention. Trying to make me forget his friend. "You—blackamoor?" (Both of my hands are full of reins; I can't let go of either horse. One horse on each side, like towers on a gate, and what am I going to do? I'm anchored.) "You—Infidel?" Meanwhile, Wart-Face is behind me, fumbling in a saddlebag.

Time to fight, or they'll strip the horses clean.

My feet are my only defense. A quick kick in the groin, and Gap-Tooth's on his knees, yelping. Wart-Face nearly bolts with a book, but—whoops! He's too slow to turn. Not like me. The gray mare's reins come in handy; they slip over his head like a hangman's noose. One quick jerk and his feet fly out from under him.

He falls backward, almost onto my feet. His head hits the cobbles. The horses don't like it; they're skittish and toss their heads. Gap-Tooth is on his feet again, behind me, bent almost double. Wart-Face is rolling about on the ground, shielding his face from dancing hooves.

He's dropped the book, God curse him. As if it's a boot. As if it's a chewed bone, instead of a window into Heaven.

If that book gets trampled, I'm dead. The priest will kill me. I can't afford to mess around.

Gap-Tooth has to go. He's still bent double, so—*whack*—my knee slams up into his forehead. Ow! That's done him. I might be limping, but he's out of the fight. As for the other one, he's crawling away. A boot up the backside might get rid of him sooner.

"*Gaagh!*" he cries as my kick makes contact. Over by the well, someone says something—and the tone sounds very unfriendly.

Never mind. With a horse on each side of me, I'm practically indestructible.

"*Benoît?*"

It's the priest. He's calling from the church door. There are two men behind him, one of them another priest in a white robe.

Gap-Tooth begins to reel away on knees made of carded wool. Wart-Face staggers to his feet and runs. I must try to keep the horses away from that book.

"Guilabert Sagnator!" shouts the priest in white, shaking his fist at Gap-Tooth's retreating figure. *"You stay away, do you hear me?"* Turning to *my* priest—Isidore, the Doctor—he lowers his voice and says something that I can't quite hear from a distance.

I don't know if Isidore heard it, either. He's already striding toward me, his black robes billowing out behind him like a crow's wings. The priest in white (who's small and fat) has to run to keep up.

"Your book!" It comes out as a squeak before I can help myself. Lower your voice, Babylonne! "They tried to take your book. . . ."

Isidore puts a finger to his lips. He scoops up the book and tucks it back into his saddlebag.

"Ah, it is a great shame to us!" The priest in white catches up, coughing pitifully and holding his sides. "They would steal the"—cough-cough—"hair from a"—*cough-cough*—"dead man's head."

"Did they hurt you, Benoît?" Isidore wants to

123

know. He doesn't seem the least bit worried about his book. (After all the trouble I took to protect it!) "Did they attack you? No? But you're limping. You've injured your knee."

Before I can respond, the priest in white interrupts again.

"Bring him inside with us. Bruno"—*cough-cough*—"will take the horses. Bruno!" He barks at the third man, who must be a servant of some sort, to judge from the clothes he's wearing. They look as if they've spent several weeks in a goat's stomach. "Bruno, take the horses in. Go on! Give them some oats."

Bruno moves, but I can move faster. Those saddlebags aren't going with Bruno, not if they have books in them. I wouldn't trust Bruno as far as I could spew a bad mushroom.

"It's all right, Benoît." Isidore reaches out and peels my fingers off the leather stitching. "Leave them. You mustn't worry."

"But—"

"Trust me," he says.

And I'll have to, I suppose.

No matter how foolhardy it may seem.

‡CHAPTER TEN‡

A room of my own. I've never had one before.

Not that it's very big, or very fine. There's no lock on the door. The window doesn't have shutters. The bed is just a palliasse dumped on hard stone, with a couple of blankets tossed over it.

But there's a latch. And a chest. And a glazed piss-pot. And the priests have stretched some kind of pale cloth across the window to keep out the rain.

I can't believe that it's *mine*. All of it! For tonight, anyway.

I should put my things in this chest: my boots and my money and my scissors. The trouble is, this chest doesn't have a lock. And I wouldn't feel safe leaving my most precious possessions in an unlocked chest. Suppose someone gets in? The door will be latched, but suppose there's another entrance that I don't know about?

I think I'll sleep on my money. And my scissors. And my pepper. I don't want to sleep undefended.

Knock-knock-knock.

"Oh!" A visitor! My very first visitor. "Come in." It's the priest, of course. Isidore. He went off to find food, and now he's back with . . . What's that in his hands?

"Bread," he announces, laying a small, wrapped bundle on the chest. "Goat's cheese. And this is a jug of mulled wine."

Goat's cheese! "Is this . . . is this all for me?"

"It is. And I want you to eat it. You're much too thin."

Goat's cheese. I suppose it's no worse than a hen's egg. It wasn't killed, after all; why shouldn't I eat it?

"What's wrong?" he asks. (He must have been watching me again. The way he does. Like a hawk watching a fieldmouse.) "Don't you like goat's cheese?"

"I—I've never eaten cheese. Any kind of cheese."

"It's good. You'll like it."

"It's the product of fornication."

"Ah. Yes." He nods. "I remember. But it's Perfects who aren't allowed to eat such things, surely? And you're not a Perfect."

Good point. I'm not a Perfect. I'm not even in training. After all, Gran and Navarre were going to marry me off.

"I suppose it's all right." I won't contaminate them by eating cheese in their house. Not anymore. "I can eat cheese now because nobody minds." Except God, perhaps. Curse it. What should I do? "Some believers eat cheese. It's not good, but it's not . . . it's not really bad. I don't think."

"It seems to me, Babylonne, that God made cheese for one purpose only. I mean to say, you can't burn it, can you? Or wear it? Or build churches out of it?" Isidore sets the wine down carefully next to the bread. "There's nothing you *can* do with the stuff, except eat it."

You know what? He's right. It's *true*. What else can cheese possibly be for? Why would God have bothered to create cheese if no one were going to eat it?

Unless the Devil was responsible for cheese?

"I also brought you this," Isidore continues, dragging something out from under his arm. I didn't notice it before, but it's a kind of hood. A blue hood. "You must wear it tomorrow."

I don't believe this. He remembered. He said that he'd get me a hat, and he did.

It feels clean, too.

"Now," Isidore continues, calmly closing the door, "a few words about tonight before I leave you. We have to be circumspect. Do you understand? This isn't a big place, and if you leave this room, you're bound to run into someone. Someone who's curious. That's why I want you to stay here, no matter what."

Yes, yes. I understand.

"You must be exhausted, in any case," he says, using his gentlest voice. His prayer-before-bedtime voice. "It's been a long day. Did they give you a— um—a receptacle?"

"Yes." See? "It's over there."

"Good. So there's no need to come out until tomorrow morning." He puts his hand on the door latch. "I'm sorry, Babylonne, but it's safer this way. I wouldn't risk subjecting your disguise to close scrutiny."

Why not? "What's wrong with it?"

"Oh, my dear." He seems mildly amused, to judge from his half smile. "You're much too pretty to be a boy." The smile fades. "Except when you scowl like that, of course. When you scowl like that, you resemble a basilisk."

He turns to go. But I've just thought of something—wait!

"Wait!"

He stops. Looks around.

"Wait." Where's my purse? Ah. Here. "How much for the food?"

"What?"

"The food. How much do I owe you?"

Every trace of expression leaves his face. It takes on a familiar chiseled-stone look.

"The canons gave me that food," he replies flatly. "You owe me nothing."

"And the hood?"

"I bought the hood from one of the other guests. But it's a gift."

"How much did you pay?"

"It's a gift, Babylonne."

"Here." Here's a *Caorsin*. Probably more than the hood is worth, but I don't have anything smaller. "Here, take it."

Isidore doesn't reply. He simply looks away. Opens the door.

"If you don't take the money, I won't wear the

hood!" I'm not standing beholden to you, my friend. Not at any price. "I mean that! I do!"

He pauses. Thinks. When at last he turns back to me, he's doing his imitation of a church-door statue: hard, cold, immovable.

"What are you afraid of?" he says. "That I'll ask for something in return? You still think that of me?"

Maybe. How should I know?

"This is a gift, Babylonne. For your father's sake."

Ha! "I will accept *nothing* for my father's sake!"

This time it's frightening. This time he doesn't even blink—just stares at me with those pale, heavy eyes and slowly leans against the door until it shuts behind him, blocking my escape.

Oh, no. He's not going to beat me, is he?

Help!

"Do you know what your father did in Carcassonne?" he says, folding his arms.

As if I care what my father did in Carcassonne!

"He was a great man, Babylonne, and worthy of your respect. He went with the Viscount to plead with the French and rode back ahead of the French army at the Viscount's side," Isidore narrates. "He had the stalls torn out of the cathedral to build barricades and mangonels. He rallied the people when their hearts were failing, and fought them off with his tongue when they tried to steal water from the city wells. He would have drawn his sword in defense of Carcassonne, had he been able. But he was a little man, and not strong. Not strong in his body. His strength was in his spirit." Suddenly Isidore closes his eyes. His color changes; he looks quite gray. Is he going to faint? No. No, he's not going to faint. His eyes are open now.

"He would have gone with the Viscount and died in prison, had events not conspired against him," Isidore explains wearily. "Had the death of his friend not . . . not left him disabled, for a short time."

"His friend?" Oh! I know! "You mean the one he was still grieving for, when he went to Lavaur?"

"Yes. That one."

"Who was the friend?" I can't help being interested. I don't want to be, but—well, it's important, isn't it? It's important to find out. "Did you know him?"

"I knew him. He was Roland Roucy de Bram, Pagan's lord. Pagan served him in Jerusalem before Lord Roland entered a monastery."

A *monastery*? I don't understand this. These people—they were all monks. Priests. Servants of the Church of Rome. What were they doing fighting the French army? Fighting the Pope's own legate, who came here with that army?

And Bram. I know Bram. "I heard about the people of Bram." (Gran told me once. Or was it Bernard Oth?) "Simon de Montfort took one hundred of them and cut off their noses and their ears and their lips. He gouged out their eyes. Then he chained them together and sent them off to Cabaret, led by a man who'd been left with one eye for the purpose of guiding them."

Isidore sighs. "Yes," he says. "I heard about that, too."

"And their lord. Lord Jordan." Gran mentioned him, as well. "He died in prison. With the Viscount."

"Yes. Lord Jordan was Roland's brother."

"So my father was a *friend* of Lord Jordan?"

"Why do you think he was running from the French?" Isidore sounds so tired. "He was running because he was in danger. A traitor priest. Only God knows what would have happened to him had Simon de Montfort hunted him down."

Only God knows? Perhaps. But I can certainly guess what might have happened. "Probably the same thing that happened to the traitor priest of Montréal who helped my uncle Aimery." Simon de

132

Montfort didn't spare *him*. "He was dragged by the heels of a horse until his face was scraped off."

Isidore winces. "By the blood of the Lamb, girl, why do you dwell on these things?" he demands. "All these horrible things?"

Why? Why do you think? "Because they must be remembered. Always. Because they must be avenged."

"They will not make you happy, Babylonne."

"Happy?" When I shrug, he looks even more pained (if that's possible). "Who can be happy in Hell?"

"You think this world is Hell?" he says.

"It must be."

"Why?"

"Because . . ." Well, look around you! "It's a terrible place. It's the Devil's realm." And all the wonderful things in it—all the songs and the colors and the soft clothes and the sweet food—well, they must be lures. Lures of the Devil.

"Babylonne, this world is not Hell."

Now it's my turn to sigh. "Are you going to preach to me?" I knew it. "Is that what this is all about?"

"No. I'm not a preacher. I don't preach." He nods at the food on the chest: at the wine and the bread and the cheese. "But I am going to tell you a story.

Eat your meal, Babylonne, while I tell you a bed-time story."

"A *bedtime* story?"

"Why not? Have you anything else to do?"

No. Not at present. Even so . . . "If it's a story about some Roman saint, I don't want to hear it."

"It's not about a saint. It's about a knight. A golden-haired knight who went to Jerusalem to fight the Infidels." He settles more comfortably against the door, propping it shut with his shoulders. "Go on. Sit down, eat up, and I'll tell you."

Very well, then. It can't do me any harm. And I'm so *hungry*. That scrap of bread at midday—that wasn't enough.

Oh! How good this cheese smells!

"The golden-haired knight was a noble soul," says Isidore. "When he was only a few years older than you, Babylonne, he decided that he didn't want to kill people anymore. He didn't think it was a good thing, killing people. He didn't think it would bring him closer to God."

Mmmm! The cheese!

"So he went to an abbot, and the abbot sent him to fight for Jerusalem," Isidore relates. "But when he reached Jerusalem, he found that it was full of thieves and whores and lepers. He didn't understand why he should be fighting for them. That's why he joined the Order of the Temple. He became a Knight Templar because he thought that it would bring him closer to God—Babylonne, slow down! You'll choke!"

"It's good . . ." (Gulp.) "Good cheese . . ."

"It won't be if you choke on it. Always remember to chew before you swallow." He tries to recover his place. "Now. Where was I?"

"The Order of the Temple."

"Yes. The Order of the Temple. The knight became a Templar, and soon afterward, Saladin attacked Jerusalem. He besieged Jerusalem. And after a lot of hard fighting, Jerusalem finally fell." The priest's gaze is blank as he watches me lick my fingers. (No point wasting a crumb of this cheese!) "The defenders were afraid that Saladin would slaughter them all," he adds. "But that didn't happen. Instead an agreement was reached about ransoms. As long as they could be ransomed, the Christians were free to leave."

"What about the poor people?" Poor people like me, for instance. "What happened to them?"

"They were ransomed, too. The noble knight emptied the Templar coffers to pay money for the poor. And he decided that he wouldn't ransom himself, because his ransom would save the lives of ten women. Or fifty children. He decided to sacrifice his one life to save fifty others."

Really? Is that true? But that's so noble. It's like something out of a *jongleur*'s tale; like a sermon about a saint. How could any falsehearted Roman have been so good? "Did—did Saladin kill him?"

"No." Isidore shakes his head. "Your father pleaded for the knight's life. He threw himself on his knees before Saladin and used that nimble tongue of his to free Lord Roland."

Ah. It was Roland, then. Lord Roland Roucy de Bram was the golden-haired knight.

"Your father told me that story a long time ago," Isidore murmurs. "It happened when he was a squire, before Lord Roland threw his sword away and became a monk. Lord Roland had learned, you see, that there can be no salvation through the shedding of blood. That there can be no peace from war." All at once, Isidore unfolds his arms. He shifts his weight and pulls the door open. (Don't tell me he's leaving?) "Please try to remember that, Babylonne. It's very important."

And he's gone. Like a puff of smoke. Before telling me the rest! I want to know—did my father kill anyone? Did he become a monk as well? And if so, how did he end up as Archdeacon of Carcassonne?

Oh, well, I don't care. Why should I care about my father? He didn't care about me.

Of course, he didn't actually *know* about me, but . . . anyway, it doesn't matter. I've finished my meal now. I think I'll go to bed.

To bed. In my very own room. When I blow out the candle, I'll be able to imagine that I'm anywhere in the world, from the richest chamber to the lowest cell. Because there won't be anyone nearby snoring or farting or fidgeting to remind me where I *really* am.

For the first time ever, I'll be able to dream exactly what I want.

Off with the boots first. Where shall I put them? Inside the chest? Under the blankets, perhaps. At the bottom of the bed. That way, I'll be keeping them within reach.

Next, off with the hose. And my girdle. I should probably sleep on my hose.

Knock-knock-knock.

What in the name of—?

"Who is it?"

A voice replies from the other side of my door.

"It's me. Father Isidore. I'm sorry. There's something I forgot to give you."

And what might that be, exactly? I don't like the sound of this. It's getting dark outside. I can hardly see.

"Please don't be concerned." Isidore's tone is apologetic. "I'm not going to attack you. You have your pepper, do you not? I shan't even come in."

He's right. I have my pepper. And my scissors. He won't be expecting them.

I can feel the weight of the scissors in my right hand as I unlatch the door with my left. And slowly drag it open.

He's in the corridor outside, bearing a tallow candle. It throws strange shadows across his hollow cheeks and deep-set eyes.

"Gloria Patri et Filio!" he exclaims, crossing himself. He's staring at my bare legs. "What happened to you?"

What? Oh, that.

"That was my aunt. She threw scalding water at me."

He mutters something else in Latin before saying, "No wonder you think the world is Hell."

"What do you want?" I'm not going to call you

138

Father. I'm not going to call you anything. "You said that you had something for me."

"Yes. This." He opens his hand, and there's a plait in it. A small, dark plait of hair. "This belonged to your mother," he says quietly. "She gave it to your father, and he gave it to me. It's a lock of hair that she cut from her head. As a gift for him. Before he left."

A lock of—?

Oh, no. It can't be.

"Take it. Go on." He's letting it dangle. "You must take it, Babylonne; it's your inheritance. Who else should rightfully have it? You are your father's true heir, not I. So take it."

It sits in my palm like a feather.

"When you can read," he says, "I'll give you the books as well. But only then. Your father would not want you to sell them—and they're of no use to you at present." He waits, but I can't speak. So he steps back. "Good night," he whispers. "Sleep well."

And he drifts away like a shadow, down the long, stone corridor, taking the light with him. All of a sudden everything's dark. I can hardly see my hand, let alone what it's holding. My mother's hair. *My mother's hair.*

He kept it. All those years, and my father kept it. Could he—could he have loved her after all? Really loved her? If he took her hair, maybe he would have taken her with him, too. Had she truly wanted to go.

The plait feels so soft in my clenched fist. I don't want to crush it, but I have to be careful. I don't want to lose it in the dark. One puff of air as I shut the door, and it could blow away.

The hinges creak. The latch drops. There—I'm safe. I'm alone with my mother's hair. Plaited in the middle, bound at either end. Each end finishing in a little silken brush.

The feathery lock touches my jaw like a kiss. Like my mother's soft cheek. They smell of lavender. . . . Oh, no. No, I can't cry. Not here. Not now.

Someone might be listening.

‡CHAPTER ELEVEN‡

"It will get better," says the priest. "Every day, it will get a little better."

Is that supposed to cheer me up? Each time the horse moves, a jolt of pain shoots through my knees. There are red-hot skewers in my thighs, and as for my buttocks—I don't even want to think about them.

What's the good of knowing that things will get better in the future? I want them to get better *now*!

I wasn't made to ride a horse. I don't think I have the right build. Isidore's different: he's tall, with long arms and legs. His wrists are strong, and so is his back. No wonder he has such an easy time of it.

"You're improving," he adds, making a feeble attempt to encourage me. "I can see it already. The way you're sitting—it's much better."

The way I'm sitting? You mean, the way I'm sitting as if someone's poking me in the spine with a sharpened lance? (That's what it feels like, anyway.)

"We must be grateful for the weather," Isidore points out. "Think how much worse this would be if it were raining!"

Yes. Let's think about that. Let's think about *something* besides the pain in my hips. If there were rain, it would be worse. If there were snowy mountains, it would also be worse. But the mountains are a long way ahead. Everything hereabouts is flat, flat, flat. River flats. Marshlands. Fields of barley. The occasional wooden bridge, like the one that we crossed this morning in front of Muret. We were so late getting out of Muret. Isidore blamed the canons of Saint Sernin ("Talkative" was his only comment), but I know that I was partly responsible. We would have left earlier if I'd been able to move more quickly. If my joints hadn't been so stiff and sore.

This isn't going to work. There's not enough distraction in the sluggish river, or the clumps of

142

trees, or the half-cleared meadows. I'll have to think of something else.

"Why did you bring that lock of hair?" If I don't speak, I'll scream instead—and there's only one subject that springs to mind. "Why did you bring it on pilgrimage with you?"

A brief silence. Isidore is staring straight ahead as if fascinated by the distant, smoky horizon. "I brought everything that your father gave me," he replies at last. "Including the books."

"But why?" I still don't understand. "Why bring them all this way? Why not leave them in that house you were telling me about?" Your house in Bologna, which sounds like a dream come true, with its carved chairs and its upstairs brazier. If I had my very own house in a great big city like Bologna, I would never move from it. Ever.

"I could not leave them in my house, Babylonne." He throws me a strange look. "I did not have them when I left my house. I have not seen Bologna in six months, at least."

"What?" But that means—you can't mean—

"When I left Bologna, it was to say good-bye to your father. At his monastery near Montpellier." His voice is so tense that it would shatter if you were able to touch it. "From Montpellier, I traveled straight to Toulouse. It was only after Pagan . . . that is, I decided to go on pilgrimage after we said our final farewells. I couldn't go straight back, you see. I felt that I—I had to do something. Something that might help me . . ."

He trails off.

Wait just a moment. Are you saying—?

"When did my father die?"

Isidore swallows. I can actually see his throat move. "One month ago," he replies hoarsely.

A month ago.

My father was living near Montpellier until four weeks ago. *Living.* Still alive.

I don't believe it.

We could have met. It would have been easy. Montpellier . . . that's not far. How many days from Toulouse? Four? Five? I could have walked right up and . . . and what?

Slapped his face, that's what.

But I missed my chance. By one miserable month! God *curse* it, what sort of luck is this? Not God's luck, that's for sure. The Devil's luck.

I was assuming that he'd died years ago—I don't know why. Was it Isidore? Did he give me that impression? Thinking back, he never said that my father was long dead. And when you consider what he looks like . . .

Glancing sideways, I can't see his face. It's shrouded by his hood; his head is bowed. All the same, I can picture very clearly his haggard features: the fleshless cheeks, the sharp nose, the dark smudges under his eyes. Could it be that he isn't always so thin or so grave? Could it be that he's still grieving?

The best cure for grief is talk—or so I've heard. If I ask this priest a question, I'll be doing him a kindness.

Though I'm not sure that kindness is what he truly deserves.

"Tell me about my mother." *She's* the one who interests me. Not my faithless, immoral father. "What did my mother look like?" According to Navarre, she was as fair as the sun. According to Gran, appearances mean nothing. But if I knew what she looked like, I might see her more clearly in my dreams. "Was she very beautiful?"

Isidore turns his face toward me. "Don't you know?" he says, frowning—but continues before I can point out that if I *did* know, I wouldn't be making inquiries, would I? "She was pretty," he says. "Wide-eyed, like a kitten. She had straight hair and white skin and dainty hands. She was too thin, though." He sighed. "Like you. She didn't eat enough."

Only a greedy priest of Rome would say such a thing. "Fasting is holy." In case you didn't realize. "Being thin is good."

"There's more to holiness than fasting," Isidore rejoins. Although his voice is stern, his expression softens suddenly; I don't know why. "Forgive me, Babylonne—I didn't know your mother well. I thought her biddable. Obedient. I thought her pliant and placid. Clearly I was wrong." He shakes his head. "Had she been weak, she would not have held to her beliefs so stubbornly," he concedes. "Had she been passive, you would not be here." With an apologetic smile, he concludes his description. "There must have been more to your mother than met the eye. And that is all I can tell you."

Which is as good as nothing. I'd hoped for more. My mother remains a ghost to me, pale and peaceful; I still don't know what songs she liked to sing or how tidy she was or whether she preferred the country to the city. I still don't know what she used to do when she wasn't praying.

But at least I have her hair now. At least that has been restored to me.

"You, there! Stop!"

God! Brigands!

The horse shies—whoops! No. I'm still on top. Clinging to its mane and . . .

Praise God. They're not brigands.

"Sorry! I'm sorry! Don't be afraid!" A short, solid, balding man in a handsome green tunic has popped out of the undergrowth like a fast-growing leek. What on earth is he doing there? And who's that beside him? His wife? "We're not brigands!" he announces, in the kind of *langue d'oc* that generally comes from Gascony. (It always sounds as if it's being pushed to the front of the mouth by a curled tongue.) "Have no fear! We're only pilgrims!"

Pilgrims?

Isidore has grabbed my reins. He says nothing, but his gaze flits around as more pilgrims start appearing, almost magically. Some crawl out from behind a fallen log. Some stick their heads around the sides of tree trunks. They all look dusty and disheveled and very, very tired.

"We heard your hoofbeats," the man in green explains, beaming all over his round, red face. "We thought that you might be marauding knights or some such thing. So we hid." He stumbles down onto the road, his fine tunic catching on twigs and

147

clawing branches. "I am Bremond. Bremond d'Agen. Do you understand me, Father? Do you speak this language?"

"I do," Isidore replies coolly. He still hasn't relaxed his guard. But that doesn't seem to worry Bremond, who babbles away like the Garonne at full flood.

"This is my wife, Galerna," he indicates. "And that is our mule, you see? A useful creature, but not as useful as a horse. Are you heading south, Father? Because if you are, we could proceed together. There being safety in numbers, as the old saying goes."

Isidore hesitates. He's still holding my reins, and he doesn't like this unexpected meeting; I can tell. When he opens his mouth to respond, however, he's interrupted. A little old woman surges forward, muttering something. She has a face like a withered apple, and her back is bowed—perhaps by the weight of the amulets hanging on cords around her neck.

She grabs Isidore's foot and kisses it: once, twice, three times.

You have to laugh at the look on his face.

"This is Petronilla," says Bremond as she backs away, genuflecting. Isidore, I notice, is wiping his foot on his horse's ribs. "Petronilla is very devout.

A God-fearing woman. She gave all her worldly possessions to a nunnery and became a lay sister before she set forth."

"She probably thinks that you're a bishop," Galerna adds. Galerna is short and round like her husband, but serene rather than buoyant. "Because of your gold ring."

Bremond seems startled. His smile begins to fade. "You're surely *not* a bishop, Father?" he says. "With only one attendant?" (I know exactly what he's thinking. He's thinking: *Oh, no! Have I offended a bishop?*)

Once again, Isidore doesn't have to reply. Instead the answer comes from another pilgrim—another priest—who's been picking his way out of a patch of nettle and chestnut. He's small and skinny and spotty, with two enormous front teeth almost big enough to use as city gates. They make him look like a hare. A white hare, because he's dressed in grubby white robes.

"That is not a bishop's ring," he says in a high, nasal voice. "Unless I am mistaken, that is a graduation ring. Is it not, Father? Are you a university graduate?"

"I am," Isidore rejoins.

"From which university, I pray you?"

"From Bologna," says Isidore reluctantly. The spotty priest nods as if he knows everything there is to know about Bologna and isn't impressed by any of it.

"I did a year's study at Montpellier myself," he observes, "but I didn't graduate. I didn't feel the need. I learned all that I required for my particular calling."

"Indeed," says Isidore.

"Oh, yes. My calling is to further the salvation of souls through pilgrimage. My name is Boniface Batejet, from Le Puy. I am a canon of the Cathedral of the Blessed Mary, in Marseille. You may have read my work, *In the Steps of the Magdalene?*"

"Uh . . . no," says Isidore.

"Oh. Well, you will no doubt read my next guide when I finish it." Boniface sounds absolutely convinced of that. "It is to be called *In the Steps of Saint James,* and it will concern this very pilgrimage to Compostela."

Compostela? Isidore catches my eye. (Don't tell me they're heading for Compostela, too!) Boniface takes a deep breath, but before he can continue, he's cut short by a burst of giggling.

Two young matrons have emerged from behind

a tree. They're both very fair, with skin as white as Isidore's; fine strands of golden hair are escaping from beneath their veils. They're with a noisy fellow in a stylish gray tunic, who's making them laugh. He has one of those wolfish *jongleur's* faces, all scrubby beard and flashing grin.

He doesn't look like a pilgrim at *all*.

But he must be well read, because he hails Isidore in Latin. Isidore responds with more Latin, and there's a brief exchange as Bremond stands there beaming, as Petronilla mutters over her amulets, and as Galerna attends to her mule. For my part, I think I'll keep watch. I don't like the look of some of these pilgrims. That man over there, for instance—the one with the yellow face and the withered hand and the squint. He has a sly expression that doesn't sit well with me. The one next to him is obviously a simpleton; you can tell by the vacant look on his misshapen face, which has the appearance of something that's been pounded with an anvil just a few too many times. As for that ragged old tree-root of a man over there—what's he doing? What's he *saying*? He seems to be preaching at a pothole.

One by one, everybody turns to regard him.

"No one can understand our aged companion,"

Bremond remarks apologetically. "We don't know his name, or where he came from."

"It sounds as if he might come from the Rhinelands," Isidore volunteers thoughtfully, and Bremond brightens.

"Ah! You can understand him, then?"

"I fear not." Isidore shakes his head. "I am familiar only with the sound of his tongue. I have taught students from that part of the world."

"Taught?" It's Boniface. Alert and on guard, he looks more like a hare than ever. "You're a master, then?"

"I am a doctor of canon law," says Isidore. Ha! That's unwelcome news to the pimply priest. See how he screws up his rabbit's nose! (So much for *In the Steps of the Magdalene!*)

"You have a genuine tower of Babel here," Isidore continues—perhaps in an attempt to divert attention from his own accomplishments. "Or should I say, a caravan of Babel? You come from all corners of the earth."

"Yes, indeed." Bremond nods enthusiastically and starts throwing his hands around. "My wife and I are from the Agenais, though we've settled in Bordeaux. When my daughter gave birth to a son after eight years of barrenness, she promised to make this pilgrimage—but we're doing it in her place because she's so busy."

"What with looking after the baby and everything," Galerna interjects.

"Of course," her husband agrees. "She wasn't fit to go. Agnes and Constance are from England." He points to the two young matrons. "A butcher's widow and a bookbinder's widow. I can understand them pretty well—I'm in the wine trade, you see. We ship a lot of Gascon wine to England out of Bordeaux."

"Ah." Isidore actually seems mildly interested. "So is that English they're speaking now?"

"It is, Father," says Bremond. "And the fellow who's making them laugh—Gervaise, his name is. He's English, too. Though I believe he studied for a while in Paris."

"Before he was expelled from the university," Galerna mutters. "Before his family sent him on pilgrimage as a last resort."

"Yes. Ahem." Bremond gives her a nudge to shut her up. "And Petronilla is also English. And Agnes brought her servant, Gilbert, who's English as well."

He gestures at the simpleton, whose finger is

shoved so far up his flattened nose that he seems to be trying to pull his brain out of one nostril (if he has any brain at all).

"And I'm from Provence," the pimply priest interrupts—as if he can't bear to be left out of the conversation. "And my servant, Drogo, here was originally from Lombardy, though he has long since abandoned his barbarous tongue."

Ho-hum. Why all these introductions? We won't be needing their names, surely?

But Isidore is lingering. He's matching their pace, for some reason. I know that we're hemmed in on all sides, but we could easily break through. Surely we're not going to *join* these people? We'll never get anywhere if we do.

I can't even tug at Isidore's sleeve, in case I lose my balance.

"Have you ever been to Vézelay, Father?" Boniface the priest is asking, as he walks along beside Isidore's gray palfrey.

"No, I fear not."

"You're aware that the monks there claim to have the relics of Mary Magdalene?"

"Uh—"

"They say that after the Magdalene and Lazarus

landed at Aix-en-Provence, a monk of Vézelay took their bones back to his country," Boniface drones. "And that he left the Magdalene's bones at Vézelay and the bones of Lazarus at Autun. But that is a terrible lie. For Lazarus—who was the first Bishop of Marseille—was interred at Saint Victor de Marseille and lies there still."

"Really," says Isidore, and we exchange a quick glance. Why doesn't he just kick his horse into a gallop? We can't stay here—just look at these people! Petronilla is shuffling along behind me, murmuring to herself and kissing something that could be a finger bone (or possibly a very old toenail). Gervaise is twiddling his index finger in a lascivious way to amuse the witless matrons; they shriek and slap his arm and giggle together. Gilbert the Fool is gawping at this horse as if it's a miraculous vision. Bremond and his wife are clunking along with strange wooden soles strapped to their boots. The mad old man from the Rhinelands is haranguing a stump.

They're all insane.

"Furthermore, the monks at Vézelay still claim that they have the bones of Saint Martha," Boniface waffles, "when those remains actually lie at Tarascon, in Provence. It can be proved, too, for did not Saint Martha tame the river monster of the Rhone and lead it around on a leash?"

"Did she?" Isidore's beginning to sound a little desperate. "I had no idea. But—"

"Also, many years ago, a visit to Saint Martha's tomb in Tarascon cured King Clovis of a kidney ailment . . ."

"Eh!" Someone taps my leg. "Boy!"

Curse it. Drogo. The man with the yellow face. What does *he* want?

"Are you his student or his servant?" Drogo queries, squinting up at me. He's like a horsefly, hovering around my palfrey's hindquarters.

I don't want to talk to you, pizzle-wit.

"You look too poor to be a student," he says in heavily accented *langue d'oc*. "But whoever heard of a servant riding a mount like this?"

Go away. I'm not interested.

"Or maybe you're his catamite," Drogo remarks slyly. "You know—his pretty boy."

What?

My foot seems to lash out of its own accord. It catches him in the brow and my horse reacts sharply, swerving. (Help!) It nearly tramples the witless Gilbert, who runs like a startled deer.

"Whoa!" Isidore catches my reins. Everyone else scatters, some to a safer distance than others. Gilbert's cowering behind a bush. The madman is running around in circles.

"Calm down . . . tha-a-at's it." I don't know if Isidore is speaking to me or to the horse. "Shh, now. Shh."

"What happened?" Bremond gasps from behind his mule. "What's wrong?"

Isidore's breathing heavily. But he has things under control and is able to answer the wine merchant with a fair degree of politeness.

"I fear, Master Bremond, that this horse is not accustomed to traveling in crowds," he says. "Also, my servant isn't much of a horseman. It might be hard to match your pace, I think—we should probably press on without you."

Aha! Well put! But the spotty priest objects. "Can't you just get down and walk?" he whines from halfway up a tree.

To which Bremond responds, "Walk? When they have horses? No, no. How foolish would that be?"

"But with horses, there's more protection for all of us," Boniface protests. (The whimpering coward!)

"On the contrary," says Isidore in smooth tones. "I am concerned that our presence will make you

157

more of a target. Horses are always a guarantee of wealth, are they not? Truly, you are better off without us."

You can't help admiring him. How quickly he thought up that argument! But he's a doctor of canon law, so I suppose he's been trained to think on his feet.

"No doubt we'll meet up again in Saverdun," he finishes, and lifts a hand to give everyone a quick blessing. Petronilla immediately falls to her knees.

Saverdun? Wait a moment. I thought we were going to that Cistercian monastery? Eaunes, or whatever it's called? That's what he told me this morning. That's what the priests of Saint Sernin advised, isn't it?

But I can't ask him yet. I'll have to wait until we put a bit of distance between ourselves and the pilgrims. Looking back, I can see them all staring after us. Even the old madman is staring after us.

He's also shaking his fist and yelling at the top of his voice.

At last a dip in the road snatches them from view.

"Don't worry," says Isidore as I open my mouth. "We're not going to Saverdun. We're going to Eaunes."

I wish he wouldn't do that. I wish he wouldn't look into my head and anticipate my questions.

"So you're laying a false trail, then?"

"I have to." He sounds tired. "I don't want them finding out who you really are. We can't afford to mix with anyone."

"We can't afford to mix with *them*." They're all mad. "Did you see the wooden shoes? Did you see all the amulets? There must have been a round dozen. And she was kissing a finger bone, did you see?"

"No. I didn't."

"Relics!" What a farce they are. "As if kissing an old toenail is going to bring you closer to God! As if *anything* on earth is going to do that!" You'd have to be stupid to believe such a thing. "I once heard someone say that if all the pieces of the 'true cross' were nailed together, you would see a whole forest instead of a single cross."

The words are hardly out of my mouth before I regret them. I'm talking too much. Not only that, but I'm challenging Isidore. He's a priest, after all; he traffics in relics and amulets.

Still, he doesn't look offended. Just fatigued.

"You think me foolish, traveling to Compostela?"

he inquires delicately. "People go there to see the saint's remains, you know."

Oh, dear. I should learn not to flap my jaw.

"Not that everyone goes for the same reason," he continues. "Your father made the pilgrimage a few years ago. My mother was killed on the same route, making the same pilgrimage. But I doubt that two such different people had similar needs or sorrows." With a sigh, he adds, "We are all on our own quests, Babylonne. And we all have our own relics." He shoots me a measured glance. "Have you discarded your mother's hair, for instance?"

By the rock that felled Montfort! That was a jab I didn't see coming. He's quick, isn't he? Much sharper than I first thought.

I'll have to watch this one.

‡CHAPTER TWELVE‡

When the beautiful princess ran away from her wicked step-mother, she traveled many leagues until, footsore and weary, she knocked on the door of a friendly brotherhood.

"Welcome," they said, beckoning her into a great hall full of tables and benches. "Welcome to our feast."

Little did the princess know that she was to be the main dish!

Oh, no. That's stupid. Nobody's going to eat me. There's nothing to be afraid of. This is just a monastery. There are no monsters. There are no bloodsucking man-beasts lurking in the shadows, waiting to pounce.

I just wish that Isidore hadn't left me alone. I keep hearing strange noises. Rushing noises like water and clanging noises like chains. And a *scritch-scritch-scritch* that might be a rat in the eaves, though this place seems too clean for rats. I can tell by their scent that the rushes were freshly laid this morning on a newly swept floor. And the whole room has been aired; there isn't so much as a whiff of smoke. And the tabletop is still damp from washing.

There are lots of wine stains around, but you can't blame the monks for that. (It's almost impossible to get red wine out of wood, even with salt. I've tried.)

Though you do wonder who's been throwing red wine at the roof. *And* who's been pissing on that wall. All I can say is, there must have been some pretty high-spirited guests passing through this guesthouse. That's probably why it's so simply furnished. The last thing you'd want, if you were an abbot, would be to have your tapestries trampled underfoot and your painted chests set on fire by a bunch of drunken pilgrims.

The door creaks, and it's Isidore. Returning.

Thank the Lord.

"Ah," he says. "There you are."

Of course I'm here. Where else would I be? You told me to stay in the guesthouse refectory.

"Bad news, I'm afraid," he continues, shutting the

door behind him. "The monks here sleep in dormitories. There are no cells. Just a couple of spare rooms in the Abbot's quarters, and he doesn't want to share them with you. With me, but not with you." Throwing out his long arms, he stretches them until they crack at the joints. "I didn't like the idea of being separated," he sighs, "so I told him that we'd sleep in the guesthouse."

I see.

Hmmm.

"There are two dormitories, Babylonne. One for men, one for women." His arms flop back to his sides. "Since we're alone, we can take one each. You can even push something up against your door, if you like."

I may, at that. Or I may not. I've changed my mind about Isidore. I don't think he'll try anything unseemly—I really don't.

Apart from anything else, he looks far too tired.

"Did they bring the baggage? Good." He comes over and begins to forage in one of his saddlebags. I can see a comb made of horn (or ivory?) and a knife with a silver hilt. I can see fur-trimmed gloves and my father's books.

My father's books. That reminds me.

"Uh—can I ask you something?" I've been thinking about this, and I have to know. Even if it means resorting to flattery. "Father?"

There. I said it. I never thought I could, but I did.

Isidore looks up, almost warily. He's suddenly still. Waiting.

"Yes?" he replies.

"Well . . ." Taking a deep breath. "You said that Lord Roland was a monk."

"That's right."

"And that he died in Carcassonne, during the siege."

"Yes."

"So how did he die? Did the French kill him? Were they killing monks? Or was it just the flux—something like that?"

Isidore glances away. His hands start to move again. He draws a tumbled garment from his saddlebag. Folds it neatly. Places it on the table.

"Lord Roland died fighting on the walls of Carcassonne," he finally says.

"A *monk*?" That's new. "Died *fighting*? But I thought you said he threw away his sword."

"He did." Isidore folds a heavy cloak, speaking flatly, as if he's discussing the route to Pamiers. "He only took it up again in my defense. We were on

164

the walls because I needed air. If he hadn't taken me up there, he wouldn't have died."

Oh.

Isidore empties his saddlebag with precise, careful movements, item by item. Everything that he picks up looks somehow more precious—more delicate—in his long white hands. Even the old heel of bread. Even the dirty socks.

"Well . . . it wasn't your fault." I have to break the silence somehow, and these are the first words that enter my head. "The French were to blame, not you. You didn't kill anyone."

For a moment he pauses in the act of arranging his quill pens. When he turns to study me, his face has softened.

I think he's about to say something. But . . .

Bang!

A door slams somewhere in the distance. There's a murmur of muffled voices. And a familiar *clonk-clonk-clonk*.

Oh, no. Those can't be—surely they're not—*wooden soles?* The horror that I feel is mirrored in Isidore's eyes as we stare at each other.

". . . Moissac? Oh yes, I know it well." That's Bremond's voice. Rapidly approaching. "We come from Agen . . ."

I don't *believe* it!

"Quick!" Isidore thrusts a wad of clothes into my arms. "Get beds!" he hisses. "Good ones! Quick!"

Beds! Right! We have to grab the best beds. And they'll have to be in the men's dormitory—oh, dear, this is bad—which one is the men's? I don't suppose it matters.

Stumbling through the first door I reach, I can hear pilgrims spilling into the room that I just vacated. (Noisy, aren't they?) In front of me stretch two rows of beds, six to a row; would we be better off near the window or the door? I wonder. Probably the door. In case we have to make a rapid escape.

There. We'll take this bed and this bed. I'll have the one closest to the wall. "Why, Father!" That's Bremond, speaking in the next room. "So you didn't make it to Saverdun after all?"

"No, I . . ." Isidore mumbles something. He sounds almost sheepish.

"What a happy chance! Now I can find out your name, because you never introduced yourself . . ."

What shall I do? Stay here? Go back?

If I stay here, I can protect our beds. Oops! And here's the first wave, swarming over the threshold: Gervaise, with his two lady friends.

166

They halt and blink at me.

"Uh . . . *hic* . . . *viri?*" Gervaise asks. But I've no idea what he's talking about.

He turns to the widows and says something in English. This time I've got a pretty good sense of what it means.

Sure enough, the widows squeal and slap his arms. Oh, yes. I'd lay a wager on it. Without question, he just said, "You girls can sleep in my bed."

"Oh." And here's Boniface the priest, with Drogo at his heels. Drogo is almost lost to view behind the baggage he's carrying. "Oh," says Boniface, "is this the arrangement? I don't know if I care for this."

"Men in one, women in the other!" Bremond calls from the refectory. The babble of English that follows must be a translation, because Gervaise immediately sags and addresses the two widows mournfully, rolling his eyes in the most exaggerated display of heartbreak I've ever seen.

Agnes and Constance burst into a fresh torrent of giggles. As they withdraw from the room, arm in arm, they throw back a comment—in English—which seems to come as a slightly unpleasant surprise to Gervaise.

He winces and says something in Latin to

Boniface (who's surveying the beds, trying to decide which one he wants).

"Oh." Boniface scowls. "Well, that's all we need."

"What's all we need?" asks Bremond, waddling in on his wooden soles. *Clonk-clonk-clonk.*

"Their servant snores," Boniface replies.

"Ah, well." Bremond shrugs. "Poor Gilbert. I'd be surprised if he didn't, with his nose in the state it is." The wine merchant collapses onto one of the beds with a groan. "He's hoping to be cured, you know, when he reaches Compostela. Agnes has promised him the face of an angel if he makes this pilgrimage."

Oh, no. How *cruel.*

"Well, be that as it may," says Boniface, who obviously wouldn't care if Gilbert's face was growing out of his backside, "I vote that we put all servants in the refectory for the night. I can't be expected to sleep in the same room as my own servant."

Whump! Drogo dumps the priest's baggage onto a bed by way of comment. And suddenly Isidore speaks.

He's right behind me. He must have slipped in like a fox, the way he does.

I didn't even notice.

"My servant is sleeping with us," he declares calmly. "In here."

And that's that. Not even Boniface has the courage to argue, though he'd like to, I'm sure. Bremond has unstrapped his wooden soles and kicked off his boots; he's now rubbing his feet, his face screwed up in ecstasy. "Ahh," he says. "You know, these sandals are my son-in-law's idea, and they wear very well, but they're mortally hard on the feet."

"Where is the old man?" Isidore inquires, and my heart turns over. Of course! The old madman!

We don't have to sleep in the same room as *him*, do we?

"Ah. Yes. Our aged friend," says Bremond. "I'm afraid he's gone."

Gone? How?

"He wandered off. I don't know why." Bremond's still rubbing his feet, which smell like something scraped out of an eel's belly. "We just looked around and he'd disappeared. Isn't that right, Father?"

He's addressing Boniface, who's busy unpacking and answers with a shrug. Gervaise has wandered out of the room, probably in search of the widows. Gilbert passes Gervaise on the threshold; he looks around in awe, as if he's never seen a roof from the inside before.

Drogo's got his head down. Hmmm. You know, I wouldn't be surprised if Drogo had strangled the old madman behind a tree.

There's something about that fellow.

"Bremond!" It's Galerna's voice from the next room. "Everyone! The food's here!"

Food? What food? Have the monks brought food?

Drogo sprints past and out the door in the blink of an eye. (It's like a flash of lightning.) Boniface bustles after him, walking very quickly but not breaking into a run. (You're probably trained to do that when you live in a cathedral cloister.) Bremond hobbles off with his boots in his hand, lured back into the refectory by a warm, spicy smell that makes my stomach rumble.

Isidore waits. He waits until the very last man has left the room before sitting down beside me on my bed.

"Will you be all right?" he whispers. "Is this all right for you?"

"I—I think so." After all, no one knows that I'm a girl, so why should I be bothered during the night? And I don't have to use a piss-pot around here.

There are latrines. We passed them on the way in. "I just won't talk. Or take too many clothes off."

"I'm sorry, Babylonne."

"Benoît. Remember? *Benoît*."

He nods. Rises. Leads me into the refectory, where two monks are serving out food. One of them is an even sadder sight than Gilbert; he looks as if his face has been turned inside out and left to dry in the sun for a year before being worn as a shoe. I suppose that's what Agnes is giggling at over there. Unless Gervaise just pinched her.

I notice that Gervaise has wedged himself neatly between the two of them—between Agnes and Constance. No surprises there. Beside Constance, on the right-hand bench, sits Galerna, then Bremond. Boniface has chosen a place on the opposite side of the table; he waves at Isidore, and I know what that means.

"Come!" says the spotty priest. "Please do us the honor, Father Isidore. I've saved a seat for you."

Though not for me, apparently. I'm supposed to eat down at the other end of the table with Drogo and Gilbert. Isidore hesitates, but there's not much he can do. If he insists that I sit beside him, it will look as if I *am* his pretty boy.

I suppose I'm lucky that I don't have to eat off the floor.

Speaking of meals off the floor, what's Petronilla doing? She's on her knees in front of the gargoyle-faced monk, her hands clasped together in prayer. When he tries to step around her, she crawls after him.

She must be expressing her gratitude. That's the only explanation.

"Silly old bitch," Drogo mutters as I slide onto the bench next to him—keeping a good three hand-spans of naked wood between us. "She'll trip him up in a moment, and then what will happen? We'll lose our soup."

No comment from me. No comment from Gilbert, who probably can't understand. (Who probably can't *talk*, in fact.) The ugly monk is handing out trenchers of bread, murmuring some kind of prayer as he does so. It looks as if—yes, it will be one trencher each. That's good. But only four large bowls of stew, so I'll be sharing one with Gilbert and Drogo. That's *not* good.

"My next pilgrimage will be to Canterbury," Boniface is saying as he picks at his bread. He's talking to Isidore, naturally, but Isidore isn't listening. Not really. He nods and grunts, but all his attention is on me. I can feel it. He keeps glancing my way. He keeps frowning, even when Boniface is laughing. "Oh, yes, Father, the *state* of the beds in that abbey . . ." The pimply priest bores on.

Hello.

Did I just see what I thought I saw?

Drogo made the sign. Over his food. Here was I, telling myself *not* to make the sign, and he did it himself, without thinking.

Well, well, well. So Drogo's a Good Christian, is he? Or is he?

I might be mistaken. It was very quick. Perhaps where he comes from—Lombardy, is it?—that's not a believer's sign at all.

"So, Benoît," he remarks as he scoops up stew with a piece of bread. (Mmmm. Bacon and beans.) "You look like a Moor. Are you a Moor?"

I have to shake my head. It will seem odd if I don't.

"No? You're as black as mud, though; you must be something." He stuffs the bread in his mouth, but it doesn't shut him up. "Jew?" he mumbles, chewing. "Are you circumcised?"

I won't dignify that question with an answer. It's not right to talk so rough, not at the table. Gilbert's making noises like fifteen pigs at a trough. It's not his fault, I suppose—with a face like his, it must be hard to eat—but that doesn't make him any nicer to listen to. Boniface is still droning away. "Better food in Nîmes . . . plenary indulgence . . . blah, blah, blah . . ." Bremond is banging the table with his goblet.

"A prayer before we eat, Father, I beg you," he says to Isidore. "A prayer of thanks for our safe arrival."

Ha! Look at Drogo. With a shifty, sideways glance, he stops chewing and swallows. Isidore gets up. He gives us a prayer in Latin, his voice as gentle as a drift of silk. It certainly seems to calm the widows, who fold their hands and bow their heads in pious unison.

Gervaise is scratching his backside. The two monks wait, shuffling their feet; having served up the food, they're now holding jugs of wine.

". . . *cum Sancto Spiritu in gloria Dei Patris. Amen,*" Isidore finishes. Everyone murmurs "Amen" except Gilbert, who honks it like a goose. Isidore settles back onto his seat with a glance in my direction. (It's all right, Isidore, I'm coping.) Petronilla approaches Isidore on her knees, babbling something in English.

"I think she wants your blessing, Father," Bremond advises from across the table. "She'll only eat if she has your blessing."

Isidore sighs and traces a cross over her head.

The monks start pouring wine.

Drogo pokes me in the ribs with his good hand. "Where *do* you come from?" he mutters. "Don't worry, I can keep a secret. Are you something he picked up in the Holy Land? One of those Infidel bastards?"

Closer than you think, piss-face, but you still don't deserve an answer. Besides, I'm busy. Busy eating. Ouch! His hand is like a smith's clamp. Right on my upper thigh. Digging in. "I like a boy who can keep his mouth shut," he leers.

Get off! The table shudders as I jump up, knocking against it; wine flows from a fallen cup. Everyone gapes at me.

"Benoît?" Isidore rises, too. "What's wrong?"

Speechless.

What can I say? I can't speak. I mustn't.

"Are you ill?" says Isidore.

Yes. Yes, I'm ill. That's it. Drogo has turned my stomach.

A nod will do the trick.

"Leave him," says Boniface, catching at Isidore's sleeve. "He'll be fine."

Oh, no, I won't. Where shall I go? Back to bed? Yes. Back to bed.

I don't want anyone to see me like this, shaking and sweating. I don't know what to do. Is that greasy, smirking Lombard trying to tell me something? Does he know that I'm a girl? Or does he like young boys? Maybe he's trying to scare me by making me *think* that he likes young boys.

Here I am, back in the dormitory. Safe. There's a candle burning—who lit that? One of the monks? Shut the door. . . .

My knees are giving way, but that's all right. The bed's here. Sit down, Babylonne. Sit down and think.

"Benoît?" The door creaks. It's Isidore. He slips inside, pushing the door shut behind him. Ignoring my frantic gestures.

"No! No!" As softly as I can. "Go back! They'll wonder!"

"What is it?" He's barely audible. "What's wrong?"

"Nothing."

"Tell me."

"Nothing."

"Are you ill? Or is it something else?" He narrows his eyes, crouching beside me. "Is it Drogo?"

By the balls of the Beast, he's quick. How did he work that out?

"What did he do?" Isidore breathes. "Why did you kick him, back there on the road? What's he been saying?"

Knock-knock-knock.

"Hello?" It's Bremond. "May I come in?" Without waiting for an answer, he thrusts his head into the room. Isidore immediately springs to his feet, stepping in front of me. Shielding me.

"If it's the flux," says Bremond, "my wife has a good draught that the boy can take. It's very effective."

"No, thank you." Isidore speaks firmly. "He'll be fine."

"Or the monks might help. They have an infirmary here."

"Benoît's fine. He's very tired. All he needs is rest. But thank you." Isidore turns back to me. "You go to bed, Benoît. Sleep is the cure. I'll be in soon." As Bremond's head disappears, Isidore leans forward and lowers his voice. "I'm *here*. Understand? I'm here." (It's amazing how much strength he can force into a whisper.) "I won't let him near you."

And all at once the room is empty. All at once I'm alone with the candle. Maybe I should get undressed before anyone else comes in.

Or maybe I shouldn't get undressed at all.

CHAPTER THIRTEEN

"Wake up."

Wha—? Who—?

"Shh!"

Isidore. Yes. That's Isidore, and I'm—where am I?

His hand's on my mouth. Gagging me. The light's very dim, but I can just make out his dark shape against the paler shadows beyond.

What's that awful noise?

"Shh." His hand falls away from my face as he puts his mouth to my ear. "We're going. Now."

Now? It's a bit early, isn't it?

"Before the others wake up," he adds, under his breath, and of course he's right. God forbid that we should have to endure another day full of pilgrims.

Pilgrims like Gilbert, for instance. That noise must be him. Snoring.

He sounds like an ox drowning in a cesspit.

Isidore straightens, and his knees crack. (It's a nasty moment, but no one stirs.) He hands me something—Oh! What are these? My boots? I can hardly see in this light.

"Bring them," he whispers.

It's good that I didn't really get undressed last night. Just kicked off my boots and dived under the blankets. Now that I think about it, I didn't even hear the others come in. I must have been dead to the world. What time is it?

Ouch! Ah! My legs! My backside!

"Shh." He's hushing me again. Oh, dear. Did I whimper? But I couldn't help it—I'm still as stiff as a lance. Sore, too. Whoops! The door creaks. There's a sleepy sigh; once again, however, no one moves. Perhaps no one heard us through Gilbert's snoring.

In my hose, it's easy to move like a fox, padding on silent feet. Yuck! These rushes! They're all wet! (I hope no one's been vomiting.)

"The bags!" I hiss, but Isidore doesn't answer. Instead he stops at the table and picks up two irregular black shapes.

The saddlebags, obviously.

He must have been up for a while, packing and dressing—unless he did it all last night. *I* certainly wouldn't have noticed. I wouldn't have noticed the Last Trump.

He leads the way through the second door into a cramped little cloister that's illumined by the first faint glow of daybreak. I can hear a restless bird twittering somewhere nearby. But no monks. Where are they?

"Are the monks up?"

"I should think so," he replies. "Didn't you hear the bell for lauds?"

"No." I was fast asleep. "Where are we going? To the stables?"

"First I have to make my farewells to the Abbot." Isidore peers around, as if in search of something. "Do you remember where the stables are?"

"Yes, but—"

"I'll meet you there, then. See if you can rouse one of the stable hands. There's bound to be a few of them sleeping in the byres."

"Wait." I have to grab him. I don't want to but I have to, because he's already moving away. "I need to go somewhere first." *You* know what I mean. "For a quick visit."

"The latrines?"

"Yes."

"Go, then. Don't dawdle."

And off he strides, his black skirts swinging. Don't dawdle. Right. I'll just pull on my boots (ouch!) and—let's see, now. Where are the latrines? Ah, yes. Over there. Pray God that nobody's in them.

Normally you can follow your nose to a latrine, but not in this monastery. There was a latrine at Laurac, and people used to pass out in mid-flow, despite all the lavender and rosemary that was tossed around the floor. In these monastery latrines, however, you can breathe quite easily—perhaps there's water underneath the holes.

Yes, there it is. I can hear it rippling along down there, although the light's too poor to see anything much. I've been told about this kind of latrine. Fresh water in ditches, carrying the refuse away. Who would have thought that I'd actually use one?

My trickle sounds awfully loud, hitting the water. Echoing off the stone. And now what am I supposed to do? Anything? Am I allowed to use this straw? Can I throw it into the water, or am I supposed to put it somewhere else?

Maybe I won't use the straw. I don't really need to. I'll just pull up my drawers, tie up my hose—there!—and be on my way.

"Well, well, well."

Oh, God.

It's Drogo.

"I thought as much," he sneers, standing in the doorway with the dormitory candle. "Last night I said to myself: There's precious little between those legs. I asked myself: Is he a girl or a eunuch? And here's my answer."

Stupid latrines! The running water—it must have masked his footsteps.

How long has he been watching me?

"Nothing to say for yourself?" He moves forward, closing the gap between us. "That's all right. Women should be seen but not heard. If *you* can keep a secret, so can I."

My pepper. My scissors.

They're here in my purse.

"No point making a fuss, or someone might come," he drawls. "And you don't want *that* to happen, do you? Oops! No, you don't." He grabs me with one hand as I try to push past. "You're staying right here until—*Aaaagh!*"

Pepper, straight in the eyes. The candle falls. He's coughing and cursing, but he's already behind me. Run. *Run!*

Out the door. Round the corner. Turn right and right again. Where next? Quick! Where am I?

Wait. I know where I am. That's the forecourt up ahead, and the stables are on the right. It's much lighter now, and—yes! The forecourt. With the stables over there, not far, just a short expanse of beaten earth and pray *God* that someone's inside. . . .

"Hello?" When I burst in, I'm greeted by the whinnying of startled horses. It's dark in here, though—I can't really see. Everything smells of hay and manure. "Hello?"

"Who's that?" A sleepy voice from somewhere to the left.

"I'm a guest." Quick, quick! "My master is Father Isidore, from Bologna. We want to leave. Now."

"Now?"

"We need our horses saddled. At once."

There's a grunt and a rustle. Something moves over there in the corner. Light's beginning to creep through chinks in the roof; it's gleaming on a glossy roan hide, and glinting off—what's that?

A hatchet?

Just what I need.

I have to go back. I have to stop that stinking, slimy scumbucket before he tells the others. Before he opens his mouth and blabs. I can do it.

After all, I'm not the only one nursing a secret around here.

Someone's beginning to tramp past the horses, tripping over pails and cursing at rats. He's too busy to notice if I take this hatchet. I'll bring it straight back; I just need it for protection while I present my demands. I won't be long.

The air in the forecourt is fresh and cool. A cock is crowing not far away, but I don't want to think about that. I don't want to think about fowl houses or floppy dead chickens. I have to concentrate. I have to be strong and quick and clear in my mind. Now—here's the first corridor. It's like a cloister walk, with stone vaults springing up overhead. Dark as a well, but I can still make out where I'm going. Raising my hatchet, because he might be just around the next corner.

No—nothing. More corridor, with a light at the end where it opens into that little cloister. I can't see a soul.

I can hear someone, though. Two people. Low voices, muttering.

Where are they?

As I creep along, hugging the cold, stone wall—trying to ignore the pain in my thighs (ouch!)—the voices become clearer. One of them belongs to Drogo; unless I'm mistaken, he's still near the latrines. Is he spilling his guts? To Boniface, perhaps?

No. That's not Boniface.

That's Isidore.

"Don't know what you're talking about," Isidore's saying, whereupon Drogo snorts.

"You know what I'm talking about, Father. You and that little chicken of yours, cozying up together."

"You're mistaken."

"You want me to tell the rest of 'em? Father Boniface, maybe? I will. I will unless you make it worth my while not to."

"Where's Benoît?"

"I've seen your books. How many do you have—three? Maybe I'll take one of those."

"Where's Benoît?"

"Here I am." Anyone would think that I'd knocked over a pile of iron pots. Isidore jumps like a rabbit. Drogo drops his candle again. They both whirl to face me. "Here I am, Father." (Swinging my hatchet.) "Our horses are nearly ready."

"Just listen to her!" Drogo taunts. "She only has to open her mouth, and she betrays herself!"

"I won't betray myself." You cur. "And you won't betray me, either. Not if you're smart."

"Oh-ho! And who's to stop me, eh? You?"

"Benoît," says Isidore, so calmly that I *know* he must be strung as tight as a *vielle*. (I think he's worried that I'm going to throw this hatchet at Drogo's head.) "Please, Benoît, let me deal with this. Something can be arranged."

"You're right. Something *can* be arranged." And this will be the arrangement. "If Drogo keeps quiet about us, we'll keep quiet about him." The spineless maggot's jaw drops as I advance on him, balancing the hatchet in both hands. "Do you want your employer to know that you're a heretic? Is that what you want?"

Isidore stiffens. Drogo catches his breath.

"Because I'll tell him, Drogo. As soon as you let drop the slightest hint about me—"

"I'm not a heretic!" he croaks. "Not anymore!" Ha! Look at him squirm. Look at him wriggle. "That was years ago, I swear it was! In Lombardy!"

"Do you think Boniface would care if it was years ago? It's a deadly sin, whenever it happened." And Drogo knows it, too. I can tell by the way his veins stand out on his forehead. "Someone like Father Boniface—he wouldn't touch you with gloves on if he knew."

"You can't tell him! You can't!"

"I won't. I won't if you keep quiet about us."

There's a pause. Drogo is panting. I'm worried about the rest of the pilgrims; is that the clatter of a wooden sole hitting a stone floor in the distance?

I hope not.

"We'll go now." Come on, Father. Stir your stumps. "And you'd better not try to stop us, Drogo, or you'll suffer for it."

"He understands," Isidore says suddenly. He moves past Drogo on soundless feet. "You understand, do you not, my son?"

"Yes, yes." Drogo spits it out. "Damn you to Hell for your sins!"

I *could* say something about being in Hell already, but I won't. I don't have time. We must leave now, before Bremond comes looking for a place to empty his bladder.

"You've a shepherd's taste in women, Father!" Drogo hisses after us. "Black as a crow, skinny as a whip, and a tongue like a scorpion's tail! Bedding her must be like bedding a scythe!"

No comment from Isidore. He probably didn't even hear.

He's in too much of a hurry.

‡CHAPTER FOURTEEN‡

You'll find that it gets easier. What a lie that was.

My knees won't bend properly. My backside feels as if it belongs to someone else. My thighs would be screaming if they had mouths to do it with.

This isn't what *I* would call easier, Isidore.

Not that you're the slightest bit worried about me. Oh, no. I can tell exactly what's troubling you, and it's not the state of my muscles. You're worried about your reputation.

"It's all right, you know." In case you haven't worked it out. "Drogo won't say anything. He'll be too frightened in case we happen to run into them all again and say something about his murky past." So cheer up, can't you? "He's a coward, that one. I can smell it on him."

Isidore says nothing. He looks very grave and thoughtful; though he's staring straight ahead, it's obvious that he doesn't see the dusty road unrolling in front of us or the little copses clustered about meandering streams or the pathetic remnants of someone's failed attempt to raise oats: upended stumps, piles of rocks, overgrown furrows.

His gaze is turned inward.

"In fact I wouldn't be surprised if he had more to hide than the true faith." (I refuse to call it *heresy*— not when I don't have to.) "I'd be willing to lay a wager that he's been a thief in his time, with that sly look of his. And whatever happened to that old madman? Why did he disappear so suddenly? If you ask me, Drogo had something to do with it. He looks like the sort of person you get working on barges down by the wharves in Toulouse; they're all of them exiles. It's no coincidence that the river keeps spewing up corpses around the water mills. If you want a hired assassin, you always head for the wharves."

Isidore remains silent. And it's beginning to annoy me. I *refuse* to be condemned out of hand without being given the chance to defend myself.

"It wasn't my fault!" Are you blaming me for all this? "*I* didn't do anything wrong!"

"I know you didn't," says Isidore, shedding his preoccupied air like a wet cloak. "I'm not accusing you of anything, Babylonne."

"Then why are you angry with me?"

"I'm not."

"You are!"

"No." He shakes his head. "No, I'm simply beginning to wonder if I've done the right thing."

Oh, curse it.

He's having second thoughts. He *is* fretting about his reputation. He'll abandon me at the next town, and I'll have to go on by myself with only my scissors to protect me—because I used up all my pepper on Drogo.

Do you think he'd give me this horse if I asked for it nicely? Probably not. And anyway, how would I feed it? Not with the money I've got in my purse, that's for sure.

I don't know why I'm so scared suddenly. Why my stomach just turned over. It's stupid, because I don't need this priest. In many ways, I'm better off without him.

"If you want to travel alone, I don't care." Except that . . . except that I don't want him to go. "I can look after myself."

"Oh, Babylonne." He sounds startled. "I'm not

going to leave you. I would never do that. I just feel . . . well, you must see yourself that this isn't the best course."

"What do you mean?" If I wasn't so nervous, I'd feel sick with relief. "What isn't?"

He's a little ahead of me, the way he often is, and drops back so that he can peer straight into my face without having to twist in the saddle. I envy the way he can do that—namely, look sideways while he's riding.

If I try to glance sideways for more than an instant, I start pulling my horse's head around in the same direction. I can't help it.

"Babylonne," he says quietly, "you must know that this is an empty dream."

What?

"You're not a stupid girl. What do you really expect to find in Aragon? How do you expect to live there?"

What do you mean? "I told you. I'm going to serve the *faidit* knights."

"In what way?"

I *told* you this! "By cooking and cleaning and—"

"You are being simple." His voice is hard and dry, like the rocks beneath us. "Even if you reach these men, they are not angels in armor. They are not monks, laboring away under vows of chastity. What kind of service do you think they will expect from a woman?"

Oh!

How *dare* you? They are good men! Noble men!

"They are fighting men, exiled," Isidore continues. "What makes you think that they'll be any different from Drogo? They'll upend you at the first opportunity."

My spit hits his cheek, and I'm away. One swift kick in the ribs and—help! My horse bolts like a hare—I never expected this—whoops! Whoa!

This is no good. I have to use the reins; I can't keep my arms wrapped around its neck. But if I let go, I'll fall off. . . .

"Babylonne!"

Ah. A rise. Quite a steep rise, and we're slowing. I can do this now. If I grab the reins . . . That's it . . . That's it.

The priest's drawing level. He's reaching out, but I'm fine. Go away. Can't you see it's all under control?

"Dominus Deus!" Isidore exclaims, and his horse shies beside me.

Good. He's not trying to snatch at my reins anymore, and now I have the upper hand. With the slope falling away in front of us and small stones tumbling from under my palfrey's staggering hooves, I can—

Oh, God.

I don't believe it.

Spread out in the distance, heaving and glittering, speckled with bright colors, lies a vast pool like a stretch of floodwater. Only it's not water—it's chain mail.

"Get back!" God help us, they must be the French! Humbert de Beaujeu's plundering savages! "Quick! Turn around, or they'll see us!"

I'm trying to remember. How many knights? People used to talk about them back in Toulouse—didn't I hear something about fifty squads of bowmen? There must be at *least* that many, judging from all the fluttering standards. And the great, straggling mess of carts. And the horses! Did you see all the *horses*? (Unless some of them were mules. . . .)

This horse is so utterly confused, it doesn't know what it's doing.

"Here." Isidore has managed to maneuver his own horse into position beside mine, bringing the two animals shoulder to shoulder. I don't know how he does it. (He's much more nimble on horseback than he is on the ground.) Catching my bridle, he guides us all back over the ridge to safety.

"It's the French army; it must be!" I couldn't make out the standards, but a force that size has to be the French. "They're taking this road!"

"Shh. Calm down."

"We can't let them see us!" They're still a long way off. They might not have spotted us—two lonely horsemen up on a hill. And now the hill stands between us and the army; we'll be well concealed until they breast it. "We must leave the road. We must hide somewhere—in a ditch or a copse."

"But why?" He seems genuinely puzzled. "I am a man of the Church and a pilgrim to boot. I am not a local lord, or a heretic." (There's that word again.) "Why would they harm me?"

"Why?" You fool. "Because they can, that's why! You told me yourself that the French killed Lord Roland—and he was a monk!"

"But that was an entirely different situation, Babylonne."

Ha! "And you call *me* simple? Father, they're fighting men, exiled! It doesn't matter who we are, don't you understand? We're here! We're weak! We have money!" He's still not convinced, so it's time for the clinching argument. "And on top of everything else, they probably haven't been paid in six months. Why wouldn't they just ride straight over us?"

Now he's thinking. I can tell by his puckered brow.

"Anyway, I thought we were trying to avoid people who might find out who I am! If they steal my clothes, they'll certainly work out that *something's* wrong." Oh, come on, will you? We have to get out of here! "Please, Father, let's go. We can't stay on this road; we have to head across country."

"You're right." (Hooray!) "You're right; we can't be certain of their goodwill." He hesitates, chewing his bottom lip as he scans the surrounding trees and rocks and bushes. "But there are so many of them. They won't keep to the road. They'll spread out."

"I know. That's why we have to go right around them. *All the way* around."

Which could be leagues. Realization dawns in his face, and abruptly he kicks his horse into a canter, veering off the road. Heading east.

This is going to be hard.

I'm not a good rider. I'm bad enough on the road; what am I going to be like on rough terrain? Horrendous, that's what. Certainly not good enough to match his pace. Ouch! And there's the proof, if you need it. I didn't even see that branch coming.

"Father!"

He looks around. His palfrey slows. "What happened to your face?" he demands.

"I just hit something." Whoops! And that ditch nearly unseated me. Isidore clicks his tongue.

"We'll have to get down," he says. "You can't manage this."

"Yes, I can. I have to." We must put some distance between ourselves and the French. "If we walk, they might catch us."

"If we don't walk, you might break every bone in your body." Isidore swings himself to the ground in one fluid movement. "Come," he says. "Don't dawdle."

I can't really argue. Not when he's right. *Yeowch!* And of course I make a complete mess of dismounting because my knees have lost their strength; one of them buckles as I put my weight on it, and I have to grab for the nearest strap.

"It's all right." He's there behind me. (How did he cover so much ground in such a short time?) "I've got you."

"Let go."

"Are you sure you can stand?"

"Let *go!*" It all comes back to me in a rush. He called me simple. He compared the noble *faidit* knights to Drogo the talking eel. He can go and eat slime off the Bazacle piers.

When I push him away, he steps back, relinquishing his hold. He knows better than to cross me. He knows that I still have my scissors. *Crunch-crunch-crunch.* Dry sticks break under my feet. You see? I can stand. I can even walk. And the horse is coming, too.

Down into this gully, don't you think? That would be the safest route. It's also going in the right direction, more or less.

I just hope that we don't get lost.

"Babylonne."

Shut up. I'm not talking to you.

"Babylonne, please." I can hear him fumbling down the slope behind me as he leads his horse into the gully. There's still some water lying in pools among the smooth, gray rocks. A tiny bird flits out of my way. "Listen," he says, keeping his voice low. "You don't need those exiled lords any longer. You have me now. I'll look after you."

"Oh, yes? In what way?" Don't make me laugh.

"You expect me to spend the rest of my life in boys' clothes? Washing your drawers? No, thank you." If I have to wash drawers, they're going to belong to brave young men in gleaming armor.

"Of course, we couldn't continue in this fashion. I never intended it." If he's offended, he's not letting it show. Not in his voice, at any rate. I can't see his face because I'm walking ahead of him. "I'll take you back to Bologna. Babylonne? Are you listening? We can turn around right now. Go north. Make for Bologna."

In your dreams, my friend.

"Babylonne, you might be headstrong, but you're not stupid. Consider what you're proposing." He's speaking very calmly and reasonably, without a spark of impatience. "You are a woman, not a soldier. You have no training with a sword or a bow. You cannot read or write. You can't even ride with any confidence. Of what use can you possibly be to the *faidit* resistance?"

"Mind your own business!" Ferret-face! "I'm more useful than *you* are!"

"How? Tell me."

But I'm not going to talk to him. He can go and jump in the nearest well. I know what I'm doing. I'm not stupid. I'm going to watch my feet and keep alert, and if the shadows start falling differently, it will mean that the gully has changed its direction.

And after we're clear of the French, I'll . . . well, I'll think about that later.

"Perhaps you intend to continue with this perilous deception of yours," Isidore adds. "If you do, the Viscount of Carcassonne might take you on as a humble foot soldier, so that he can throw you into an assault to protect himself from the spears and arrows of his enemies. Unless, of course, the other soldiers discover your secret first. And you know what will happen *then*."

Every word is like a nail being hammered into my guts. I can't stand it anymore. The Viscount won't betray me. Olivier de Termes won't betray me, nor will any of the others.

"Just hold your tongue!" You whining mosquito! "I know exactly what I'm doing!"

"Do you? Really?" He's not taunting me. He's in earnest. "I don't believe you do. I don't believe you've thought this through at all. Please think, Babylonne. *Think*. It won't work."

Yes, it will. It has to.

What else is there?

"This ceaseless war is no place for you," he argues softly. "You have other choices now. You can come with me to Bologna. Arrangements can be made. . . ."

"Such as what?" (You expect me to live in a chest under your staircase?) "How am I supposed to share a house with you? Everyone will think I'm a whore!"

Wait. He's stopped. Why isn't he moving?

Oh. Of course. It's because I've stopped, too.

"I can find you somewhere else to stay," he says, with a little less confidence than usual. "Perhaps a nunnery."

"A *nunnery*?" You must be joking. "You expect me to become a *nun*?"

"Shh. Not so loud."

"I knew it would come to this!" At last the truth is revealed. He's two-faced, just like every other Roman priest. "All this time you've been humoring me, in the hope that I'll convert to your misguided faith!"

His face takes on a rigid expression. "I wish only to keep you safe, Babylonne—"

"Safe in the arms of Rome, you mean!"

"This is hardly the time to debate theological principles." He's about to say more, but something stops him. The noise of a distant horn, faint on the breeze. If it were the Last Trump, sounding the Day of Judgment, it couldn't be less welcome. I can see my own dismay reflected in the gaze that he turns on me.

Isidore is right. This isn't the time or the place to talk religion.

We have to get out of here.

‡CHAPTER FIFTEEN‡

There are two stone structures and one made of wood and daub. But the mud has almost washed away; the wood is split and sun-blistered; the stone is scattered and crumbling. Thorny plants have grown up inside former rooms, which are now open to the sky; I can even see black scorch marks on the walls, so it's not hard to guess what happened to the thatch. Or to the vanished inhabitants.

"A deserted village?" Isidore speculates in a low voice.

"No. Too small." Someone's been grazing his sheep here recently. There are pellets all over the ground. "See those stone fences? Those mark the boundary. This looks like a *forcia* to me. A fortified farm."

"Not fortified enough, apparently," says Isidore, his gaze fixed on the scorch marks.

"No." Someone went through this place, all right—went through it like a thunderstorm. Could have been anyone. Anytime in the last twenty years. "There's a well, though, see? Do you think it's been filled with dirt?"

"We can always check." Isidore squints around, shading his eyes from the hot afternoon sun. Nothing stirs. Even the air is still. "Perhaps we might rest here for a short time," he adds. "Refresh ourselves. The Abbot gave me bread and cheese and some pickled olives."

Pickled olives! Mmmm. But let me just have a look at this well first, because there's something about it . . .

There. I thought so.

"Father!" When I start hauling on the rope, it comes up so quickly that there can't be anything on the end of it. No. No bucket. Even so, it's in a suspiciously pristine state. "Father, this rope's almost new. Someone's been here very recently." Sure enough, the end of the rope is wet. "We can use this ourselves. To water the horses. Is there anything we can use as a bucket?"

"We could finish the wine in the first wineskin," Isidore suggests, joining me at the rim of the well. "Tie that to the end of this rope."

"I suppose we could even soak a piece of clothing. Soak it and wring it out."

"Into what?"

"I don't know. Is there an old trough anywhere?" Scanning the ruins to our left, I can see nothing that resembles a trough. Or a pot. Or even a hollowed-out stone. But that overgrown patch in the corner—could that be what I think it is?

"Look!" Of course. I should have been keeping an eye out for lush greenery. Every farm must have its kitchen garden, and every kitchen garden must be fed with manure. It's the kind of treatment that bears fruit for years, even without constant tendance. "Look, Father, beans!"

"Beans?"

"We can pick them!"

But some have been picked already. There's been a bit of weeding, too. Not much: just a little space cleared around the roots of the bean stalks.

By passing shepherds, perhaps?

"Here. Hold out your skirts. Like this." I'd better

demonstrate, because he seems confused. "To put the beans in. We can take them with us."

"To eat?"

"Why not?" You'd think I was suggesting that we stick them up our noses. "Nobody owns them."

"Babylonne, it's not safe to eat things fresh from the ground." He's still speaking quietly, as if he's afraid of being overheard. "You can make yourself very sick doing that."

"We'll cook them, then. It's better than letting them go to waste." They're a little spindly, but they're a good color. (And they snap when they break, too.) I wonder why the sheep didn't get to them. Because the garden's tucked away behind a stone wall? "Come closer, please. I can't reach you."

They must have sown other crops, the people who tilled this garden. Turnips, perhaps? Cabbages? I can't see a trace of either. Everything's so choked with weeds, I wouldn't expect to find more. The beans are miracle enough.

What's that?

Isidore catches his breath. My muscles seize up; I can't move.

Someone's having a muted discussion nearby.

God save us! The horses!

Beans scatter as Isidore drops his skirt. Before

I can catch him, he strides out to confront whatever lies beyond the ruinous wall that shields us. (Wait, you fool! It could be anyone! Brigands! Frenchmen!)

Ah.

But we're lucky.

"Who are you?" says Isidore. The two men by the horses stare at him like rats trapped in a corn bin. They wear dark robes and sandals.

One of them carries a bucket.

"Well?" says Isidore, imperiously. He sounds like a bishop questioning a cowherd. "Who are you? Do you live here?"

"It's all right." Let's calm down, everyone. There's no need to panic. "They won't kill us, Father: they can't. They're not allowed to kill anything." And to demonstrate our goodwill, here's the full *melioramentum*: hands clasped, knees bent, head to the ground, three full bows. "Bless us, bless us, bless us. Good Christians, give us God's blessing and yours. Pray the Lord for us that God may keep us from an evil death and bring us to a good end or into the hands of faithful Christians."

"Uh . . . from God and from us you have the benediction." The older Perfect has a faint, feeble

208

voice like a lamb's fart. "And may God bless you and save your soul from an evil death and bring you to a good end."

I don't recognize him. I don't recognize either of them, thank God. The older one is a sad sight: a burned-out candle of a man, all waxy skin and guttering strength. His hair is silver; his back is bent; his hands shake as he makes the sign of the benediction. His friend is about Isidore's age, but much smaller. He has the worst case of boils I've ever seen: great open sores, seeping scabs, oozing pus. . . . He looks like a pile of offal left to breed maggots in a slaughterman's yard. There's even a sore on his bottom lip.

"You're a believer?" he says hoarsely, fixing me with a red-rimmed gaze. "From where?"

"Uh—from Castelnaudary." I must remember to keep my own voice hoarse and low. "My name is Benoît. This is Father Isidore."

They both stare at him, horrified, as he pushes back his hood. (A Roman priest! In the flesh!) The look on their faces—it almost makes me laugh.

"Father Isidore is no bent stick." Good work, Babylonne. You don't sound like yourself *at all*. "He is my good master. We are both running from the

French army because it's coming this way. And no one is safe from an army."

"That is true," wheezes the older Perfect. "No one is safe. They tear up vines and burn houses—"

"We have heard the drums," his friend interrupts. "You saw it yourself, this force?"

"Taking the road from Saverdun," Isidore replies before I can open my mouth. He touches my shoulder gently. "But it cannot keep to the road. It's too big for that."

"You're right. There will be scouts. Looking for food and women." Boil-Face turns to his waxy friend. "We must hide. At once."

"Hide?" says Isidore. "Hide where?"

The two Perfects look at him. They remind me of two fledglings, fallen from a nest. As they blink and sway, a horn bleats in the distance.

The four of us turn as one.

"There!" the old man squeaks. "It's coming! The army of Satan!"

"We must go," says Isidore. He reaches for his palfrey's bridle. "We must be quick. Can you ride, Benoît?"

"I . . ." I don't know. Perhaps. I can certainly try. As I hesitate, the Perfects begin to steal away, kicking up dust with their sandals. Isidore calls after them.

"Wait!" If he had cracked a whip, it would have had the same effect. Both Perfects halt. And turn. "Wait," Isidore continues. "Where are you hiding? Will you show us? Will you hide our horses, too?"

The Perfects exchange glances. They don't like Isidore. I can tell.

"Please, Holy Fathers." If I have to kiss their pustulant feet, I'll do it. "Please let us come with you. We have food here, and wine."

"We cannot hide the horses," Boil-Face replies. "There is no place for them."

"Are you sure?" We can't leave the horses. It would be like leaving fresh tracks in snow. "Is there no thicket? No hidden byre?"

"If by chance we are discovered," Isidore adds, "these horses will bear two men apiece. With the horses, we might escape. Without them, we'll have no hope."

That's a good point. It certainly impresses Boil-Face. He strikes me as the sharper of the two. "All right," he says at last. "You can come. And you can bring the horses. There is a place. . . . It might work. . . ."

211

Praise the Lord and all his angels. This is a lucky chance. As we begin to move, the horn sounds again—closer, this time. The old man whimpers.

"Courage, Brother," his friend says softly. "We are in God's hands."

I certainly hope so. Beyond the northern wall of the *forcia*, the land drops away quite steeply into a tangle of brush and thorn and vine that looks impenetrable from up here: a dense, silvery grove at the bottom of a cleft. This cleft, I feel certain, marks the passage of a watercourse, though not one that flows in the heat of high summer.

"There." Boil-Face points at a goat's track that careens down into the cleft. (I hope our horses can manage it.) "We take this trail."

"Before we do, would you object to giving us your name, fellow traveler?" Isidore inquires. "Since we have given you ours."

Boil-Face looks wary, but finds the courage to speak. "I am Gui. This is Imbert," he replies. "We must hurry."

Easier said than done, my friend. It's a tricky descent, made even trickier by the horses, which refuse to be rushed on such a narrow, winding, unstable path. My mount, in particular, balks at the task expected of it; I can sense that it's a beast of the river flats. It snorts and jibes at the bit.

"Shh!" says Gui—as if I have it in my power to stop a horse from snorting. (What does he want me to do, stick rocks in its nostrils?) Imbert moves more quickly than I would ever have imagined. He takes the lead, disappearing suddenly beneath a canopy of grayish leaves, bucket in hand.

"There is no water down here," Gui murmurs, tossing the remark over his shoulder as he reaches the bottom of the cleft, where a dry watercourse is all but choked with eager plants. "Not in the summer. That is why we must use the well."

And the garden, presumably. But how long have they been here, these Perfects, hiding like mice in the undergrowth? Are they using this place as an inn, or have they made themselves a permanent home? I remember how Arnaude used to talk about the four months she spent in somebody's cellar during one of the summer campaigns, when Simon de Montfort seemed to be everywhere at once and no Perfect within his reach was safe from burning.

These two look as if they've been doing the same thing. They have the scurrying, sun-dazed appearance of men who have spent far too much time crawling around rocks like lizards. They're skinny and dirty and weathered and worried. Not like Isidore, who strides along with a firm tread, his pale face smooth and almost luminous above the darkness of his robe.

But the Perfects are more holy. I have to remember that. You don't get close to God by eating pickled olives and reading expensive books. You do it by fasting and praying and not washing very much.

Ahead of me, Gui has followed the creek bed to a thick hedge of wild oak and nettles, which suddenly rises up like a wall in his face. The creek bed disappears straight into it, under overhanging branches. "Here," he says. "The entrance is here."

"We'll never get the horses through that," Isidore observes from behind me.

"The horses aren't going in there," Gui rejoins. "They must go around and up again. I'll show you."

Whereupon he moves off to the left of the watercourse, plunging into a patch of waist-high grass. Isidore and I exchange glances.

"I can't lead both horses," Isidore mutters. "Not through that."

"Then I'll come with you."

"But let me go first, Benoît."

"Yes, yes." Hurry, or we'll lose Gui. He's already vanished into the bushes, though I can hear his footsteps—*crunch, crunch, crunch*. Our valley is very narrow by now; there are low, crumbling cliffs closing in on both sides, converging ahead of us behind the screen of wild oak and nettles. Old Imbert seems to have gone to ground somewhere beyond that tangle of growth. But Gui has managed to skirt it, plotting a narrow course between the left-hand wall of the cleft and the reaching, clawing branches of wild oak to his right.

It's a matter of dodging the ones that slap back after being pushed aside by Isidore's palfrey— ouch! You really have to keep your wits about you.

And there's Gui again. He's climbed out of the scrub in front of us, slowly mounting the tumble of rocks and earth that marks the end of our cleft and the beginning of higher ground. It seems to me that we're standing at the base of what might, in heavy rains, become a waterfall; the actual cascade would largely be hidden by all that wild oak to my right. Unless I'm mistaken, Imbert must be hiding in the cliff face somewhere—perhaps there's a cave behind the waterfall (or where the waterfall should be, at least). And the path to the top of the falls has been picked out along a slightly gentler slope directly ahead of Isidore, to the left of the nonexistent cascade.

Of course, though it might be a gentler slope than the sheer drop of the waterfall, it's not exactly a river wharf, either.

"We'll never get the horses up there." What does Gui think they are—goats? "It's too steep."

"We must try," says Isidore.

"But—"

"There's no time to go back."

Did you hear that, horse? There's no time to go back. And it's no good rolling your eyes at me, because I'm not in charge here. I'm just doing what I'm told.

Gui is already at the top, peering down at us. The path isn't *quite* as bad as I expected. It's more like a set of stairs than anything else. The rocks are fixed hard in the baked earth, not rolling around underfoot. And with Isidore's beast leading the way, my own seems more amenable.

Yeow! God! Except when he steps on my foot!

"What is it?" says Isidore, trying to look back.

"Nothing." It comes out sounding like the creak of a hinge.

"What happened? Are you hurt?"

"No." As far as I can tell, I'm not about to lose any toes. "Quick. Hurry."

And here we are, at last. There's more growth up here than I expected—must be something to do with the creek bed, which is all fissured mud and dry pebbles. There's even a wild olive, I notice. And beyond it, over to the south, a glimpse of the *forcia*, back on our level.

Now I understand where we are.

"There's a rear entrance just up here," says Gui, whose boils look worse than ever against the sweaty red flush that's engulfed his face. "If we leave the horses in this copse, they might not be seen. And even if they are," he adds, "the back entrance is practically invisible."

"We'll have to unload everything," says Isidore. "We'll have to bring the saddles and the halters—"

"Hurry, then. Can't you hear it?"

I can hear it, all right. The roll of drums. Quick! We have to move!

"I've nothing to tie the horses with." Isidore frowns, already unstrapping the saddlebags. "No ropes or thongs."

"We shouldn't tie them." Keeping my voice down serves to disguise it. "If we tie them, we're leaving a trail."

"But—"

"If we let them loose, they might easily have wandered."

"If we let them loose, they will wander," Isidore protests, working away furiously. "And then we'll lose them."

"Better to lose our horses than to lose our lives."

"Will you please hurry?" Gui hisses from over near a patch of nettles. "We haven't *time* for this!"

"We'll leave the halters on," Isidore suddenly decides, hauling the saddle off his palfrey. "Just drape your bridle over that branch as if it's snagged there accidentally—"

"And leave the other one free." Of course! "If my horse has been caught, his friend might stay."

"Yes."

"Good idea."

"Come *on!*" grunts Gui, who's struggling with a great weight. A rock, is it? He's crouched near a patch of pink flowers—and he's not the only one struggling with a great weight. "This saddle is too heavy for me."

"In here." Gui has rolled aside several rocks to reveal a hole in the ground. A very small, dark hole in the ground. "If you crawl through this tunnel," he explains, "you'll come to the cave where Imbert is hiding. I'll roll the rocks back after you and return the other way."

But—

"Quick! *Quick!*" Gui's boils are practically erupting, he's so frightened. "Get *in!*"

"I'll go first," says Isidore, who's brought up the rear with his saddle *and* his saddlebags. (I hope they're all going to fit.) "You can follow me, Benoît."

"Couldn't we—um—light a candle or something?" It looks awfully murky in there.

"You won't need a candle. There are fissures and cracks that let in the light until you're nearly at the cave. Then you'll see Imbert's lamp." Gui gives me a push. "Go on!"

Isidore's already crawling into the hole, which is like a burrow. It seems to ease him down gently. Once his hands and face have been swallowed up, the rest of his black shape simply merges with the shadows, disappearing more quickly than I would have thought possible. I can't help thinking of gullets. And graves. And wolves' eyes shining yellow in the darkness.

"Go on," Gui repeats, already poised to cover the gaping, toothless mouth.

Now it's my turn.

✢CHAPTER SIXTEEN✢

There once was a beautiful princess who was swallowed by a giant whale. For three long days she wriggled down its throat, and on the fourth day she emerged into its stomach, which was as big as a cathedral. All around her were gold and silver and precious gems, because the whale had swallowed more kings and kingdoms than there were stars in the sky. And the princess took the treasure and traveled to the end of the world, and laid her priceless gift before the band of noble knights who awaited her in their ivory castle. . . .

I almost wish that this *were* a whale's throat. At least it would be softer on the knees. (Ouch!) And now Isidore has stopped again, for about the tenth time. Surely he's skinny enough to get through this tunnel? I'm not crawling out of here backward—I don't care how small it gets.

"What is it?" Go on! "Why are you stopping?"

"Wait," he gasps. There's a flurry of feet and skirts and all at once he's disappeared. Disappeared!

In his place I can see a flickering light, dancing about like an insect.

"Come," croaks Imbert. "There's a bit of a drop."

As if to demonstrate, the saddle that I've been pushing in front of me suddenly falls away. Vanishes. *Thump.* Hands reach for me—Isidore's hands—and fasten themselves to my arms. Ow! Wait! Don't pull yet—I'm—

Whoops!

I'm on the ground. All tangled up in Isidore's soft black robe. Above me, the mouth of the tunnel yawns like the end of a pipe: a round, dark hole punched into the wall.

"Are you hurt?" Isidore demands.

"No." You broke my fall. "Is this it?"

"Apparently." He doesn't sound very enthusiastic, and I don't blame him. It's not nearly as big as I expected. The ceiling is so low that even I can barely stand upright. The ground is so uneven that there's only enough flat space to allow one person a good night's sleep. (You *might* fit two people, providing that they slept nose to nose, with their arms wrapped around each other.) Everything else is jagged rock, some of it too sharp to sit on. There's a blanket and a bucket and a few little rag-wrapped bundles that might be food. There's also a jug that's missing a handle. I hope the jug is a piss-pot. I'd hate to think that the Perfects were using their water bucket to piss in.

"Welcome," says Imbert timidly. He settles onto one of the rocks, folding his hands in his lap. Isidore begins to stack the saddles and baggage on a kind of stony shelf, and I suppose that I'd better sit opposite the Perfect. Leaving as much distance between us as I can, naturally.

At last Isidore finishes. Sidling past Imbert, he wedges himself next to me, barking his shin in the process.

I wonder what happens now.

"We must be very quiet," Imbert mutters. "If we speak too loudly, it will be heard outside. Just as we can hear the people who pass overhead."

"We are in no danger yet, I think," says Isidore. "The hoofbeats of so many horses would shake the very ground, would they not?"

Imbert doesn't reply. He's listening hard—for

Gui, probably. Gui must be retracing his steps, coming back down the side of the valley and entering via the front entrance, which is almost certainly around that corner over there.

In the silence, my stomach rumbles.

"Sorry." How embarrassing.

"Would you like some food, Benoît?" Isidore murmurs.

My nod propels him to his feet again; he's rummaging through his saddlebags when a noise from outside makes Imbert stiffen. Oh, dear. What was that?

We ought to have a sword, you know. Or at least a big stick. Something to use if an armed man ever penetrates this fastness. We could ambush him. Cut off his head as soon as he stuck it around that corner.

An unconvincing owl's hoot seems to reassure Imbert, who releases a great sigh. The owl's hoot must have been a signal.

"Gui," says the old man as Isidore turns from the baggage, bread in one hand, cheese in the other.

Sure enough, Gui suddenly appears. His thin hair is full of straw and burrs. He collapses onto a spire-shaped rock that must be *very* uncomfortable, though perhaps not for a holy man like Gui. Gui probably sleeps on iron spikes when he can find them.

"Nothing yet," he gasps. "But the drums are getting louder." His gaze follows Isidore, who's stumbling back to his seat. Damn, damn, damn.

How can I eat cheese in front of these Perfects?

"You are welcome to our food," says Isidore, as if he's suddenly become conscious of all the attention he's attracting. "Our food is your food, now that you've shared your hearth with us."

"We do not eat cheese," Gui replies. "It is a sin to eat cheese."

Oh, dear, oh, dear. We're not going to discuss religion, are we? Isidore regards Gui for a moment, his eyes calm and thoughtful under pale, heavy eyelids. Finally he begins to wrap the cheese back up in its linen swaddling cloth, saying, "I would not offend mine host in his own domicile."

"You are not offending me, but the Lord," Gui rejoins, wincing as he shifts about, trying to find a more comfortable spot. "Cheese comes from milk, and milk is the product of fornication, which is anathema to God. For Saint Paul said, 'Flee fornication,' by which he enjoins us to flee all things that stem from it—like milk, and cheese, and

224

eggs, and meat. Saint Paul said, 'It is good neither to eat flesh nor to drink wine.' Therefore we live according to the injunctions of Saint Paul."

Ho-hum. I must have heard *that* more times than I've trimmed my toenails. I could almost be back in my grandmother's house; this whole place puts me in mind of it, what with the dry bread and water and the uncomfortable seats and the fact that there aren't enough blankets.

"Saint Paul did say, 'It is good neither to eat flesh nor to drink wine,'" Isidore agrees quietly, breaking his bread into equal portions. "But he finished with the words 'nor anything whereby thy brother stumbleth or is offended, or is made weak.' It is all of a piece with his other rulings; he tells us, for example, 'Wherefore if meat make my brother to offend, I will eat no flesh while the world standeth, lest I make my brother to offend.' He does not describe it as wrong in itself, I think, except insofar that it might trouble others. And therefore I will put my cheese away."

"But you *do* offend," Gui insists, "in that you do offense against all people."

"I think not," says Isidore.

"No, I assure you! Eating meat is wrong." (Gui is beginning to preach. I can hear the strength

225

building in his voice.) "Because you should not kill a living thing, nor condemn its spirit to another earthly body."

"But Saint Paul would not have it so." Isidore doesn't speak like a preacher. He passes me a piece of bread, his tone gentle and soothing. "He said, in his first epistle to Saint Timothy, 'Now the Spirit speaketh expressly, that in the latter times some shall depart from the faith, giving head to seducing spirits and doctrines of evil; speaking lies in hypocrisy; having their conscience seared with a hot iron; forbidding to marry, and commanding to abstain from meats, which God hath created to be received with thanksgiving of them which believe and know the truth. For every creature of God is good, and nothing is to be refused, if received with thanksgiving.' "

Hmmm.

How beautifully he speaks. And the words that fall from his mouth—are they truthful? Did Saint Paul really write them?

If they *are* the words of Saint Paul, then . . . then perhaps we *shouldn't* be abstaining from meats.

Even Imbert looks a bit startled.

"Ah!" Gui exclaims "But you're speaking about two different worlds. Nothing is to be refused in the world of the *spirit*, by the truly faithful souls of the Saved. Saint Paul is not referring to this world, for this world is the realm of the Devil. Because if 'every creature of God is good,' then how could God have created the bad things, like wicked dragons and poisonous snakes? Remember, as the Blessed John says, 'God is light and in Him there is no darkness.' So this world is not of God. This world is full of darkness, and full of the Devil."

Well? What do you say to that, Father Priest? Isidore gives a piece of bread to Imbert, who stuffs it down almost guiltily, chewing awkwardly on unreliable teeth.

"If this world is not God's creation," Isidore replies, "then why does Saint Paul say of Christ that he is 'the image of the invisible God, the firstborn of every creature, for in him were all things created in Heaven and on earth, visible and invisible'?"

Yes. Why does he say that, if this world is really the Devil's realm? Gui is beginning to look cross. He hesitates, his mouth working. Hasn't he an answer to this argument?

"Saint Paul also says that 'there be gods many and lords many,'" he finally splutters. "And Saint Matthew says, 'No man can serve two masters,' meaning that Satan is the lord and master of this world."

"Oh, my friend." The pity in Isidore's voice seems to surprise everyone—even Isidore. He catches himself and moderates his tone. "You must know that a master is not a god," he continues. "In the same text of which you speak, Saint Paul tells us, 'For though there be those that are called gods, either in Heaven or on earth, yet to us there is but one God, the Father, of whom are all things.' All things, you see. In Heaven *and* on earth."

I've never heard anyone argue like this before; I've only heard preaching. It makes you think, doesn't it? It makes you wonder. I've always thought that it was holier not to eat meat. But if the Scriptures say it isn't—if Saint Paul says it isn't—then could the Perfects be wrong? Could the Romans be *right*?

Surely not. Surely the *Romans* couldn't be right!

Though I have to admit, Isidore certainly seems to know the Scriptures very well. Better than Gui, who only uses small snatches of text—not big slabs of it, like Isidore. Unless Isidore is lying? Unless he's quoting from false Scriptures? There *are* false Scriptures, I know. The Perfects always talk of them. But

Gui didn't accuse Isidore of falsifying the words of Saint Paul. Perhaps Gui doesn't even know the Scriptures well enough to recognize falsehoods.

Oh, dear. I wish I could read. Then I could read the Scriptures for myself, and work out who's right.

"But Christ said, 'My kingdom is not of this world,'" Gui proclaims, as if he's about to wave his hand in the air. "Therefore Christ is not king of this world!"

"It is confusing, is it not?" says Isidore sympathetically. "It could be argued, however, that Christ, in using the word 'of,' was not using it in the sense of 'over this world' but 'from this world.' In which case He was reminding us that the world did not give Him His power—"

"Shh!" It's Imbert. He's sitting up straight, staring at the rocky ceiling. His eyes are wide and scared in the light of his oil lamp. "Listen!"

I can hear them myself now. Muffled shouts and rhythmic thumps. All very faint, but clear enough to raise the hairs on the back of my neck.

"It's them," Gui breathes. He's rigid, his argument forgotten. "They're coming."

"The *forcia* might lure them away," Isidore whispers, but Imbert flaps a nervous hand at him.

229

"Shh! No talking!" the old man hisses.

Please, God, don't let Humbert find the horses. Let him loot the beans in the *forcia* and ride past satisfied, without stopping. How late is it now? Surely not too late. Without the sun, it's hard to say. But I'm certain the sun hasn't set yet. It can't be time for vespers. If the French ride hard, they would reach Eaunes before nightfall. Camping around Eaunes would be much more comfortable than camping in this out-of-the-way spot, even if it does have a working well.

How hard it is, sitting here. Not knowing where the soldiers are or what they're up to. Though I have to admit, it sounds as if they might be right overhead now. I can actually hear voices: honks and barks and hoots filtering through the layers of rock that shield us. Suddenly, there's a patter near my foot.

Help!

"Shh." Isidore's hand closes on mine. "It's earth," he hisses. "Earth falling from the roof."

Dislodged by the impact of a heavy object? Someone directly above us must have jumped off his horse. Or dropped a load of weapons.

A metallic jingle sounds so close that Gui sucks air through his teeth in alarm. Someone's crashing

230

around in the brush outside the front entrance of our hole. A man's voice shouts something about firewood.

Oh, no. Firewood?

They must be settling in for the night.

‡CHAPTER SEVENTEEN‡

My mother's hair slips silently through my fingers. Even when I flick it against my palm, it doesn't make a sound. It's the one thing I can fiddle with that won't betray us—as long as I keep it away from my nose, of course. Or it might make me sneeze.

I can't believe that it's come to this. I'm actually counting my own breaths, just to keep my mind off my bladder. It's going to rupture soon if I don't get some relief.

A hundred and eighty-four. A hundred and eighty-five. A hundred and eighty-six . . .

"Psst!"

Is that Isidore? It must be. I can hear him scuffling around at the entrance.

"Psst!" he says. "They're gone!"

Gone?

"You can come out now," he declares.

Glory to God. Glory to *God*. Praise the Lord for all his mercies—at last I can take a piss!

Baggage first, though. Got to get the baggage.

"What are you doing?" asks Gui, watching me edge toward the shelf above Imbert's head. Silly fool. What does he think I'm doing?

"Leaving." Bog-brain. "Aren't you coming, too?"

"Oh, no." The very thought seems to appall him. "It can't even be noon yet. They only left around sunrise—they can't have gone very far. Suppose they see you? You should stay a little longer."

After sitting on a full bladder all night? No thanks.

It's all very well for people who can piss standing up. Those of us who can't would have a hard time disguising the fact in a space this size.

And here's Isidore, looking ruffled and out of breath. His skirts are studded with grass seeds; he has a smear of dirt on his cheek.

"Don't bother with the saddles," he says abruptly. "We won't be needing them."

What?

No.

233

"The horses are gone?" Gui says it before I can. Isidore looks tired and dejected. I'd be surprised if he got much sleep last night.

"The horses are gone," he confirms.

"Oh, *no!*" They found the horses! They took them away! My poor brown horse—the gentle horse that Isidore bought for me with his own money!

But I won't cry. I have to be brave. It's not a good time for tears, just now.

"They may have found the horses, but at least they didn't find us." Isidore is suddenly beside me, helping to drag down the saddlebags—though not the saddles. "We can still make our way, Benoît. We have food and money."

But can we carry it all? It's going to slow us up. Gui and Imbert mutely watch us sharing out our load; they eye Isidore's ivory comb with grave displeasure. When we come to the books, Isidore hesitates. They're very heavy. He knows that.

At last he turns to Gui, cradling the thickest of the books.

"Master Gui," he says quietly, "we are of different minds, you and I, but our discussion last night put me in mind of happier days, before the French came to this country—days when men such as yourself, and men such as I, used to debate our theologies without resorting to violence. I cannot agree with your beliefs, Master Gui, but I can see that they are faithfully and honestly held. And I would wish that a man of your generosity and fervor might open his heart to the truth." As Gui goggles like a dead fish, Isidore offers him the book in his hand. "Please honor me by accepting this pledge of my gratitude," Isidore continues, "which, if you sell it, will provide you with every article that you could possibly require for your continued existence—and which, if you do *not* sell it, will provide you with an even greater gift. For the mind and the soul are less easily fed than the body. And this book is a fount of spiritual wisdom from which no man can safely turn away."

Sometimes, when Isidore speaks, it's as if the angels themselves are singing. Is this something you learn at university? I wonder. Gui is so overwhelmed—so astonished—that he accepts the book without a murmur.

Imbert says, "But he cannot read."

What? Isidore blinks. Gui says savagely, "He means that I cannot read Latin. I can read our language well enough."

"Then perhaps you should have someone read this book to you," Isidore suggests. "Before you let it pass from your sight." He jerks his chin at me and moves back toward the entrance, his saddle-bag flung over his shoulder.

Gui rises.

"Farewell, then," he says awkwardly, laying the book on the ground. Before I can stop him, he puts both hands on my cheeks and inclines his head three times. "Your blessing, your blessing, your blessing," he mutters. "You should tread with care, boy. He may be your good master, as you say, but his honey is poisoned. For Rome has inserted a black needle into his heart, and all his noble kindness is cankered with the bitterness of lies."

So I've heard tell, my friend. But do you know, as I cast my mind back, I can't think of one lie that he has told me yet? Not one.

Now I'd better get out, or you'll start wondering why there isn't a trace of down on my upper lip.

"Wait! Father!" Don't forget about me. "I'm coming!"

The entrance is closer than I thought—around the corner, five short steps and here I am. It's a wide fissure in the cliff face, hidden by a trailing curtain of vines that drag at my hair as I push through. The undergrowth beyond it seems to be armored; it's like walking through a crop of miniature spears.

(Ouch!) The low trees look as if they're crouching, ready to spring, their gnarled arms spread wide.

Isidore has used the creek bed as a path. He stands in a pool of shade, his hood pulled up and his load carefully balanced.

"I am sorry that we had to relinquish that book," he says. "I had no choice—the other two are all we can manage. One each."

"I know."

"I will find you another, I promise. Even if I have to sell one of my own."

The whole business seems to be bothering him immensely. I suppose I can understand why, though I'm happy enough to have saved the old man with the lion. "It doesn't matter to me, Father." Not much, anyway. "I can't even read. And I just want to take a piss, do you mind? Over there."

He can't exactly object. In fact he practically falls over his own feet, trying to get out of my way. "Yes . . . yes, of course," he mumbles. "I'll wait behind the . . . I'll just . . . yes."

Yes. This bush will do nicely.

Ahhhhh.

It's like a fleeting glimpse of Heaven.

"Where are we going, do you have any idea?" Talking loudly might cover up any embarrassing noises. "The sun's over there, so south must be that way. Back past the *forcia*."

"Um . . . yes." He has his back turned, so he won't see me emerge from behind my bush. "But we have to reconsider our options, Babylonne. We are on foot now, and very vulnerable. Whether it's to the south or not, we have to find the nearest place of safety and seek refuge there before deciding on our final destination. Don't you agree?"

Agree with what? "So you're saying . . ."

"I'm saying that we should head for the monastery of Boulbonne. We know where it is, thanks to what Gui was saying last night, and it's closer than anything else—even the Saverdun road. From Boulbonne we can make our way to . . . well, wherever it is we decide to go. North to Bologna or south to Aragon." He swings around and waits for me to adjust my girdle. "You know my feelings on *that* subject, but this is neither the time nor the place to discuss them."

Discuss them? There's nothing to discuss. Not now, not ever. I'm going south, whether you like it or not.

You're right, though, first things first. "Very well." Boulbonne it is, then. "So we should be striking out to the east, if we're heading for Boulbonne. East from the top of the waterfall."

"I believe those were Gui's instructions."

"And we'll have to climb up that cliff again?"

"Much easier this time, Babylonne. Without the horses."

Without the horses. Yes. I feel so bad about the horses. It still hurts my heart to think of them, stolen away by the cruel and greedy French. Please, God, the French aren't hungry. Please, God, they need pack animals more than they need meat. Fifty squads of bowmen—that's a lot of mouths to feed. I fear what might happen if they run out of farms to pillage and flocks to slaughter.

Speaking of the French, I can see where they've been. They must have passed so close to us last night; there are many flattened fronds and freshly turned stones hereabouts. Even a footprint in the dust. Not to mention the smell of stale piss, carried on a fitful breeze.

But no ashes. They must have lit their fires up above. Near the back entrance of the cave, or over in the *forcia*.

"Can you carry that bag? Is it too heavy?" Isidore wants to know. He's paused at the foot of the stony rise that we mounted yesterday on our way to the cave's back entrance. "I can take more."

"No, no." You already have twice as much as I do. "I'm fine."

"Pull up your hood, Babylonne. It will protect you from the sun."

"Nutshells."

"I *beg* your pardon?"

"Nutshells. These weren't here yesterday." Nor was all this horse dung. Why on earth would any horse want to drop a load halfway up a cliff? Fear, perhaps? Or do malicious French horses simply like to annoy people by blocking narrow paths with piles of excrement?

Oh, well, at least it's horse dung, and not the human variety. I wouldn't put anything past those French. I'm sure they take a squat wherever they please, whether it's on a path, a road, or the back of a wagon.

And here we are, at last. The campsite.

Filthy, of course.

"I've not much of a talent for reading tracks," Isidore remarks, instinctively lowering his voice in the presence of so many warm, smoking ashes, fresh piles of dung, and gleaming gobs of spittle. "But it looks to me as if they swung around to the west, don't you think? The ground over there is very much torn up."

"Yes."

"It would make sense, if they're following the road from Saverdun," Isidore adds. "Another reason why we should avoid it, don't you agree?"

I do. Though if the army's heading north, and we're heading south, the risk of our running into each other wouldn't be high, even if we did take the road to Saverdun. We'd probably hit that road long after the French had passed. As Isidore turns and strides off toward the east, along the shaded bed of the dry watercourse, an unwelcome picture springs to mind. Will the French overtake Bremond and his company? Would Lord Humbert dare to plunder and murder a party of Roman pilgrims?

Might as well ask if a wolf would kill a sheep.

"Gui said that we should follow this dry stream to a path that leads off to the right," Isidore remarks from some distance ahead. He stops and turns, waiting for me to catch up. "Then we take that path to the first of the monastery vineyards."

"*Mmmph.*" I'm not deaf. I heard what Gui said.

"Are you sure that you're not overburdened, Babylonne?"

"I told you. I'm fine."

"I could take that wineskin."

"I'm *fine*." Is he always like this? Doesn't he realize that I've spent my whole life dragging around great loads of firewood and wet laundry? "I'm just slower than you because my legs are shorter." In case you hadn't noticed.

"Your boots are thinner, too," he says, matching my pace. "They're poor, cheap things." (Don't let Gran hear you say that! She'd have your guts for a girdle.) "I wish now that I had bought you a new pair of boots at Muret."

"Oh, well." Try not to pant, Babylonne, or he'll probably offer to carry *you*. "Maybe I should hollow out two small logs and wear those instead. Like Bremond."

Isidore laughs. (Come to think of it, I've never heard him laugh before.) "And then," he drawls, "if we come to a river, you can simply float across it. Really, what a sensible and practical alternative it would be to an ordinary shoe."

"Especially when you have to fend off sword thrusts or start fires." I can't help grinning as I catch his eye. But the smile on his own face disappears instantly, swallowed by an expression of the most profound pain. "What is it?" Did you step on a thorn? "What's the matter?"

"Nothing." He turns away.

"Was it something I said?"

"No, no."

"You look as if you just bit down on a nut and broke your tooth."

He shakes his head. All right, then. If that's the way you're going to be, I won't talk, either.

He's right about these boots, though. They're too soft for terrain like this. I can feel every sharp stone prodding at my instep.

Maybe wooden soles wouldn't be such a bad idea after all.

"It's the first time I've seen you smile," Isidore suddenly explains in a tight voice. He's still not looking at me. "You have Pagan's smile."

Is that meant to be a compliment?

"When you look up at me like that, and smile . . ." He swallows. "I'm sorry. It was such a terrible loss, and such a recent one—but I mustn't burden you with my sorrows." A pause. "I only wish that you had known him, Babylonne. He was a great man. He had the finest mind and the biggest heart. . . . He was the bravest, most eloquent, most accomplished teacher . . . so funny and quick . . . such a devoted friend and noble spirit . . ."

Isidore's voice cracks. He can't even speak. I

never realized, until this moment, how deeply he must have loved my father. A "father in all but blood"—that's what he said. I thought it simply a turn of speech, but I was wrong.

Have I *ever* loved anyone as much?

My mother, perhaps, when I was a baby. The mother I never knew. But how can you *really* love a person you've never known? Or even known much about?

How can you love someone who isn't clear in your head?

"Forgive me." He's speaking more firmly now. "Your own loss is far greater than mine, of course. You never met him, whereas I enjoyed his company for many years. At least I had that blessing. You did not."

True. On the other hand, I can think of many other things that I've wanted a great deal more than my father's company.

"Well . . ." What can I say? "You can't miss what you never knew." And never particularly wanted to know, either. But the sadness in Isidore's face makes me sad as well. He doesn't deserve to be so miserable—not really. Though he might be a Roman priest, he's also a good man. I can see that now. *He* wouldn't have stood around watching my mother die; I'm sure of it. "For your sake, I wish that my father was alive." There. I said it. "Just so that you would be happy again and not grieve so much."

Isidore stops in his tracks. He peers around at me, his expression softening.

As up ahead, someone shouts.

‡CHAPTER EIGHTEEN‡

Horses. Men on horses.

Run!

"Wait." Isidore catches my arm. "You cannot outrun them," he says under his breath. "Don't even try."

"But—"

"Shh." He lifts a hand in greeting while placing himself between me and the mounted men. There are six of them—no, eight. Their horses are big, powerful beasts, well caparisoned and hung about with all manner of things: rolled blankets, leather bags, halberds, maces, spiked mauls, even pot helmets. They clank and jingle as they pick their way between the smooth river rocks, laying their hooves down with a delicacy that you wouldn't expect in such huge, heavily laden animals.

The men riding them are no less well equipped. Some even wear chain mail under their surcoats, and quilted *hacquetons* under their chain mail; their cloaks are stained and faded from long days in the sun. There's a short sword on every belt and a beard on every face.

Slowly they fan out, as if to surround us— though I didn't hear any order being given. The very young man on the sturdy chestnut, who has leather vambraces strapped to his forearms, says, "Who are you?"

Hooray! He speaks the *langue d'oc*! Not only that, he speaks it *well*.

This is no Frenchman. Whatever else he is, he's no Frenchman.

Isidore bows. "I am Father Isidore Orbus, of the University of Bologna," he replies, his tone as calm and sweet as I've ever heard it. "I am a pilgrim on the road to Compostela."

"Compostela?" Vambraces lifts an eyebrow. His eyes are large and brown and set wide apart in a sallow, triangular face. "Then you are well off your road, Father."

"I know it, my dear son," Isidore says. "But at present we are directing our steps toward the monastery of Boulbonne, which is not far from here."

I don't know if he's trying to point out, in a subtle way, that any brutal murder in broad daylight is unlikely to go unnoticed by the large number of Cistercian monks who live nearby. If that's his purpose, I doubt it will do any good. Men like this would see no threat in the proximity of a monk. Or, indeed, of a hundred monks.

Oh, God.

Oh, no.

That face over there—I recognize that face! The scarred cheek, the broken nose, the little screwed-up eyes . . .

It's Pons de Villeneuve! Cousin Bernard's old friend!

Perhaps if I put my head down and stay behind Isidore—but no. Pons has spotted me. Jerking his head and stiffening in the saddle, he addresses Isidore without wrenching his gaze from my profile.

"What is a priest from Bologna doing with the granddaughter of Blanche de Laurac?" he asks in a low, rumbling voice.

Isidore catches his breath. Vambraces turns to stare at his friend. "*Whose* granddaughter?" he demands.

"She's Mabelia's by-blow," Lord Pons rejoins. Damn him! Damn him to Hell and all his broken bones along with him! He's going to ruin everything—he's going to *tell* them everything! "I've seen her in Toulouse, and in Laurac, too, before Bernard Oth threw the Lady Blanche out on her ear. I'd recognize this one anywhere: they say she has Arab blood."

"Is this true?" Vambraces is speaking to me now. "Are you indeed a girl?"

How can I deny it? They could prove it for themselves easily enough, and I don't want *that* to happen. "Yes, my lord."

"What is your name?"

"Babylonne."

"That's it! Babylonne!" The gates of Lord Pons's memory have been opened. He slaps his forehead. "Her father was a Roman priest—though not this one, I wouldn't think, to look at him."

"No," says Isidore, before I can open my mouth. His fingers have closed around my elbow. "I am merely her father's heir. And you, my lord? Whom do I have the honor of addressing?"

He's very brave, is the priest. Here we are, surrounded by armed and mounted knights, and he demands their names as coolly as you would demand a dish of soup from an innkeeper.

Vambraces eyes him somberly.

249

"You are addressing Lord Olivier de Termes," he replies, "and Lord Pons de Villeneuve, and Lord Loup de Montguiscard, and this is Lord Guillaume de Minerve . . ."

Olivier de Termes! Son of Lord Raymond de Termes! I don't believe it!

Here he is, in the flesh. Olivier de Termes.

I've heard so many stories: When he and his father were defending Termes against Simon de Montfort, they used to raid his camp and capture his flags, which they hung from the castle ramparts. And they once killed the man standing beside Simon with a crossbow bolt. And one night, when they had run out of water and had agreed to open their gates the very next morning, a shower of rain straight from Heaven filled their cisterns again.

He died though, poor Lord Raymond. Simon de Montfort overcame Termes at last, and Lord Raymond died in a cell below his own citadel. Leaving his son to become one of the noblest and bravest of all the disinherited *faidits*.

Lord Olivier. The man himself.

I thought he'd be bigger.

"My lord." Even if I dropped to one knee, it wouldn't be enough. By rights we should both be groveling, Isidore and I. "My lord, I am your humble and devoted servant."

"Did you abduct Mabelia's daughter?" Lord Pons asks of Isidore (ignoring me). Almost at once, I can feel them all tensing. Perhaps it's the creak of leather as their muscles tighten or the way their hands drop casually to their sword hilts.

Oh, dear.

"No, no!" You don't understand! "No, I ran away! Truly! Lady Blanche was going to marry me to Hugues Saquet!"

A honk of laughter from Lord Pons. Lord Olivier says, "Who is Hugues Saquet?"

"Oh, a toothless old lump of suet from Lanta," Lord Pons replies. "You could cut off his head and it wouldn't make much difference."

"They want me to marry him because I would never have children or do anything wrong." (I wish that Lord Pons would stop laughing.) "But I don't want to marry him, I *can't!*"

"Don't blame you," says Lord Pons.

"So you ran off with a *priest?*" Lord Olivier's sounding more and more perplexed.

"I—I—" I don't know what to say. Isidore releases my elbow and puts a hand on my shoulder instead.

"I knew her father," he explains quietly. "Upon finding her in pursuit of a fool's errand, I took her under my wing. For her father's sake, I owe her my protection."

Fool's errand? Why you—you—

"Protection, do you call it?" Lord Pons leers. "We call it something else in this part of the country. Trust a Roman priest to get himself a bedfellow. Even on pilgrimage."

Bedfellow!

Isidore's grip tightens.

"You are mistaken," he murmurs as Lord Olivier frowns.

"Fool's errand? What fool's errand?" he wants to know.

"It was *not* a fool's errand!" (How *dare* they call it that!) "I wished to join the *faidits* in Aragon and offer them my service! Is that so foolish?"

Lord Pons obviously thinks so. He almost falls off his horse, trying to stifle his laughter. The other knights also look amused. One of them smirks. Another rolls his eyes and shakes his head sadly at my blind stupidity.

At my fruitless hopes . . .

These men don't want me. They would never

want me. How could I have imagined that they would? To them, I'm nothing but a nuisance.

Isidore was right. Just look at their faces. Just look at Olivier's astonished expression.

"You're going to Aragon?" he splutters. "On *foot?*"

"We had horses," Isidore interjects. "They were taken last night by the French."

If he had suddenly sprouted dragon's wings, his words couldn't have had a more alarming effect. On all sides there's a tossing of horses' heads as hands jerk at reins and backsides shift in saddles. Blades flash in the sunlight, half drawn from their scabbards. Eyes scan the surrounding hills.

"The French?" Lord Olivier snaps, his unlined face suddenly hard and alert. "You mean Humbert's crew?"

"Some of them. They camped near the *forcia* back there." I have to tell him this. It will be important to him. "It's not far, but they're gone now. We think they went west this morning."

"West?" Lord Olivier frowns. "Back to the Saverdun road, you mean?"

"We think so."

"God's grace," Lord Pons mutters. "That would have been a merry meeting!"

253

"Too soon for my taste," Lord Olivier agrees under his breath.

"We'll be hard put to outrun them at this rate. What if they arrive there before we do?" Lord Pons is addressing Lord Olivier, who flashes him such a fierce look that even the battle-scarred Pons flinches.

Suddenly, for the first time, Lord Loup speaks out.

"We cannot delay," he declares. He's very dark—almost as dark as I am—with cascades of shiny black hair, one thick eyebrow across his forehead, and brown smudges beneath his eyes. He's not as big as Lord Pons, but he looks just as dangerous. "If they passed near here this morning . . ."

"You're right," says Lord Olivier. "We cannot linger. We must go."

"And these?" Lord Guillaume's voice is a big surprise. It's high up in his nose—almost a whine, in fact—and it doesn't suit the rest of him, because he's the oldest and largest of the lot, red-faced and broad-chested, with a belly spilling out over his sword belt and feet the size of Garonne barges.

It's like hearing an ox cheep.

"We can't leave *her* here," Lord Pons interrupts, nodding at me. "Blanche will have my head if we do. Bernard as well. I'll never hear the end of it. Blanche will tell every Perfect from here to Montségur, and *they'll* be at me as well."

Lord Olivier sighs. "All right," he says. "You can bring her. I suppose we'll have to sort something out. Send her back to the Lady Blanche somehow."

What? Oh, no. Not Gran. You can't. If you don't want me, then leave me here—don't send me back to *Gran*!

"As for you, priest," Lord Olivier continues, circling Isidore, "I could kill you here, but I won't. If your story is true, then for watching over the daughter of Mabelia de Laurac you deserve to live, at the very least. Get on your way. Get out of this country."

"No, wait! My lord!" You don't understand! "I don't want to go back to Toulouse! You won't take me back, will you? I don't want to marry Hugues Saquet!" But Olivier isn't listening! And Lord Pons is bearing down on me—help!

"My lord!" Isidore sees Pons coming, too. He grabs me with both hands. "Lord Olivier, please, you must let me come with you!"

"No," says Olivier, and there's a flurry of movement as Pons surges past, his horse's hooves ringing against hard stone, his harness creaking, his body swinging, his arm reaching—

"Aagh!" Let go! Let go!

"No, please!" It's Isidore's voice, and he must be clinging to my tunic! God, I'll be torn apart!

"Ow! Ouch!" Ah. That's better. Except . . .

Except that it's not better! Because I'm up here on the horse in front of Pons, and Isidore is down there!

"No! You can't do this! Let me go!" You brigand, you— "Get *off* me!"

"A kindly warning, priest," Olivier says. "I have many friends between here and the court of Aragon. If I find that you have told anyone about meeting us here, my vengeance will be visited upon you."

"Wait—my lord, please." It's Isidore speaking. If I twist around—there! I can see him, hanging off Olivier's stirrup. He's dropped his saddlebag. He *can't* let them take me. "My lord," he pleads, "I owe a duty to her father—"

"And I owe a duty to her cousin, for all that he's a sniveling turncoat," Olivier replies, kicking hard to release Isidore's grip. Isidore stumbles backward; he nearly falls. "Go on your way, priest, and leave this country. You are not welcome here."

"Wait! Please!" Isidore's voice cracks. "Where are you going? Let me follow—let me come after you!"

"Father!" (I can't get down! You must help me!) "My lord, please, he's my friend, I can't—I can't leave him!" Not with the French so close . . . "Over here—Father—I don't want to go!" Get me down, hurry, *please*!

Isidore lunges. He grabs at the horse underneath me; he catches at the girth with one hand and the stirrup with the other.

My hand! Grab my hand!

Pons moves. I can feel his whole body convulse. There's a flash of silver. A splash of red.

A scream.

"Father!" Oh, God! Oh, God, what happened? He's cut! He's hurt! Pons just slashed him with a knife! "You cur! You turd! Let me *go*!" I'll kill you! God damn you to Hell, I'll rip out your eyes for that!

A roar from Pons because—yes! I got him! I scratched his cheek!

"Ooof!"

Wha—who—?

Dizzy.

Going to fall?

No. There's an arm in the way.

"Behave yourself," Pons growls, his rib cage vibrating, "or you'll get another one." Another what? Oh. He must have hit me. Hit me. Isidore! I have to crane my neck, but I can still see him. He's already so far behind, staggering and holding his arm, shouting something—I can't hear it. Pons must have cut his arm. He's bleeding. *Bleeding*. "Isidore!"

Oh, God. God help me, what shall I do? They cast him down in the dust. He's hurt and abandoned. I've lost him.

He's disappeared from sight.

‡CHAPTER NINETEEN‡

Once upon a time there was a beautiful princess who was abducted by a cruel giant. The giant had a dung heap for a nose, a cesspit for a mouth, and hair like a heap of dry entrails. Whenever he spoke, those around him would flee in terror, thanks to the stench of his breath and the stupidity of his words.

But the beautiful princess saved herself from the cruel giant with the help of . . . of . . .

Of a saint dressed all in white, with beautiful pearly teeth and the gentlest face in the whole world.

When are they ever going to stop?

Can they really be human? I'm so tired and sore and thirsty—my bladder is full and my stomach is howling—but they keep riding and riding without pause. How can they do it? They haven't even passed around a wineskin, let alone stopped to stretch their legs.

They *must* be thirsty. Pons has been sweating like a cellar wall. He hasn't been crying, of course (like me), but he's been losing enough salt water to float a merchant ship, steaming pile of pigs' offal that he is. I could kill him. I could kill them all. Curse them and their issue, how could they do this? When I think about Isidore . . . When I picture him all alone, lost and wounded . . .

But I can't. I have to stop thinking about him, or I'll go mad. After all, the monks were nearby. They'll take care of him. He can recover at Boulbonne and press on from there to Compostela, the way he planned. He won't have to buy me another horse. He won't have to hide from everyone because of me. He's better off, really. I just wish . . . I just wish . . .

Oh, God, I can't bear it.

"Are you sniveling again?" Pons rasps. "If you are, I swear, I'll drag you along by the heels."

I'm not. Look. I'm not crying—it's just my nose. It's stopped bleeding now, but it's still running. What do you expect, when you throw punches at it?

My sleeves are a mess.

"Where are we going, anyway?" I *know* that we crossed the road to Carcassonne awhile back. "Didn't we pass the Abbey of Saint Papoul on the right?"

"Shut up."

"I lived in Castelnaudary for a few months, but I've never been to the Black Mountains. Are we going to Saissac?"

"Shut your mouth or I'll shut it for you."

He means it, unfortunately. If I don't want my teeth punched through the back of my skull, I'd better keep quiet.

I'm right, though. This is all so familiar. We're in the foothills of the Black Mountains and over there on the left—that's the hill to the north of Castelnaudary. I keep catching glimpses of it through the trees. And we're slowing now because of the steepness of the road. Even Olivier is slowing, though he's the lightest horseman and the fastest, as well as the most accomplished. You almost forget, watching him, that he and his mount are two separate creatures.

Mind you, that wiry little sergeant—Vasco—he's a good rider, too. It's funny: I never knew that sergeants rode horses. But they do. Of the eight men in this company, only four are knights. The rest are sergeants or squires or some such thing. (No one's bothered to introduce me, but it's clear enough who gives the orders around here.) I think one of them may even be Catalan. I certainly can't understand a word he says.

"Hold," says Olivier with a gesture that everyone else seems to understand, and he swerves off the path toward slightly higher ground. Pons follows. There are branches to dodge and rocks to avoid, and why are we heading in this direction? This won't lead us anywhere, except over the edge of a cliff.

Ah. I see. A clearing.

And beyond it—what a sight! The lands of the Lauragais, spread out before us. There's Castelnaudary way off in the distance, clinging to a silver ribbon of river (I recognize the church spire) and— oh! There's Saint-Martin-Lalande! A tiny huddle of roofs, small enough to hold in your palm, set in a spider's web of white roads. There are stripy vineyards and straggling woods, and what's that over there? That dark mass spilling across a field, glinting as it moves?

God help us. Is it *Humbert*?

"The French!" Look there! "It's them—I know it is!"

"Shut up," says Pons before turning to Olivier. (He's hardly even out of breath.) "They're moving fast, don't you think? For a force that size."

Olivier shrugs. "Seven leagues in two days?" he retorts. "It's not such a great accomplishment."

"They won't be able to resist Saint-Martin, surely?" Loup actually sounds tired. "A little place like that? They're bound to attack it. And if they do, it will slow them down."

"Perhaps." Olivier's eyes are narrowed to dark slits as he stares out over the Lauragais country-side, one hand resting lightly on his hip, the other twisted around his reins. "Mark their route, though. It's wide of Castelnaudary."

"Oh, they'll never attempt Castelnaudary." Guillaume dismisses the notion with a snort. "There aren't enough of them. They wouldn't reach halfway around the walls."

"Then we are well placed," Olivier declares with a glance at Pons. And suddenly we're moving again. Again! Lord help me! I thought we might at *least* stop at the clearing, but I was wrong. Plunging back onto the road, which is getting less like a road and more like the scar of an endless rockfall, Olivier takes the lead ahead of Loup, Guillaume, and the sergeants. As for Pons, he's last in line.

My weight is slowing him down.

"Are we going to Saissac?" I've never been there, but I thought it was more to the east—and the setting sun is on our left now. "Will we reach it before nightfall?"

"One more word and I'll cut out your tongue," Pons snarls.

No help there. But I don't think that we're going to Saissac. We're not heading the right way. If it weren't pure madness, I'd say that we were riding to intercept the French—though for what purpose, I can't imagine. Four knights against an army? Even Olivier de Termes wouldn't risk those odds.

No, there's more to it than that. Olivier is bent on reaching a goal. A destination. And it's not Saissac, and it's not Castelnaudary, and Montferrand is much too far.

Where's La Bécède?

I could ask Pons, but it wouldn't be wise. La Bécède. I'm sure it's around here somewhere. I've never been there, and I don't know much about it, but people from La Bécède used to sell squirrel skins at the Castelnaudary markets.

A poor village, no doubt, but at least it's not Toulouse. I can't go back to Toulouse. If I'm going to die, I'd rather be killed by the French than by

Aunt Navarre. Because she'll kill me—I know she will. She'll never forgive me for taking her scissors.

My scissors, now. I still have them in my purse, so I'm not entirely defenseless. No pepper, though; I wish I hadn't wasted it all on Drogo. What am I going to do tonight? It's getting dim under the trees—there's a greenish twilight creeping out of the thickets that we pass. Birds are calling and wheeling. Sometimes we hit pockets of cool air flowing out of low, dank, shadowy places. Soon we'll have to stop and camp. Soon it will be night.

Oh, God, how I wish that Isidore were here!

Isidore. What's happened to him? Has he reached Boulbonne yet? I hope so. Lord Jesus our Savior, please let him be safe. Let him be resting on a bed somewhere, with his arm bandaged and a jug of wine at his side. (Wine! I'm *so* thirsty!) Surely he reached Boulbonne? Surely he's all right now? Except that he couldn't have carried his saddlebags, not with that wounded arm. Not both saddlebags, anyway.

Please, God, let his books be safe, too. If he loses them, it will break his heart. And mine.

Please, God, preserve him from the French.

"Stop leaning on me," Pons rumbles, and—ouch!—prods me in the ribs.

"Sorry."

"Sit up straight, what's the matter with you?"

What's the *matter* with me? I'm in agony—that's what's the matter with me! "My back's sore. . . ."

"Something else will be sore if you don't stop whining." And suddenly, after half a day's silence, Pons begins to talk. I don't know why. Is fatigue making him light-headed? "When did you last see your cousin?" he asks.

My cousin? "Which cousin?"

"Don't get smart with me," he barks, snapping my cheek with his fingers. "You know which cousin, your cousin Bernard!"

"Oh." *That* cousin. "Well . . . not for a long time. Not since we left Laurac."

Pons grunts. After a while, he says, "Haven't seen him myself since winter. Keeping his head low these days."

I'm not surprised. After making his submission to the King of France, Bernard Oth can't have many friends left.

"And his wife?" Pons continues. "You haven't seen anything of her?"

Nova? "No."

"She didn't join your little crew? That gaggle

of women Blanche has been dragging around with her?"

Our convent, you mean? "No." This is interesting. "Why, was she going to?"

A bark of laughter. "Not if she could help it, no," says Pons. "Bernard Oth wanted her to—or so he told me. But she wouldn't be persuaded."

I don't understand. "Why would he want her to do such a thing?"

"Why? Because it would put an end to their marriage, that's why."

Ah. I see.

"He'll get rid of her somehow, though, you mark my words," Pons muses, more to himself than to me. "He has a stubborn streak, does Bernard. Mind you, I don't blame him. There's nothing worse than a woman with a big mouth."

This is aimed at me, I'm sure. It means that I'm to speak only when I'm spoken to.

Suddenly, up ahead, someone shouts. Dusk has been settling like smoke, and it's harder than ever to see Olivier, who's still in the lead. Only Loup's white horse and Vasco's white surcoat are clearly visible. But there's something rearing up in front of us all, jagged and dark against the red-streaked sky.

It's studded with flickering lights, and there's a flag snapping over it, coiling and unfurling in the wind.

By the bargemen of Bazacle! Can it be La Bécède?

"In the name of the Count!" Olivier cries, and there's an exchange of greetings with one of the garrison. Yes, this must be La Bécède. (What else could it be?) It's a citadel, like Muret's, only smaller. Even in the dim light I can see stone walls that tower above us, their battlements swathed in shadow save where torches have been lit. There's a smell of cess and animals; the woods have been cleared all around us and replaced by little terraced gardens, with here and there a stunted fruit tree or poor thatched house. As for the citadel, it seems to be well placed—up high, with bald, rocky approaches on at least two sides. (Perhaps on three, but it's hard to tell in this light.) A village is huddled beneath it, behind the wall that we're skirting now: a wall that could be higher and better preserved, but which presents a formidable barrier even so.

And here's the garrison. Or some of it, anyway. Men are spilling from what must be a gate—yes, it's a barbican—wearing helmets and *bacquetons* and even chain-mail hauberks. They seem ecstatic that Olivier's arrived, kissing his feet or throwing themselves on their knees in gratitude. Olivier ignores most of them. He fixes his attention on one man only, an older fellow in blue, who's attended by two torchbearers and who seems to take charge of the whole procession.

Because we're a procession now: a line of horses, flanked by milling foot soldiers and led by a silver-haired official (a steward, perhaps?), winding its way through the village—which isn't a big village. You could practically spit from one end of it to the other. There isn't even a church that I can see. Just a handful of houses, all tightly packed, and one or two gardens. Pigs squeal somewhere off in the shadows.

If there are women around, they're not showing their faces.

"Welcome to La Bécède!" someone yells, so I was right. And the Lord of La Bécède is . . . who? I can't remember. My mind's blank.

I'm so tired and thirsty.

"Bernard Bontard!" Pons exclaims. He's peering at a fellow with unruly black hair like a ram's fleece. "Is that you? Is your master here?"

"He is, my lord," comes the reply.

"Well, that's a mercy," Pons mutters. Then he

raises his voice, which is hoarse with fatigue: "Loup! Do you hear? Guillaume de Puylaurens has already brought his men!"

"God be praised," Loup responds dully. And here we are at the castle. Our horses' hooves clatter over some kind of bridge; there's a short, steep climb to the second gate, which is small and high and squeezed between two monstrous towers. More foot soldiers greet us with joyful shouts as we pass under the portcullis. At last we reach the great stone bailey that would probably seem bigger if its walls weren't lined with ramshackle structures made of wood and daub and flapping blankets.

But there's a keep, too, and it looks invincible: large, tall, and practically windowless, with a narrow tower on each corner.

Do they have a well in this place? I certainly hope so.

"The Lord of Termes!" someone cries. "What a blessing!" Whoever he is, this noisy fellow, he's advancing on Olivier with his long arms spread wide, wearing a green surcoat that must have been good once, to judge from the silky gleam on its lining. (His boots are very handsome, too.) When Olivier dismounts, the two men embrace, and it becomes obvious that I'm in the presence of another lord. The Lord of La Bécède, probably. He's a tall man with the most beautiful hair I've ever seen, thick and wavy and touched with gold, like the hair of certain painted angels in the church of Saint Etienne. He also has the biggest nose I've ever seen, which spoils his beauty somewhat; it sticks out like a crow's beak or a boat's rudder.

Beside him, Olivier looks almost dainty and very, very tired.

"Off you get." Pons prods me in the ribs, and—whoops! Help!

But hands reach out and catch me, easing me to the ground. It's hard not to stagger like a drunkard. If I wasn't being held up, I'd be flat on my face.

"Thank you." It comes out as a croak because I'm so thirsty. And here's wine! A whole cup! "Thank you . . . Bless you . . ."

God, that's good!

Pons drops from his horse beside me, as heavy as a load of firewood. "Give me that," he says, snatching the cup from my hand. As he drains it, Lord Big-Nose approaches. (His nose comes first, followed by the rest of him.)

"Pons, my brother!" he says, taking Pons by surprise. Pons is still wiping his mouth when Big-Nose embraces him; the whole exchange is a bit clumsy.

271

"My lord Pagan," says Pons.

Pagan? Lord *Pagan*? The name sends a chill down my spine—as though I'm suddenly confronting my own father. But I'm not, of course. This is just Lord Pagan of La Bécède. I remember his name now. Navarre has mentioned it. Cousin Bernard, too. I suppose it's not an uncommon name hereabouts.

Still, I'm glad that Isidore isn't with me. Just for an instant, I'm glad he's far away. Because I know how much anguish that name would cause him, if only for a little while.

Oh, Isidore.

"And this?" Lord Pagan is almost giddy with joy; I can see it in the pale, glittering eye that he's turned on me. He's so happy that he's even deigned to notice the varlets. "Who is this, your squire?"

"Hell, no." Pons sounds alarmed at the very thought. "This is the niece of Bernard Oth, Lord of Montréal."

"The *niece*?" Lord Pagan exclaims, and there's a rippling murmur all around us.

"She was living with Lady Blanche de Laurac, in Toulouse, but she ran away," Pons continues. "We picked her up this morning down near the Abbey of Boulbonne, silly bitch."

272

Stinking pig. Keep a courteous tongue in your head, why don't you? Lord Pagan's high spirits have all drained away. He's wearing a troubled expression.

"Maybe you should have left her," he says. "We're living lean here, my friend."

But Pons shakes his head.

"Have you ever *met* Blanche de Laurac?" he retorts. "She'd tear strips off me if it ever came out that I left her granddaughter on the road to Compostela. With a *Roman priest*."

"A Roman priest?" Lord Pagan echoes. "But I thought half that family were Good Christians."

"They are. That's what I mean. You can't turn around in this part of the world without bumping into one of 'em, and they're mostly believers." Pons accepts a second cup of wine. "Even Bernard Oth isn't too friendly with his local bishops, though he's been flying the King's colors lately, of course. I don't want him turning on me if the wind changes and we find ourselves defending the same keep. Like this one, for instance." He nods at Lord Pagan's inner defenses. "He's got a mad temper, has Bernard Oth."

"Very well, then." Lord Pagan has stopped listening. He beckons to the silver-haired steward before turning back to Pons. "Isn't Lady Blanche a Perfect?" he asks. "Living with Perfects?"

"In a kind of nunnery," Pons confirms. "People send their daughters to her."

"That's what I thought." Lord Pagan addresses Silver-Top: "Take this girl to the chapel. She can sleep with Gerard de la Motta and the other Perfects."

With whom? With *Gerard de la Motta*?

Oh, no.

I don't believe this.

I spend four days traveling across the length and breadth of the Lauragais, and I end up with *Arnaude's cousin*!

‡CHAPTER TWENTY‡

So that's Gerard de la Motta. He doesn't look much like his cousin Arnaude. But he does remind me of someone. Who is it?

Oh, yes. He reminds me of Bernard Oth's lymer hound. The one with the dewlaps and the drooping cheeks and the rolls of loose skin over its eyes.

Even the set of his shoulders looks glum.

"What is your name?" he asks in a spiritless voice.

"Babylonne." It's nice of Silver-Top to abandon me at the door with barely a word of explanation. I feel as if I've been dumped in a corner. Discarded like a grape pip. "My mother was Mabelia de Laurac."

"Ah." He's heard about her. I can tell by the way his gaze skitters away from me, toward the chapel altar—which is bare, of course. A bare block of stone under a small, high, unglazed window. There's ribbed vaulting overhead, but nothing else to distinguish this chapel from an armory or a guardroom or even a rather large latrine that happens to have been requisitioned as a dormitory.

Four thin palliasses are laid out on the floor around a single oil lamp. Three other Perfects are huddled together on one of these palliasses like sheep on a raft. I recognize the young Perfect with the shaved head and the lazy eye. He's from Montréal, and he lived in Laurac for a while. His name is Peitavin. The others I don't recognize. There's a tall one and a short one, but they're both skinny, of course. (I've yet to meet a fat Perfect.) The short one has that wrung-out, sweaty look of someone enduring a painful dose of the flux. The tall one stares at me bug-eyed, as if I'm the Fourth Horseman of the Apocalypse. Even with a great stretch of stone floor lying between us, he's obviously afraid that I'm going to corrupt him somehow.

"Why did you run away from the Lady Blanche?" Gerard asks me suspiciously, without bothering to introduce his friends. "To commit fornication?"

"No!" (You twisted scrap of boiled ox-tripe, how dare you?) "To *avoid* fornication! My grandmother was trying to marry me off!"

Gerard blinks. "I can't believe that," he says. "Lady Blanche is a Good Woman. She is no friend to matrimony."

"For me, she is." (Anyway, what would you know? I've never seen *you* in her house, for all that your cousin's been living with her for a year. I've heard of you, naturally, because Arnaude's always dropping your name, but I've never seen you. How would you know anything about my grandmother?) "That's why I don't want to go back to Toulouse."

"What you want is of no importance," Gerard replies gloomily. "It is the Lady Blanche's wishes that must be respected. Perhaps she has despaired of you, owing to your want of proper reverence. You do not strike me as a fit candidate for the *consolamentum*."

And you don't strike me as a fit candidate for the human race, my friend. Frankly, when I compare you to Isidore, it's like comparing lilies to pond slime.

That's why I can't stay here. That's why I *must* find Isidore.

Tomorrow, perhaps. I'll leave first thing tomorrow, while Pons isn't looking.

"Who is your affianced?" Peitavin suddenly pipes up. (Smart little horsefly.) "Is he a believer?"

Gerard frowns him down. Clearly, he's not meant to be talking to women.

"He is not my affianced." (Fart-Face.) "I shall never marry him."

"You were asked for his name, girl!" Gerard snaps. "Now give it to me and speak in a civil manner while you're about it!"

"He is Hugues Saquet. Of Lanta." If it means anything. I can see that it doesn't—not to old Droopy-Drawers. But Peitavin snickers.

"Hugues Saquet is very old," he explains when Gerard shoots him an inquiring glance. "He is so old that he is incapable of sinning. He couldn't even eat meat or cheese, not having the teeth for it."

"Ah." Gerard nods. "I understand. Well—that makes sense. A marriage is no sin unless it is consummated. Your grandmother is a wise woman. You must go back to her and present your apologies for your prideful disobedience."

Over my dead body. "And how am I to do that, with a French army between me and Toulouse?"

Ha! *That's* scared 'em! They all stretch their necks

as if they're about to crow like cockerels. The short one even groans and clutches his belly.

"The French?" Gerard gasps. "They're coming?"

"Didn't you know?" (Where have you been living, at the bottom of a well?) "Lord Olivier seems to think that they might be heading this way."

"Lord Olivier?" It's Peitavin again. He seems to have forgotten that I'm a girl and unworthy of his address. "Lord Olivier de Termes? Is he here?"

"I came with him. And with Guillaume de Minerve and Pons de Villeneuve and—"

"Then they're rallying," Peitavin interrupts. For all that he looks like a botched job, there's something quick about him. He turns back to Gerard. "Lord Pagan was right. He *said* La Bécède would be the target, because there are so many Perfects here. That's why he sent for help. He could see it coming."

"Then we must go!" At last the tall Perfect speaks. He sounds as if he's talking through a mouthful of pebbles. "We must go at once, before they arrive!"

"In the dark?" Gerard retorts savagely. "Don't be a fool, Brother. If we go, it must be tomorrow. At first light."

You'll be lucky. There's a pause as the short Perfect scrambles to his feet and staggers past me, bent double. (Just as I thought: an attack of the

279

flux.) Being forced to step aside for him, I can't exactly help it if one of my feet crosses the threshold, can I?

Apparently, however, I'm forbidden to enter the chapel. Gerard says, "You can't come in here."

"Lord Pagan said that I was to sleep in here. With you." It's not my idea of a happy conjunction, either, but where else am I supposed to go?

Gerard shakes his head vigorously, so that his dewlaps jiggle.

"No, no," he says. "This is no place for a woman. You must go with the other women."

"What other women?" *I* haven't seen any.

"I'll take you. Here. Come with me."

And suddenly he's out of the chapel, heading down the stairs. For a man who looks as if he'd always be tripping over his own loose skin, he's surprisingly fast on his feet. I'm going to have to hurry if I want to catch up.

The circular staircase makes me dizzy. They always do when I'm due for a feed—especially if they smell of urine. I remember coming up these stairs, but I entered them from the Great Hall. This time we don't seem to be going anywhere near the Great Hall, presumably because it's now full of knights discussing important matters. Instead

Gerard leads me down and around and up again, past the latrines (no mistaking *that* smell), through a storeroom (mostly lumber and flax), into a wine cellar where the air alone could make you drunk.

From the wine cellar, more stairs lead up into what must be the buttery: dirty men snap at us as we squeeze by because they're trying to pour wine and carve meat for the new arrivals.

If I were alone, I might grab one of those cakes. But Gerard would see me chewing. And Isidore wouldn't want me to steal. I can just picture his expression—sorrowful and disappointed—if he spotted me filching a honey cake.

When we meet again (and we *will* meet again), I want to look him in the eye with a clear conscience. So I'll keep my hands off the food.

God, I'm hungry, though.

"This way," Gerard declares as if he can read my mind. Perhaps he saw me eyeing the pig's trotters. I'm half expecting that we'll plunge into the kitchens next—you generally find them next to butteries—but all at once we're in the bailey again.

I can't believe it. How did we get here?

"Hurry," says Gerard, snapping his fingers. And now I can smell the kitchens. They're off to the right and very close—about ten to fifteen paces

281

from the keep. (Wisely placed, I suppose, if you're concerned about fires.) They also seem to be stone-built against the rampart walls, but it's hard to see in the darkness. Gerard isn't interested in them anyway. He doesn't want me fed. He just wants me out of his sight.

Someone makes lewd sucking noises, but I don't know whether they're aimed at me or at the Perfect. It's the Perfect, after all, who's wearing long skirts. I can't see who made the noises, either, because there are quite a few dim, faceless figures moving about, and they're all of them men.

It's my experience that you can never find a corner to yourself in a castle like this.

"There is much sin around us," Gerard mutters. "You must guard your eyes and pray that God will keep you from all temptation." Like cakes, you mean? "Here," he adds, waving me into another structure jammed up against the walls. "In here."

It's very confusing. All at once I'm in a room with a thatched roof, and there's a lot of smoke everywhere because a fire is burning in a brazier over near the open window. Something's boiling on the fire in an iron pot, but this isn't a kitchen. At least, I don't think it is. There aren't any tables or knives or dangling hams. Instead there's a lot of firewood heaped about, and something that might be a big stone trough, and there are wooden buckets, and piles of rags, and many tunics and table-cloths hanging from ropes strung high across the room.

Whatever's cooking in that pot, it smells *abominable.*

"Woman!" says Gerard. "Ah! There you are."

There she is. A mountainous great lump of lard spilling over the sides of a three-legged stool. Her big round face is flushed, and her thin hair is plastered to her scalp with sweat, and she's picking peas from a pod, popping them, one by one, into her rather small mouth.

She doesn't bother getting up, I notice.

"This is Babylonne, from Toulouse," Gerard announces. He hates speaking directly to any woman, let alone one with breasts like two melons in a sack, so he addresses himself to the wall over her right shoulder, carefully avoiding her eye. "Babylonne is related to Lord Bernard Oth," he explains. "She needs modest clothes and a place to sleep. You must assist her until she can be returned to her family."

And that's that. He's said all he's going to. Abruptly, he turns on his heel and walks out, leaving me abandoned like a chewed bone in a dish.

There's a long pause. I can see another woman perched on a wood stack; she's mending a cloak. There's also a boy, about ten years old. He seems to be trying to delouse himself.

"If that fellow was trampled in running water and dried," the fat woman observes at last, "he'd feel a lot happier in his own skin, because it would shrink to fit his bones." She tosses her empty peapod onto the floor, where a wandering dog snaffles it up. "What did he say your name was? Babylonne?"

"Yes."

"I'm Maura." The fat woman gestures at the woman on the wood stack. "That's Grazide. Are you some kind of bastard, then?"

"Yes." If it's any of your business.

"I thought so. They wouldn't be throwing you in here with us if you weren't. Not someone with your relations." Maura turns to Grazide. "See if you can find her a scrap to wear, will you, my dove? Something with long skirts." She turns back to me. "I suppose that's what he meant by 'modest,' is it?"

How should I know? When I shrug, she smiles.

284

She has terrifying teeth, all black and jagged like burned battlements.

"You neither know nor care," she says in her booming voice. "I understand. But perhaps you can tell me if you're meant to be fed?" Seeing me glance at the steaming pot, she laughs and slaps her knee. "No, no, that's not for you, my piglet! That's for our brave sergeants, to make them strong!" By now Grazide is laughing as well. She's a scythe of a woman, all sharp angles and narrow limbs.

"And to keep them clean in thought and deed," she adds, to Maura's great amusement. They shriek together for a while, until Maura finally gasps, "We're boiling soap. Fat and ashes. You wouldn't enjoy it, Babylonne; it's an acquired taste."

Oh. Right. I see.

"Go on, Grazide, get off your bony rump and find the poor girl some clothes!" Maura continues. Whereupon Grazide puts down her sewing and goes to do as she's bid. Maura beckons to me. "I can offer you some bread and a bit of cheese," she says, studying my face with narrowed eyes. "How would that suit you?"

"It would suit me very well." I'm trying to be polite here, because there's something formidable about Maura. I don't sense any fear in her at all—

285

not of anyone or anything. "Thank you for your kindness."

"Oh, it's not kindness to feed a skinny little sprout like you," she replies. "It just makes people uncomfortable, seeing the condition you're in. You need feeding up, my lamb."

"That's right," Grazide interjects from over near a pile of clean washing. "Men like a bit of flesh with their bones, don't they, Maura? They like something they can chew on."

Ha! That sounds funny, coming from *you*, Spindle-Shanks. Maura catches my eye and winks. "Grazide's had most of hers chewed off already." She smirks. "Haven't you, Grazide? Grazide's very popular hereabouts." She waits for a moment before adding, "Now that there isn't much choice."

"Oh, you don't know anything!" Grazide retorts crossly. She flings two garments across the room with such force that—ouch! They sting when they hit my chest. One's a scab-colored *bliaud;* the other's a cesspit-green gown to go under it. Both of them look well worn.

"What do you mean, 'Now that there isn't much choice'?" This gown has no end. It's going to be much too long, I can tell. "Do you mean that there aren't any other women here?"

"A few in the village," Maura replies. "But the ladies of the family and all their attendants—they left weeks ago. They didn't stay long."

"Because the French are coming?" It seems like a sensible question to me. I don't know why Maura thinks I'm so hilarious.

"The French?" She titters. "God help us, the French would be a fine distraction! No, no, you can't blame the French. The French never built this place."

"The ladies never linger here," Grazide interrupts. "They only stop on their way to somewhere else."

"I mean, it's not exactly Narbonne, is it?" Maura shifts in her seat and breaks wind so loudly that the dog scurries behind a woodpile. When she speaks again, she seems to be imitating a person of high birth—to judge from the pursed lips and fluting accent. "Imagine sitting through a siege in a place like this! No baker's oven. No proper forge. Leaky cisterns. Blocked latrines."

"At least there's a well, though," Grazide points out. "There's not a single well inside the Castelnaudary defenses."

"We wouldn't be here ourselves," Maura continues, ignoring her friend, "if the men could wash their own clothes, poor helpless souls that they are."

"Or sew their own seams," Grazide remarks.

"Though they can ply a needle well enough if Grazide's around, eh, my poppet?"

More shrieking laughter and slapped thighs. (These women can't seem to get their minds out of their drawers.) But I have to admit, it sounds as if I've stumbled on to what is, basically, a fortress. Not a court's cradle or a young township or even a well-defended farm, but a stark, grim stronghold, which has been stripped down to its fundamentals so that it might serve as a shield mounted high for the French to joust at. The question is—when will they strike their first blow? And will I be able to escape from this place before the blow falls?

I can't stay here. I have to find Isidore. I have to make sure that he's safe and well.

First thing tomorrow, I'm leaving.

‡CHAPTER TWENTY-ONE‡

Isidore?

No, he's not here. It was a dream. He seemed so real, but I was dreaming.

Where am I now? What's all that noise? Whose blanket is this?

Wait, I remember. La Bécède. I'm in La Bécède. And I must have fallen asleep. . . . Yes, that's right. In the corner of this room. Maura let me have a blanket and a pile of old bandages and palliasse covers to sleep on.

She's not here now, though. Neither is Grazide. The brazier's out, and the lines overhead have been stripped of wet washing. Outside, it's very bright. Full day. How high is the sun? What time is it? Why is everyone making so much noise?

Oof, my back!

It's so confusing because of the dream. I can still see Isidore's house; it had a Great Hall like the one here, only there were paintings on the walls. Paintings of saints and angels. Though my eyes might be looking at smoke-stained rafters and discarded peapods and torn, smelly clothes, my head's full of golden wings and glass goblets.

I have to get out of this pigsty. I have to get out and find Isidore before the French come. Only I don't have much time. . . .

Damn. It's just as I thought—this gown is too long. If I don't want to trip over the hem, I'll have to bunch it up around my waist under my girdle, and that will make me look pregnant. As for the *bliaud*, it's much too short. It barely covers my backside.

Oh, well. Who cares? I'm not exactly on the prowl for a husband.

Yeow!

God, the light is bright! And the sun—it's way up there! I can't believe it's so late. How can I have slept for such a long time? It must be nearly noon. *Anything* could have happened!

In fact, something already has happened. I can tell, just by one glance at the bailey. There are too many people. Men are running everywhere, shouting and gesturing and swarming all over a half-built wooden frame, pounding in nails with mallets. There are women, too, huddled near doorways with their children. Armed soldiers are stamping about in full chain mail. There's a dreadful screeching noise as someone sharpens a blade on a whetstone. There's even a small flock of sheep squeezed into a makeshift pen over by the eastern tower; their anguished bleats are adding to the confusion.

I can hear a lot of shouting, too. Faint cries of "whoreson dung-eaters" and "go suck up your own pizzle" are drifting down from the battlements.

Wait! Who's that over there? He looks familiar.

"You! Boy!" It's that boy from last night. The one who was trying to pick lice off his own scalp. Seeing him in broad daylight, I now understand why no one else would do it. He's one of those children you wouldn't touch with tongs: his eyes are leaking yellow gum, his nose is pouring green snot, and his face is covered in dry, reddish, scaly patches. "What's your name, boy?"

"Dim."

"*Dim?*" What sort of a name is that? It's worse than Babylonne. "What's going on, Dim?"

"Don't you know?" He gawps at me, blinking

through blobs of pus, poor child. He looks frightened. "The French are here."

Oh, no. *No.*

Isidore.

"Here?" What do you mean, *here?* I don't see any French. "Where are they? Show me."

"Out there." He points. "Beyond the walls."

Beyond the walls. As he runs off (to hide, no doubt), everything becomes clearer. Of course. It all makes sense now. That wooden frame—it's probably going to be a trebuchet or a mangonel. Something to hurl rocks with, in any case. And all the women must have come in from the village. As for those insults, they must be aimed at the French.

Ah, God. The French.

They always come back. We beat them off and we beat them off and they never go. All my life, they've kept returning with their war machines and their bloodthirsty bishops and their endless troops— wave after wave of them—like a recurring nightmare. Why can't they leave us alone?

I'm trapped here now. I'll *never* find Isidore now!

"Fulk of Toulouse," someone says nearby, and the name stings me like a hornet. It makes me drop my hands from my face and turn, just in time to spot Vasco, the sergeant, passing me on his way to the keep. He's with someone else—someone I don't know—and they're discussing the French.

"I recognize him," Vasco continues. "He was with the French King last year."

"The Bishop of Toulouse?" his friend says. "That Fulk? The one who preached against the Count? Who took the French side at Muret?"

"If there are French about, my brother, Fulk will be with them. Kissing their arses. Trust *him* to show up with his gaggle of pet priests."

The two men disappear into the keep, and I can't hear anymore. But I don't need to. I know all there is to know about Fulk of Toulouse. I know that he was with Simon de Montfort when they murdered my mother. I know that he was cast out of Toulouse by the will of its count and its populace.

I have to see him. I have to look at the face of evil.

Oops! But not until I can see again. The sun is so bright that a plunge into the nearest tower practically blinds me. Everything's so dark. I'll have to wait for my eyes to adjust. That's it. And now I can pick out details: a brace of lances, propped against one wall. Bales of straw and flax. Empty oil pots, their mouths gleaming. Not a soul in sight.

But the staircase is more crowded. It's partly blocked by one soldier carrying a huge stone. Other

293

soldiers almost knock me over on their way down. "Move your fat arse!" one of them shouts. A glimpse of the second-floor guardroom reveals palliasses, a pile of conical helmets with attached nose plates, and a man restringing his bow.

Someone's been spitting all over these stairs — they're very slippery.

"Stand aside!" grunts the man with the rock. "Look out! Stand aside!"

And here we are at the top of the tower. It's a frenzied scene: the whole room is stuffed with men, and there's even one woman. (I can see Maura peering out through an arrow slit.) Someone's greasing up arrowheads that are wrapped in flax and tow. He's surrounded by a scattering of shields, all of them made of leather on wood with bits of horn attached, and all of them looking as if they've seen better days. The man with the rock dumps his burden on a small pile of similar rocks and turns to head downstairs again.

Without removing her eye from the arrow slit, Maura says, "What are on those oxcarts?"

"Siege machines," replies a man wearing a horn cap. "The French love their machines. I heard that Simon de Montfort spent twenty-one *livres* a day on the carpenters who worked his."

"You! Girl!" The shout's so close, it makes me jump. "What are you doing here?"

Who? Me?

"Go and make yourself useful!" A piece of gristle in quilted leather waves his arms at me. "Go and get water! Bring water!"

Oh, all right. All right, I heard you. Water. Water for the defense.

There are more stones coming up the stairs, borne by panting, red-faced men. To dodge them means delaying in the second-floor guardroom, which has an arrow slit of its own—and no line of people waiting to use it (yet). I wonder if I could just have a little peek. I don't see why not. They're not desperate for water yet, are they? And that archer doesn't seem very interested in me.

"Mind where you're treading," he says. All around on the floor are arrows stacked in bunches. But they're easy enough to avoid.

The wind cuts through the arrow slit like a knife, making my eye water. Still, I can see some things. Smoke rising. White tents. Hobbled horses. And what's that? A faraway sound. A distant voice . . .

If I put my ear to the arrow slit instead of my eye, I might be able to hear better. Yes. That's it. A few words carried on the wind: "Mercy of King Louis . . ." and "will of the Holy Spirit . . ."

Are they parleying out there? By the blood of all believers, we're not going to *surrender*, are we?

Ow!

Who did that?

"Are you waving your backside around for a reason?" leers the man who must have pinched me. Oafish churl. He reaches for me again, but stumbles on some arrows; the archer cries sharply, "Pick up your feet!" and here's my chance to duck for cover.

Garrisons are all the same. They're raw and rude, with no trace of restraint anywhere. You get tanners and salt sellers drunk with their own martial glory, turning into beasts before your very eyes. As for the mercenaries, they're even worse. There's nothing human about them. They're all pigs. Crows. Mad dogs.

Perhaps Isidore was right. Perhaps Aragon would have been the same. Why would the Viscount's garrison at Aragon have been any more upright in its conduct than the garrison of Olivier de Termes at La Bécède?

How could I have been so stupid, expecting unstained honor amongst men of war?

Whoops! And here's Gerard de la Motta, standing at the bottom of the staircase. (I knew that he'd never get out of La Bécède in time.)

"What are *you* doing here?" he asks. "This is no place for you."

"I'm fetching water."

"You should go to the kitchens. With the other women."

"I've been told to fetch water." And that's what I'm going to do, so you'd better not get in my way! "You should fetch water, too. We must all work together, if we're to defeat the French."

"Wait. Come back . . ."

But he's too late to stop me. I'm off to the laundry room, where there are buckets to be found. The question is, where's the well? Oh—there it is. Over there, near the stables. Almost hidden by the people clustered around it.

I wonder why they need water up there on the battlements. To drink? To extinguish burning bolts? To boil up and pour through deadfalls onto French heads? Onto the tonsured pate of Bishop Fulk?

I'd like to see *his* brains boil. I'd like to see the skin hanging off his flesh in long, flayed ribbons.

"Oh!" And here's Grazide, curled around a hairy man with bare legs. It's so dark in this laundry room; they're going to break someone's neck, rolling around down there. "I just—um—I have to get a bucket. Sorry." If you could just roll out of my way . . . Thanks.

So Maura was right. Grazide is popular. It's enough to turn your stomach—especially when you consider her appalling taste—but I'm not going to think about that. I've got other things to think about. The well, for instance. I must draw water from the well.

There are many, many people around the well, every one of them an armed man (though some only have knives at their belts). They're all large and loud and unshaven, lolling about as if they have nothing else to do, scratching their balls and passing around a wineskin and laughing at jokes that are probably all about lopped-off limbs or castrated husbands. One by one they stop laughing when they see me.

A few of them spit.

"Who are you?" says a man who seems to be missing most of his nose.

"I am Babylonne, cousin of Bernard Oth, Lord of Montréal." It's no good knuckling under to men like this. You have to put your chin up and look them straight in the eye. "I have come for water. They need water on the battlements."

"Bernard Oth?" someone says. "Is Bernard Oth here?"

"No, no," Master Noseless replies. "I've heard about this one. She came with Lord Pons last night."

A snort from somewhere to my left. "Pons never did have much taste in women," somebody mutters before the winch starts turning. Its squeals put a stop to any further conversation; we all just stand in silence as the smallest, weakest, youngest member of the group draws some water. His friends stare at me, some chewing, some leering, some doing lewd things with their tongues.

Why doesn't anybody ask them what the hell they're up to? Where's Lord Olivier? Where's Lord Pagan? On the battlements, probably. Parleying with Humbert de Beaujeu and that Devil's spawn Fulk.

"Here," says the Noseless Wonder. "Give me that." And he takes my bucket, which he fills from another bucket on the end of the rope. "Now," he adds, holding my bucket out of reach. "What do I get for it?"

God give me patience. If only I had my pepper!

"Well?" He leans forward. "What about a kiss, eh?"

What about a punch in the mouth, Bowels-for-Brains? "Here." Here's my payment. The first coin that comes to hand is a *Caorsin*. "Have this."

One flick and it disappears into their midst. Immediately they all go mad. They dive for it like hens on a worm, because they probably think that it's silver or gold. Noseless abandons my bucket without a second thought, wading into the fight. Quick, Babylonne! Get away, while you still can! And don't forget your bucket.

What am I going to do now? I can't go back to that well—not until someone clears all the scum away. Once I've delivered this water, I'll have to find some other method of making myself useful.

This water is heavy. It's dragging my arm out of its socket. Gerard's no longer in the tower, thank God, but there are many others, buzzing about like flies. They keep knocking into me, spilling my water onto the stairs. "Stand aside!" You morons. "Stand aside!" But nobody takes the slightest bit of notice.

Whoops! Just my luck. Another obstruction blocking my way. The last one was noseless, and this one's as drunk as a bishop. There's wine on his breath, he's sweating like a piece of cheese, and his nose is the color of cock's comb.

"Aha!" he cries. "What's this? A little fresh chicken for our comfort?"

By all that's holy. "Get out of my way."

"Got to pay the toll first, my dear." And he reaches for me.

Splash!

The water hits him so hard, he lands on his backside. (Take that, you sot.) As the crowd behind him roars with amusement, he flaps around like a landed fish, cursing and spluttering. But what's this? Help!

"Let go!"

Someone's grabbed me from behind! Get off! Stop it! Arms tighten around my chest, lifting me— pinning me—and the drunkard in front of me is lunging again!

WHOOMP!

This time the bucket fells him for good, the cur. *"Let go, damn you to Hell!"* Whoever's got me doesn't listen, though. He swings me around, through the door of the second-floor guardroom, and this is bad—this is very bad—all the men behind us are cheering and hooting . . . I can feel a foul breath on my cheek . . .

301

God, God, God, God, God—But here's Loup de Montguiscard. Straight in front of me, not six steps away.

He's head to head with the archer, in deep conversation about gut or ballistas or some such thing. He looks tired and tousled and as thin as a pike; his sword belt is almost sliding off his narrow hips, and his surcoat could do with Maura's attention.

When he sees me, he frowns.

"What the hell do you think you're doing?" he asks—but he's not addressing me. (Corpse-Breath mumbles something in my ear, the turd.) "Who gave you permission to leave your post?" Loup continues as the grip around my chest loosens. "What do you think this is, market day? Who do you think you are, the Archbishop of Narbonne? Get back up on the walls! Now!"

Release! My feet hit the floor as Corpse-Breath beats a hurried retreat; he's smaller than I thought, and older, with a face that looks as if it's been used as a whetstone for the last thirty years, all scored and pitted.

"By the by," Loup adds in a bored, impatient voice that he raises for the benefit of those on the stairs, "if you lay a hand on this one, you'll have

Pons de Villeneuve to answer to. This one's kin to Bernard Oth."

He nods at me before turning back to the archer. And here I am, on my own, abandoned again. What shall I do? Thank him? Slip out quietly, back into that crowd of rutting swine? Try to fetch another bucket of water?

Maybe I'd be better off with the women after all. Maybe Gerard de la Motta was right. God, I'm starting to shake. Like a triple-damned *coward*.

I can't do this. I can't *bear* this. I wish Isidore were here.

"Well, it's all fresh sinew," the archer is saying. "Useless until it's dried . . ."

Wait. What's that sound? Horns? Trumpets? Loup lifts his head. So does the archer. Everyone on the staircase falls silent, listening.

It's Loup who finally speaks. In a harsh drawl that matches the crooked line of his mouth, he says, "Well—there's the parley come to an end. Now at last the fight will begin."

And his chain mail clinks as he shifts his weight to his back foot.

‡CHAPTER TWENTY-TWO‡

Once there was a beautiful princess who lived trapped in a mighty castle . . . No. On second thought, I don't want to be a princess. I don't want to live in a castle.

One morning, Babylonne woke up in her own bedroom in the house of Father Isidore Orbus. When she got dressed, she put on a pair of boots and a silk-lined gown. Then she went downstairs, where Father Isidore was waiting. He smiled and said, "It's time for your reading lesson—unless you'd like to go and buy a pen and ink first?"

Father Isidore. I hope he's all right. It's been a week now—anything could have happened. Lord our Heavenly Savior, let him be all right. I'm so worried about him.

"Oh, we'll be fine," Maura's saying. She and Grazide are sitting across the room from me, near their stone trough. But they're not washing. They're just sitting and talking as they delouse each other. "Don't trouble yourself, Grazide; there's nothing to be afraid of. Nothing at all."

"But the food can't last forever." Grazide is beginning to fret. "What if it runs out? What if we have to surrender?"

Maura waves a careless hand. "Listen," she replies, "I was at the siege of Montferrand sixteen years ago. I've been through it all before, and let me tell you this: the garrison never comes out of it well, but people like us . . . pah!" She clicks her fingers. "We're not important enough to attract attention."

"But—"

"Besides, no matter what a man's fighting for, he always needs his washerwomen. Men are all the same—they can cook for themselves, they can draw water and milk cows and make bread if they have to, but they won't wash clothes. I've never met a man yet who'll scrub his own drawers. So don't worry—we're safe."

"But what if they start rationing water?" It's Dim who speaks, in his hoarse little voice. He's been hanging around a lot—I don't know why. I don't know who he belongs to or where he comes from. He just seems to spend most of his time curled up near the laundry woodpile. "I've heard that the water in the well might get low," he adds. "What if you can't wash clothes anymore?"

"Then we'll find something else to do," Maura retorts. "We'll empty crap buckets or scrape blood off the walls. Don't worry—there'll always be some unpleasant job that no one else wants to get stuck with. You watch."

"But what if the French want to empty their own crap buckets?" Dim pipes up. He's worried, and I don't blame him. If anyone looks expendable around here, it's poor Dim—what with his feeble limbs and his gluey eyes and his snotty nose. In fact, there's many a war-hardened mercenary on both sides of the castle wall who wouldn't think twice about feeding him to a hog or using him for target practice.

I should be nicer to Dim. Isidore would be, I know. He was kind to that mad old woman, Petronilla. He was kind to those pitiful, cave-bound Perfects. He was kind to me.

I should be charitable like Isidore. Because Isidore always knew what was right and what was wrong.

"If the French come, you should hide," is my advice to Dim. "You're so small; you can easily hide."

"Where?" he wants to know—though he's better placed to answer this question than I am. He's more familiar with La Bécède, after all.

"Somewhere dirty." Where do you think? "Somewhere no one would think to look."

"Under Grazide's skirts," Maura suggests, and receives a slap from Grazide. "Ow!"

Before Grazide can strike again, however, the two women are distracted. They stop what they're doing, listening hard. They turn their heads.

It's that singing again, faint and sweet. The Roman priests must be marching around outside the walls barefoot, singing their Latin songs. I saw them at it the day before yesterday, when I was up on the ramparts bringing rocks to hurl at the French.

God, I'm so tired.

"There they go," says Maura, straining to catch the sound of the distant chorus. "You'd think they'd have better things to do."

"It's the same time every day, have you noticed?" Grazide remarks. "I wonder why."

Maura shrugs. "Personally, I don't mind it," she confesses, turning her attention to Grazide's scalp.

307

"I wish they'd change their tune, though. Sing something a bit livelier. Like 'The Red-Combed Cock,' for instance."

She and Grazide laugh the way they always do when they hear a smutty joke. Grazide actually starts to sing about a red-combed cock perching in a lady's chamber, but she stops suddenly as someone sticks his head through the door.

Whoops! It's Gerard de la Motta.

With any luck he won't see me, though. I chose this seat deliberately because I'm shielded by a great big pile of dirty washing.

"Are you looking for Babylonne, Master?" Maura says cheerfully. "She's not here, I'm afraid."

"Are you sure?" I can't see Gerard's face anymore, but he sounds suspicious. "She doesn't seem to be anywhere else."

"You can have a look if you like." Maura farts before continuing. "Mind those silk drawers, though. If you touch 'em when they're wet, it will leave a stain. And I just cleaned all the stains off."

"Um—er—no, that's all right," Gerard mutters. There's a brief silence, broken at last by Grazide's guffaw. *If you touch 'em when they're wet, it will leave a stain,*" she chuckles. "You're a dirty sow, Maura!"

"It's not my fault if he's got a lecher's mind,"

Maura rejoins. "Where's the girl? Babs, my poppet, he's gone now. You can come out if you like."

Thank you, God. That's the second time today. Why can't he leave me *alone*?

"If you want to know what I think, I think he's got a yen for you, my Babsy," Maura continues, flicking a dead louse off her thumb. "Otherwise he wouldn't always be chasing you around."

"It's not that." (Can't you think about anything above the waist?) "He just doesn't like me wandering free. He wants to keep me locked up somewhere, because he's scared of my grandmother."

"Ha! Maybe that's what he *says*," Maura replies. "They might *say* that they're against a cuddle in the cow byre, but they're all cut from the same cloth."

"Not Good Men, though," Grazide objects. "Good Men really are chaste."

"Don't you believe it." Maura speaks with authority. "They all need to plant their standards, and the less they do it, the worse they are. Good Men and Roman priests alike."

You're wrong, Maura. You're wrong because you don't know Father Isidore. Father Isidore really *is* a holy man. He doesn't even notice if you're a girl or a boy.

"Anyway, if I were you, I'd keep away from those Good Men," Maura adds, dragging a nit out of Grazide's hair. "Because if this place submits, they'll be first in the fire."

"I know." How could I *not* know?

"They burned 'em at Minerve. They burned 'em at Les Casses. They'll burn 'em here," Maura continues, as if I never even opened my mouth. "There's only one lot that ever comes out of these things worse than the garrison, and that's the Perfects. You don't want anybody thinking you're one of *them*."

CRA-A-ASH!

God help us! What was *that*? It shook the very ground—I can hear someone screaming—don't tell me they've broken through!

Grazide whimpers. Even Maura frowns. As for the boy, he seems to shrivel up like a worm in the sun, cringing fearfully.

I don't know what to do. What should I do? What would *Isidore* do? I know that he'd try to offer some comfort. . . .

"Come on!" It's Maura, gesturing to me. "Come quick!"

Dim starts to climb under a pile of dirty laundry. (He'll be safe enough there, I suppose.) Outside, everything's a mess. There are people running around like startled chickens. Someone's stretched out on the ground and . . . Ah. I see.

A rock must have come over the wall and shattered in the middle of the bailey. That poor soul was hit by a flying splinter.

Unless I'm mistaken, the French have finally gotten their trebuchet to work.

"Come on," says Maura from behind me. "We'd better take this one up to the chapel." And she brushes past, shambling toward the wounded man on the ground.

I suppose I'd better help, since I'm on infirmary duty. I wish I didn't have to, though. I hate this job. I'd rather do *anything* else. I'd rather carry sand or draw water or pass bolts to the men who arm the ballista, up on the walls in full view of the French. I'd rather shovel *manure* than move the wounded.

Not that there have been many wounded yet, but there will be.

"Mercy on us," says Maura as she rolls the limp figure onto his back. God's death! That's too . . . that's too much. I can't look.

He's lost half his face.

CRA-A-ASH!

Help! Another one! But it didn't sound close—it

311

must have hit the wall. Yes, up there. It must have knocked a merlon off the ramparts.

"Come *on!*" Maura snaps. "Take his feet, will you?"

Take his feet. Yes. There's nothing wrong with his feet. If I keep my eyes fixed firmly on his feet, I won't be sick. Someone's still screaming somewhere, and here comes Olivier, running across the bailey. He's pulling a surcoat on over his chain mail, which chinks with each step. He has the ruffled hair and creased face of a man who's just woken from a heavy sleep.

If he's been sleeping, things can't be too bad. Can they?

Vasco is with him.

"...aimed at the weakest point," Vasco's saying. "But they're firing wide."

"We have to get out there somehow," Olivier mutters. "Get out there and burn it."

"Move, you slug!" says Maura, and she's talking to me. Right. Of course. This is no time to stand and stare. As we shuffle toward the keep, I can hear somebody crying. I can see shards of rock scattered around—shards that might be useful if they're collected. All the children should be made to collect those chips of rock.

Suddenly, the wounded man whimpers.

"It's all right, my lad," says Maura. (At least he's alive.) Inside the keep, there aren't many people. The Great Hall's practically empty; everyone must be up on the walls. I recognize the soldier who's asleep on a pile of straw under a bench. He's the one who took my *Caorsin* from me by the well a couple of days ago.

Doesn't he *ever* do any work?

CRA-A-ASH!

Another missile. Closer, this time. God preserve us.

"The French are in a hurry," Maura wheezes. The wounded man gurgles with each breath, and it's a terrible sound. I'd rather hear rocks hitting the walls. At the base of the stairs, Maura shifts her burden. She's beginning to pant. "Got him?" she asks.

"Yes."

"Not much farther."

Maybe not, but what good will it do? This man is dying, I'm sure of it. And taking him to Gerard de la Motta won't help. On the contrary. Gerard's no physician.

If these stairs don't kill the poor wretch, Gerard de la Motta certainly will.

"Make way!" yells Maura—because who knows what careless fool might be hurtling down toward

313

us? Oof! I must be bearing most of the weight now, and it's quite a load. He's a big man, this one; his feet are as long as my forearm. We're leaving a trail of blood behind us. (Somebody's bound to slip on it.) And here we are at the chapel.

At last.

"We've got another!" Maura announces for the benefit of the Perfects who turn to watch us come in. "Where do you want him?"

I'd be laughing if I wasn't so heartsick. Look at the way they all cringe at the sight of Maura's huge, bouncing body and sweaty face! Only the old Gascon sergeant wearing homespun doesn't seem to notice Maura. He's more interested in what she's carrying.

"Who is it?" he asks in his thick, crunchy voice. (It's like the sound of seeds being ground in a pestle.) "Does anyone know?"

No one does. At least, no one says anything. Certainly not the half dozen men lying on the floor, who are probably incapable of speech anyway. The amputee by the altar will never talk again, in my opinion. He's dying. You can smell his stump from way over here; Peitavin's been left beside him to flap the flies away. The rest of the patients simply twitch and moan or lie unconscious, their faces the color of tallow.

Gerard de la Motta ignores them, however. He's not interested in their suffering. He's far more interested in mine.

"Where have you been?" he demands, scowling at me. "I told you to stay here. At your post."

"I felt sick." This whole place makes me sick. You, especially. "I had to get some air."

"Put him over here," the old sergeant commands, taking charge. "That's it. Gently."

"You shouldn't wander about, Babylonne." Gerard's still nagging. "Why should you do such a thing? Are you *courting* the attention of lewd men?"

Oh, will you shut *up*? "I'm bringing in the wounded!" In case you haven't noticed! "Can you help me, please? Before I drop this man?"

But it's the old sergeant who catches my load as it slips from my grip—catches it and carefully lowers it onto a palliasse. "There's still a piece of stone buried in that mess," he observes, peering into the wound. "We have to get it out."

"Won't do any good," Gerard remarks gloomily. "This man isn't going to live long."

"So maybe you should just put him out of his

misery?" Maura drawls, and Gerard flushes—though he pretends that he didn't hear.

"I'll get the implements," he announces in lofty accents. God, but he's a loathsome louse. Having scraped together a few small knives, a pair of tweezers, and a razor, he won't let anyone else go near them. In his view, there's only one person entitled to wield such delicate and expensive equipment, and that's him.

"All we can do," says the old sergeant as Gerard shuffles over to his jealously guarded hoard, "is pull out the splinter, bandage him up, and pray."

"Unless you've got some comfrey," Maura interjects. She's bent double, hands on knees, still recovering from that last steep climb. "Comfrey or hawthorn. They might do him some good."

"Be silent, woman!" It's Gerard. "You have no place here! Get along!"

"No, she's right," the old sergeant rumbles—much to everyone's surprise. "Comfrey can help."

"Nonsense!" Gerard bustles up to his patient with an armload of knives and grubby bandages. "All the authorities agree that wounds must be kept open with padding until the pus drains. Any kind of herbal poultice might impede the flow of pus and prevent the fever from breaking."

"Ah, but fevers are no problem," Maura declares, straightening up and folding her arms. She really is interested; sickness of any kind is the one thing that she doesn't laugh about. "With a fever, you should pick vervain while you recite a Sunday prayer, and grind it up, and put it in some holy water to drink."

"Get out of my way!" Gerard barks, nudging her aside. "Get back to your work, you ignorant fool!"

"Where are the tweezers?" The old sergeant is crouching now, feeling around the shattered head in front of him. "We'll have to get this splinter out."

"*I'll* do that," Gerard insists. "You go and soak some bandages in egg white and pork fat, and then we'll pack the wound."

"This eye looks bad. Should we leave it there or not?" asks the sergeant, and I can't stand it anymore. I can't, I can't—I'm going to vomit if I listen to another word. Even with my hands over my ears, I can still hear the thin, high-pitched squeal of the injured man.

Oh, God, oh, God, I wish I weren't here. I feel as if my head's going to break into a thousand pieces. Why? *Why?* It's what I wanted—to fight the French—but now I can hardly put one foot in front of the other. Now I can hardly stop myself from screaming.

"Hold him down!" Gerard yelps. The clumsy, stupid, prating liver-worm! If only Father Isidore were here! *He* would do the job properly, I know he would! He's so learned and kind, with such gentle hands—he wouldn't hurt a dying man like this.

I wish he were here now. I can't believe how much I miss him. I only knew him for three days. Why do I miss him so much?

I think I'm going mad.

‡CHAPTER TWENTY-THREE‡

My mother's hair is very soft. When I brush it against my cheek, it feels like a kiss or a warm breath. Comforting. Gentle.

I'm so glad that Isidore gave me this little plait. Now, whenever I wake in the darkest hours of the night, I can hold my mother's hair close to my mouth and feel it on my skin. I can pretend that my mother is here, though it's hard. It's hard because she's just a blur to me. Navarre never talked about her much. Neither did Gran. I probably learned more from Isidore than I did from them, and even Isidore had very little to say about my mother.

If only I had asked him more. If only I hadn't been too *proud* to ask. If I should ever see him again . . . if we should ever meet one day . . .

Please, God, make that happen. I am a grievous sinner, Lord, and ignorant, and unworthy, but seeing Father Isidore again—it would make me a better person. I know it would.

Suppose he were with me now, in this room? Suppose he were lying in Maura's bed, instead of Maura? Sometimes it makes me feel better to imagine such a thing, but sometimes it makes me feel worse. When dawn breaks, and it's Maura in the bed after all . . . that's always a bad moment. I have nothing to turn to then, except the hood that he bought me. I have my mother's hair and Isidore's hood, and that's all I have to treasure.

Wait a moment. What's that noise?

There's something going on in the bailey. It's the middle of the night, but there's something going on. Where are my boots? Where's my sharp stick? I don't want to be taken by surprise. I don't want to be killed in my own bed.

Mind you, it doesn't sound like a fight, or even a scuffle. I can hear low murmurs and the clink of metal on stone: no thumps or grunts or heavy breathing. There are people milling around out

320

there, and come to think of it, I was wrong about the time. It's later than I thought. The touch of moving air on my cheek—the faint sheen in the sky—the distant, sleepy sounds of birds and farm animals . . .

I think it's near dawn.

"Shh!" someone hisses. From the door, it's easier to see what's happening. Torches are bobbing about—torches and candles. In their fitful, flickering glow, humble men are shouldering bundles of straw. Knights are donning helmets and adjusting sword belts.

There's Loup de Montferrand in full armor. He's even wearing mail vambraces.

"What's happening?" I have to know. "My lord?"

"Shh!" For a moment he doesn't recognize me; his mind is somewhere else, far beyond the walls of this fortress. But slowly recognition dawns in his eyes. "Oh," he says quietly. "It's you."

"What are you doing, my lord? Where are you going?" You're not leaving us, are you? "Please don't go!"

"Shh!" He motions frantically for silence, replying in a whisper as he does so. "Have no fear. We're going out to burn the trebuchet."

"Oh!" But how? "Not through the gates, surely?"

"No. We'll take another route." He beckons to his attendant, who passes him a pot helmet. It's a huge, heavy thing, and it transforms Lord Loup into something fearsome; only his eyes and mouth are visible now that his helmet's on. "Pray for us," he says in a muffled voice.

"Oh, yes! I will! God be with you, my lord!"

It's a raid, then. And I have to see it. I have to get upstairs. Not onto the ramparts—if there's too much activity on the ramparts, the French will be alerted—but into one of the towers. That tower over there, perhaps: it's closest to the French trebuchet. It's taken most of the blows.

Lord Loup is heading for another tower entirely. They all are—half a dozen armed men and twice that number of attendants. Is there a door that I haven't noticed, over in that stretch of wall? A little postern tucked away in a hidden corner, above a steep slope? A tunnel that leads to a copse? They can't have been *digging* a tunnel; I would have known about *that*. Perhaps all the stone that they've been bringing up onto the ramparts lately—perhaps that was stacked across the hidden door, and now it's been cleared.

I don't know. All I do know is that Lord Loup is

taking a terrible risk. Does he really think that he'll be able to approach the trebuchet, set fire to it, and return to this citadel without attracting attention? He doesn't seem to be taking many men with him, though that might be because they want to move quickly. No doubt they realize that a swift and glancing raid will be their only chance of survival.

Please, God, let them return unharmed.

Chink-chink-chink. One of the armed men has peeled off from the rest; he's heading back this way, his chain mail softly clinking with every step as he winds himself up in a dark cloak. Behind him scurries a varlet with a torch, and its flaring flame illuminates the shrouded man who's passing.

Lord Olivier.

I haven't seen much of him this last week or so; one fleeting glimpse is enough to show that he's not worn well. There are bags under his eyes, each big enough to cast a shadow. All the flesh has dropped away from beneath his cheekbones, and his chin has been pared so sharp, you could almost cut wood with it. He looks sterner and grimmer than he ever did before—a walking, talking war machine.

He disappears into the western tower, and I think that I might follow him. Discreetly. At a distance.

He must be going up there to watch events unfold.

Dear Lord Our Father, please by Your mercy bring Loup back unharmed. (I should pray, because I promised.) *Please protect his companions, O Lord, in Your infinite compassion. Amen.* There are bodies all over the floor in here—snoring, twitching, sighing bodies, most of them fully dressed and ready to be roused. It's so dark that I'll have to be careful: I don't want to tread on anyone.

The stairs are clear, though. They won't be hard to climb.

"*Sst!*"

God save us. *That* gave me a start! But it's only Pons de Villeneuve, bringing up the rear.

He doesn't bother to pick a path through the slumbering garrison, the way I did. He simply kicks them aside, causing them to roll and groan.

"What are you up to?" he whispers. "Spearfishing?"

"What?" Oh. I see. He's talking about my sharpened stick. "No, my lord."

"Been visiting your lover?"

"No!"

"I should hope not. Too many bastards in your family as it is."

Up your arse, pus-face. He swings past me, taking the stairs two at a time as he ties the strings of his hooded cloak. All these dark cloaks—they suggest that some of the knights are afraid of being seen.

They must be heading for the ramparts.

I suppose I'm allowed to go on, am I? Pons didn't tell me to go back to bed. And here's some activity, at last—archers in the second-floor guardroom. Filling their quivers and testing their bows. Squabbling in tense and muted voices.

Whoops!

"Get out of my way!" snaps the hulking great sergeant who just rounded a turn in the stairs above me. He's so big, I'll have to flatten myself against the wall to let him by. I wonder where he's going in such a hurry. Wherever it is, he's determined to get there. The look of concentration on his face—it's the same look that I saw on the faces of those archers.

I shan't be bothered by these men. They don't have time to pinch or kiss or grope. I won't need my sharpened stick this morning.

Aha! And here's Lord Pagan himself, throwing back a draught of wine at the top of the stairs. Beyond him the highest tower room is packed with people: there's Lord Pagan's steward, and his two squires, and Lord Guillaume de Puylaurens, and that fellow with the missing ears, and—

Where's Olivier?

There he is. Wrapped in his cloak, the hood pulled over his eyes. Seated on a barrel, patiently waiting. For what, I wonder. For a signal? A summons?

Pons de Villeneuve stands near him, pissing into a bucket.

"What's that girl doing here?" somebody whispers. (Curse him.) Olivier looks up. Pons spins around, adjusting his crotch. "God's sweet angels, it's you again," says Pons. Olivier jerks his chin at me, his dark eyes as grave as death.

"Out," he grunts.

No use arguing. But the staircase is suddenly impassable—stuffed full of archers. They're all heading this way, and they won't yield to anyone. Their shuffling tread sounds like leaves in a stiff wind.

Somebody pulls me aside. Suddenly it's so crowded up here that I can hardly breathe.

"Men." Olivier rises. "All of you—listen to me." His voice is low but commanding. His eyes glitter in the soft light of a nearby oil lamp. "When I give the command, we're going out onto the ramparts—crawling. I don't want any heads showing above the battlements. Do you understand?"

Nods all around. Everyone's forgotten about me. Perhaps, if I edge into this corner, out of the way . . .

"Try not to make any noise," Olivier continues. "Do not rise when I rise. I'll tell you when to rise. *Hands and knees*, my brave hearts, is that clear?"

More nods. And a hoot.

A *hoot?*

Followed by a flurry of movement. (That hoot must have been a signal.) Olivier strides to the door ahead of Pons and Pagan and the archers. One by one, they all duck their heads. One by one, they disappear into the dimness of early dawn. And what shall I do now? Depart?

Everyone who's left—steward and squire, earless or not—clusters around the doorway, peering out. Nobody's stationed at the arrow slit. Nobody tries to stop me from sidling up to it.

And I understand why, now. It's hard to see anything through this narrow opening, especially in such poor light. I can vaguely make out some dim, white shapes that must be tents. And there are pinpoints of flame here and there. And a tree. And smoke . . . is that smoke?

A sudden exclamation from behind me.

"It's begun!" someone hisses. (I don't know who.) Noises reach my ears from the ramparts, muffled by distance and the intervening stone. A shout. A curse. The crowd by the door presses forward. Part of it spills out into the morning air.

God, if only I could *see*!

Now the shouts are coming from farther afield — from the French camp, no doubt. It's a furious uproar, as clear as the toll of a bell in the stillness. But whatever is happening, it's happening beyond the range of my restricted outlook. All I can glimpse is a handful of dark figures, disappearing from view.

This is intolerable. I can't stay here. And I don't have to anymore, because this room is empty. Completely empty. They've all headed for the parapet.

I think I'll follow their example.

"Ah, no, no!" someone yells. (That doesn't sound good.) No one's bothering to be quiet up here on the walls; stepping out onto the ramparts, I'm greeted by a torrent of wails and protests, every one of them aimed at the French below. The archers are taking up their positions, one to each crenel; Olivier paces back and forth behind them, stopping every fifth or sixth step to check his targets.

"Hold," he says. "Steady . . ."

"They're dousing it," croaks Pons. "They're dousing the fire." He's leaning out into space, as if he wants to throw himself off the battlements. "It's not taken hold!"

"Come on," Lord Pagan murmurs. "Come *on*, Loup."

I still can't see anything except the backs of the men in front of me and the flushed sky beyond. Something's gone wrong with the raid—that much I can tell—but what, exactly? Is there a fight? A chase?

"Come *on*!" Lord Pagan yelps, hammering at a stone merlon with his mailed fist. "Jesus *Christ* our Savior's blood!"

"Hold fast!" Olivier cries sharply, his hand outstretched in a quelling motion as he addresses the archers. "Wait for my command!"

"Look." Someone points. "Is that him?"

"It's him!" Pons swings around to address Olivier. "He's retreating!"

Who is? Why? I must see. I *must* see! They're all so intent on the action; they won't notice if I join them, will they? Perhaps if I squeeze through over there, near Lord Pons . . .

"Hurry!" Guillaume shrieks—but not at anyone up here on the ramparts. Olivier's voice rings out ("Covering fire!" he bellows), and the score of archers move as one. It's a beautiful thing to see: as beautiful as it is terrible. Twenty arms drag together on twenty bowstrings; the *twang* of their combined release sets my teeth on edge. "Again!" shouts Lord Pagan, and there's a space directly ahead of me. If I get down low and dodge Pons de Villeneuve's dancing feet, I'll be able to peek over the top of the parapet.

"No! *No!*" he screams. A roar of despair springs from every throat. The bows creak once more, drawn tight at Olivier's command. What is it? What's happening? Pons is praying—he's actually praying aloud—and he has no idea that I'm curled down here at his feet because he's ready to tear the stone parapet apart with his bare hands; he's in utter torment, his scars a stark white against his wet, red face.

Another shower of arrows is released (it's an

indescribable sound) and at last I'm here. At last I can raise my head enough to look down, and it's all so confusing. . . . What's going on?

There's a lot of smoke over by the trebuchet. A lot of people, too. The first golden beams of sunlight are gilding the treetops, and crows are wheeling overhead.

Close by the foot of the walls, in deep shadow, a knot of tumbling, twisting men is attracting more combatants—they're running in from all over, waving weapons, shouting, gesturing. The knot itself is very tight, full of vague shapes that could be anyone or anything; it's hard to distinguish each from the other. But suddenly there's a rent in the crowd, and somebody falls, rolling, and a dozen blades are raised against him—they come down as he tries to shield himself, making a sound that jabs me in the gut. It's like hewing wood . . . Oh, God. I can't watch this.

"Who is it?" Lord Pagan groans, before his voice is swamped by other voices. "I got one! I hit one!" cries an archer. Guillaume says, "The fire's out." Pons is cursing furiously, weeping all the while. But Olivier's hard, clear tones cut through the commotion like a hot knife through fat. "Mark that ballista!" he instructs. "They're mounting a ballista, look! Keep your heads down!"

It's hard to keep my head down. I don't want to look, but something draws my eyes back toward the field of fury below. That poor man (not Loup, please, God) is being dragged away from the base of the walls. He's as limp as loose guts and soaked red; one of his forearms is dangling on a stringy piece of sinew. Around him his bloody killers skip and hoot, throwing taunts up at us, the fiends, the scum, God curse them!

"Fire!" shouts Olivier, and—ha! Now you're not laughing, are you, my fine friends? Now you're *running*, aren't you? With the arrows nipping at your heels!

I wish I had a stone. I could *brain* that blond.

"Mark the ballista," Olivier warns. "Mark it, now—is it out of range?"

"Yes, my lord," comes the reply.

"Then mark it only. We don't have long. They'll get their elevation soon."

"My lord!" It's the steward. "Look over there!"

Over where? Oh, no. No, it can't be. They're stringing up bodies. They're stringing them up in a tree, like meat, but they're too far away . . . I can't make out the faces. . . .

"Oh, Christ in Heaven!" Pagan moans, bowing his head. Pons hurls curses over the parapet as the archers take aim. But the French are retreating to a safe distance—all save those whom the arrows have already found. One or two lie still, down below. Half a dozen are struggling away from us, limping or crawling or draped over their friends.

"Fire," says Olivier coldly. *Twang* go the bowstrings. *Swish* go the arrows.

One of the walking wounded falls.

"We need our own ballista," Lord Pagan croaks. "That's the bishop, way over there; I'm sure it is. We could hit him, with a ballista."

What did you say? The bishop? Where?

"Fulk, you mean?" asks Olivier.

"There. Look there." Lord Pagan's pointing. At what? The tents? They're all in shadow—the sun's not high enough. Damn it to Hell, I can't see! But what's this, staggering out of the crowd near the trebuchet? A man. It's a naked man, white with smudges of black and red. His hands are loose. He's unsteady on his feet.

Everyone falls silent. Everyone.

Even the French.

He's stumbling toward La Bécède. His face is a

mass of blood, but now that he's closer, it's clear that his hair is black beneath all the red.

"It's Loup," Pagan whispers.

No. Oh, no, it can't be. Not Loup. No! He swerves, and a lance pokes at his side, nudging him back onto his original course. Beside me, Pons stiffens. "They cut out his eyes," says Olivier flatly. He turns to the man next to him. "Bring rope," he orders. "Quick."

They cut out his eyes. He's blinded.

I can't bear it.

"'Ware that ballista!" someone exclaims, pointing at the giant crossbow. "They're turning the winch!"

"Heads down," says Olivier. Yes. Heads down. My head is down, shielded by stone, because I can't look. I can't even see through all the tears.

But nobody else pays attention to Olivier. They're standing on tiptoes, shouting with all their might. *"Loup! This way! Loup!"* They're trying to guide him.

Lord Pagan gasps. "They'll never let him go! They'll never wait for him to get to us!"

"He won't see the rope," Pons adds, his voice cracking. But here's the rope (it looks like a full league of plaited tow) and a dozen hands reach for it. Though it seems enormous, Pons is right. No blind man could find a dangling rope—or climb it even if he did find it. Especially with that ditch in the way.

WHUMP!

"Ow!" What was that? Something sharp hit my cheek. I'm bleeding!

But not much. Just a little.

"Heads down!" Olivier roars, and everyone ducks. Of course. I understand. The ballista fired a bolt, and the bolt hit stone. I must have been scraped by a flying stone chip.

"Loup is bait," says Olivier breathlessly. (To Lord Pagan?) "They're trying to keep us up here." He's hunkered down so low that I can see his face, and it's not what I expected. It's bright—flushed—with eyes keen and sparkling. "Bring rocks!" he hisses. "Stay on your knees and roll them over here! *Now!* No—not you, Bernard. You and your brother wait for my signal."

Rocks. All right, I'll bring rocks. Where are they? Oh. I see. Piled up by the door. Someone's already reached them: the man with no ears. He's dragging a broken building block from the top of the pile. Shoving it ahead of him, toward the battlements.

I can do that.

"What the hell?" says Pons. He's staring straight at me with bloodshot eyes. (Now that everyone's on my level, I was bound to get noticed.) "What are *you* doing here?"

"I can bring rocks." Please—please let me help! "I'm strong enough!"

"Get out."

"But—"

"*Go!*"

WHUMP! Another bolt hits the wall, fired wide and striking stone harmlessly a long way below us. It distracts Pons, though; he turns and grabs one end of the rope as the other end is cast over the parapet. Four other men do the same, without much regard for the French ballista.

Perhaps they know exactly how long it takes to winch back a bolt.

"A rock to each crenel, quick!" Olivier rasps, flapping his hand at us while he peers over the edge of the wall. What's he doing? What's his plan? He'll get a bolt in the brain if he's not careful, waving his head about like that. Lord Pagan, too. Lord Pagan's silhouette must be clear against the sky.

"They're coming!" Pagan squeaks. "Loup will

never reach us! They'll stop him before he gets to the walls!"

"Let them come," Olivier replies.

"But—"

"Let them come closer."

"Loup!" Pons bawls. *"There's a rope! To your right!"*

Oh, God. I understand now. The French have sent Loup back to us so that we'll stay up here, clear targets for their ballista. But Loup's drawing close now, and the French are getting uneasy. They'll advance to retrieve him, and then—

"Now!" yells Olivier, heaving.

THUMP! THUMP-THUMP-THUMP! Half a dozen rocks hit the ground far below. There's a terrible shriek. More rocks follow the first barrage. Olivier whirls to address Bernard and his brother. "Fire!" he cries. "Quick, while you can!" The two archers jump to their feet, taking aim. The terrible shrieking continues. *WHUMP!* Another bolt from the ballista—and someone falls! The steward falls, beside me!

"Loup!" Pons wails. "We hit Loup, oh, God!" There's blood spilling onto the ramparts, but Pons doesn't see. He grabs Olivier's arm. "Loup's dead!" Pons cries. "We killed him!"

And Olivier says, calmly, "It's good that we did."

Oh, Lord our Savior, preserve us in Your mercy. I can't be here. I can't do this.

Isidore, help me. Where are you?

I can't stand it anymore.

✠CHAPTER TWENTY-FOUR✠

This man is doing better than I would have expected. It's a good sign that he can actually suck egg from my spoon. Yesterday I thought that the final fever had hit him, but he's much improved today.

Probably because his wounds weren't tended by Gerard de la Motta.

CRA-A-ASH!

Another rock hits the bailey, and another spoonful of egg hits the floor. I can't help jumping, though I should be used to it by now; that trebuchet never seems to stop.

I hope no one got hurt. We're running out of room in this chapel.

"It's all right." Peitavin's voice is shaking like a palsied crone. He's not convincing anyone—least of all the breathless man whose brow he's mopping. "Don't worry; it's all right."

All right? What a laugh. If this is all right, I'm the Sultan of Baghdad. Our water's running low. Our food is running low. We hardly have any linen left for the bandages. (Which reminds me: I must take some linen now and hide it away, before the bloody flow strikes me at the end of this month.) Even our mangonel is a paltry thing compared to the French trebuchet. Didn't I hear Vasco say that we're fighting at a disadvantage, because our machine is worked with twisted ropes instead of weights and pulleys?

Finally, on top of everything else, we have Gerard de Motta treating our wounded. God, I hate him. God, but he's a bladder-headed big-mouth. Listen to him, prating on about an amputation right in front of the poor soul who's going to lose his leg.

"Up high," Gerard's saying. "Up high, well above the green part. Only we must be careful, or the marrow will run out of the bone, and he'll die instantly. . . ."

Aaugh. I have to get out of here. I need some fresh air.

"Babylonne!" Trust Gerard. He just can't leave me alone. "Babylonne, where are you going?"

"Out."

"Babylonne!"

"Please, Holy Father, I think my monthly flow has started."

Ha! That's done it. Gerard positively blanches. Peitavin flinches. Here they are, surrounded by vile smells and oozing pus and burning, swollen skin, and the dreadful thought of female filth nearly unmans them.

"Oh—uh—yes." Gerard flutters his hands at me. "Yes, go. Go!"

If you say so, frog-face. Hell on earth, I feel dizzy. It's so hot. This keep is like an oven. And the latrines—don't even *talk* to me about them.

You have to bat your way through the flies as you pass the latrines, which smell even worse than the chapel.

CRA-A-ASH!

Oh, *stop*! Just stop it, damn you! I don't know if they're misfiring or if they're trying to frighten us, but I can feel every impact in my bowels. And this time they must have hit someone, because there's shouting from the bailey. Shouting and groaning.

I suppose that I'd better go out and help. It's my job. My appointed task. The trouble is, I . . .

God, I can't do it. Not yet. Just give me a moment while I close my eyes and breathe out, and breathe in, and lean against the wall, and think about something else. About Isidore. About his house.

Isidore would keep a clean house; I know he would. All the walls would be whitewashed. All the beds would have pots under them. He wouldn't spit on his floor, either.

And he would scatter lavender among the rushes for a nice smell.

"Babs."

I know that voice. Yes, it's Maura. She must have come out of the latrines; she's hauling herself along as if she has bricks on her back. Poor Maura. She's already lost weight.

The flux is a terrible thing.

"How are you, Maura?"

"Not good," she croaks. "It's a bad dose, this one."

"I'm sorry."

"I'll lose half my guts if it goes on."

"Isn't there medicine that you can take?"

"Not anymore. It's all gone. The fennel. The dried blackberries." She winces. "Too many sloppy bowels around here."

"Maybe you should stay away from those latrines." (*I* never use them.) "It can't be good for you, dragging yourself upstairs all the time."

But she's not listening. Her mind is on other things: namely, the fresh cramp that's just hit her. Bent double, her face contorted, she spins around and stumbles back upstairs toward the latrines.

I have to admit, I'm worried about Maura. The flux can be deadly. It killed the last King of France. It killed the last Viscount of Carcassonne. Sieges always bring it on, fast and furious; why should this siege be any different? Half the time, it's not the fighting or the lack of water that ends a siege. It's disease among the defenders.

I'm surprised that the French haven't been hurling dead animals over the walls.

"No, no!"

What the—? What on earth was that? It came from the bailey; what's happening out there? The growling doesn't sound frightened; it sounds exultant. And there's movement in the Great Hall— scraping benches and thudding footsteps—as if everyone in it is heading outside.

Yes, I thought so. The Great Hall is empty. There's nothing but overturned stools and slimy rushes and greasy tables and a month's worth of scraps: bones and rinds and fruit stones and nutshells, with a lone rat in the midst of the bounty, perched on someone's discarded helmet.

Over it all, the arched ribs of the vaulted ceiling—studded with their fine carvings of harps and vines—look impossibly pure and delicate.

"God's death!" That's Pons. Pons de Villeneuve, framed in the doorway, dark against the sun. But as he enters the Great Hall, it becomes clear that he's wounded. He's holding his wrist and grimacing. His surcoat is smeared with blood.

"My *lord*?" (Oh, no!) "What happened?"

"What happened?" He lurches to the nearest table. "We lured 'em in, that's what happened. Ambushed 'em near the barbican."

"Your arm . . ."

"It's nothing." He picks up an empty jug with his good hand and shakes it. "Any wine?"

"You should dress that. My lord? It's bleeding."

"It's *nothing*." He laughs wildly. "You should see what I did to *him*!"

To him? "To whom?"

"Go and look," he says hoarsely, nodding at the door. Through it, I can make out milling bodies wrapped in a pall of dust. There are sticks waving and swinging; screams and curses; cries of triumph.

The sun hits my scalp like a hammer and pierces my eyeballs like a knife. Whoops! Watch yourself, Babylonne, or you'll take a tumble down those stairs into the bailey. The dust is making me cough. And what's going on out here? What's all the excitement? Why all the cheers?

Oh.

Sweet mercy of Christ.

"*Mon Dieu . . .*"

It's a Frenchman. A captured Frenchman. He's on his knees, his hands lifted in supplication. He can hardly speak through the blood trickling from his swollen lips. Most of his clothes have been torn from his body.

And there's another one, dead on the ground with his throat cut. And another. Stripped. Groggy. His face pouring blood. Someone kicks him in the head, so that he topples over and lies there, his hands waving feebly. Someone else dances around, waving his bloody surcoat in the air like a flag.

That Frenchman is only a boy. He can't be any older than I am.

He's crying.

"Let's cut out *your* eyes, and see how *you* like it!" cries a beast in human form, who can't be serious— oh, no, *no*!

"Stop!" What are you doing? "You can't! Wait! My lord!" (Thank God! Here comes Olivier!) "My lord, help, please!"

Olivier is striding across the bailey toward us. He can't have taken part in this ambush, because he's not wearing his chain mail—just his *hacqueton*, loosely tied under his sword belt. All his clothes are too big for him now; he's been whittled away to almost nothing, and his eyes are looking huge in his small, sallow face.

Vasco and Guillaume de Minerve are in attendance, hurrying to keep up with him. They're both blinking with fatigue.

"Where's Pons?" Olivier demands sharply, scanning the turmoil in front of the keep.

"In there, my lord!" I have to raise my voice over all the commotion; when he spots me, Olivier frowns. "Lord Pons is in the Great Hall, my lord; he's wounded."

"Badly?"

"I—I don't think so." Not like these Frenchmen. In the name of all that's holy, can't you see what's going on? Can't you hear the pleading? How can you just *stand there*? "Please, my lord—this is not . . . not . . ."

Not what? Not fair? Not human? Of course the French must pay for their crimes—they are wicked and cruel—but surely we're better than they are? The *French* cut out people's eyes; they're famous for it. We're not like them, though. Are we?

Unless they deserve it. Perhaps they do. Perhaps I'm being weak. Female. I can't seem to think clearly anymore.

Except that . . . I know how Isidore would feel about this. And Isidore wouldn't like it. Oh, no.

Isidore would stop it somehow.

"Silence!" Olivier thunders.

And of course everyone obeys, because he's held in such respect. Everyone obeys except the French, who are still whimpering and moaning. They probably don't even understand.

You can almost see the dust settling as all movement stops.

Olivier coughs to clear his throat. He surveys

the scene before him: the filthy, panting foot soldiers with their dangling sickles and mattocks; the
boots and swords and knitted garments that have
passed from hand to hand; the naked corpse in the
pool of drying blood; the sobbing boy with his
hands wrapped around his head . . .

"These are the captives?" Olivier asks.

"Yes, my lord," someone pipes up. "God rot them,
my lord, they came and—"

Olivier lifts a hand for silence. "No other casual-
ties?" he inquires.

"No, my lord."

"But Pons was hurt?"

"In the arm, my lord."

A brief silence. Olivier runs his fingers through
his lank brown hair. He looks exhausted.

"All right," he says at last. "We'll hang these two
from the walls. I want the French to see them
kicking."

A growl of approval.

"As for the dead one . . ." Olivier turns to Vasco.
"Bring an ax. We'll chop him up and put the pieces
in the mangonel. Send him back bit by bit."

A savage roar greets this command. The Frenchmen suddenly disappear behind a rush of bodies. A
cry of alarm is cut short by a *thump.*

348

Those churls are actually fighting. Fighting over who gets the spoils and who has the honor of dragging the prisoners up to the ramparts.

I can't believe it. I thought . . . I was hoping . . . I don't know.

"Well?" It's Olivier. He's standing there, on the stair below mine. Hands on hips.

Oh! I'm blocking his path.

"*Well?*" he repeats impatiently. "What is it?"

What should I say? What's the right question? I must look like a stranded fish.

But as he begins to brush past me, the words suddenly spew from my mouth like blood from a fatal wound.

"Is this because of Loup?"

He stops. His bleak gaze fixes on me, dark and unyielding. "What?" he says.

"This . . . butchery." (There's no other way of describing it.) "Is this for Loup's sake?"

He narrows his eyes intently, as if he's seeing me for the first time. He seems interested in something, but it's not my question. My question is dismissed with a careless shrug.

"This isn't Loup," he says. "This is war."

And that's that. No more discussion; he doesn't have time. Instead he disappears into the keep,

349

moving briskly—and I might as well follow, for all that the keep is a noisome cesspit.

I can't stay here.

If I don't leave now, I might see Vasco return with the ax.

CHAPTER TWENTY-FIVE

Once upon a time there was a beautiful girl whose father died. On his deathbed, her father begged his dearest friend to care for the girl, who had no one except a cruel aunt in her life. So the friend, who was a good and gentle man, took the girl into his house and gave her nice clothes and tasty food and a room of her own. And he taught her to read and write and to look after his books, and she became his very own daughter.

CRA-A-ASH!

Oh, God. God help us. Our Father, who art in Heaven, hallowed be Thy Name—

"Here! Over here!" Someone needs my rock. He's gesturing wildly, coughing and pointing, but I can hardly see him through all the dust. Where am

I supposed to take this? Where do they need it—in the breach? Over there? Or do they want it for ammunition?

The fighting on the walls is getting desperate. The French must have thrown up ladders, and I still don't know what's going on. We seem to be holding the breach that they made in the battlements, but have they got through elsewhere yet? Have they struck another weak point, knowing that we're busy trying to mend that huge rent?

There are so many weak points. So many gaps in our defenses because of all the ill and injured. And now this hole—this great, yawning wound on the ramparts . . . *CRA-A-ASH!*

That shot was fired wide, thank God. Most of their shots seem to be aimed at the breach now, but that one hit the wall of the keep. Bounced straight off.

Luckily.

Someone snatches the rock from my hands, and it's passed to the next man in the chain, which winds its way across the bailey into the western tower and up the stairs. All the stone that fell when the breach was made—all that stone has to be returned to the ramparts so the breach can be mended. Before the French overwhelm us.

Please, God, don't let it happen. They'll be so angry. They'll cut us to pieces.

No. I won't think about that. Be strong, Babylonne. Be brave. This is only a siege. You've been in sieges before.

Thud!

"No!" Oh, God. He fell. He fell from the ramparts. Oh, God, I can't look!

He's dead, though—whoever he is, he must be dead. I can't take him inside, either, because he's too big for me to carry alone. Anyway, why bother? What would be the point? He's dead, after all. And I have to do something *useful*. I have to . . . what? Get more stone? Yes. Get more stone. They need more stone up there.

Someone else can take care of the wounded.

"You! Girl!"

Who, me?

"Bring water!" It's Lord Pagan. He's already left me behind, his voice drifting over his shoulder as he runs heavily across the bailey toward the eastern wall. Ever since the breach was made, he's been back and forth from fight to fight, covering every sudden attack or point of weakness, holding our defenses together. "Get water! Wine! Anything to drink!"

Water. Wine. Yes. I can do that. The men are laboring hard in the hot sun; they'll pass out if they get too thirsty. But there's precious little wine left, as far as I can tell. It will have to be water.

The well's closer, anyway. Closer than the wine cellar in the keep.

CRA-A-ASH!

A shower of stones, pattering down. *Ouch!* One stone must have grazed my hand, but it's not bad—it's not serious, just a scratch. Shouts and wails from every direction. From up on the walls now. *Screams from the walls.* What's happening? I can't see. . . .

Christ our Lord!

"Run! *Run!*" The wall's coming down! *"Out of the way!"*

A colossal roar, like the end of the world. The ground shakes, and I'm going to fall! No, I'm not. I'm all right. But stones are whizzing past like bees, ricocheting off the ground—good Christ, that was close!

The keep. I must get to the keep.

"La Bécède! La Bécède!" someone's shouting. It's Lord Pagan. He's turned back from the eastern wall. He's running toward the keep ahead of a small, armed phalanx, but suddenly the dust hits. It hits like a great, choking, rolling cloud of fog.

"Ah! Help! I can't breathe!"

"La Bécède!" (Cough, cough.) *"To me, La Bécède!"*

I can't see *or* breathe. The stairs nearly smack me in the mouth. But these are the stairs to the keep (I'm here! I've reached it!), so all I have to do is follow them up. And the dust is already clearing. Lord Pagan is visible now: a faint silhouette behind me. He's still calling and calling. *"La Bécède!"* Beyond him it's all dust and frantic cries and the clash of weapons.

We're lost. They've broken through.

Run!

"Oof!"

Get out of my way, you dolt! Don't you have eyes in your head?

"Babylonne?" It's old Ferrand, the infirmary sergeant. I didn't know that he was back on guard duty. "What is it? What's happening?" he says.

"It's a breach!" (Don't block the door; there'll be people coming in!) "A full breach, the wall collapsed!" Consternation. These are all garrison men in here. Simple soldiers. They must have been sleeping off their night watch in the Great Hall.

"What should we do?" says one. "Should we go and fight?"

355

"Ask Lord Pagan." He's over there, see? "Lord Pagan will know."

They all surge forward as one man, and it's difficult squeezing through their tight-pressed armor. Scraping past their chain mail. There'll be a retreat; I know there will. A retreat to this keep for the final rout, and after that . . . after that will come the massacre.

I'll have to find a place to hide.

Not in the chapel. When the French arrive, I don't want to be found up there among the Perfects and their patients. It would be instant death. The buttery will be the first destination of every hungry Frenchman, and as for the latrines—if I hide in the latrines, I'll be dead before the French even reach me.

There'll be fighting in the Great Hall. Fighting in the towers. The storerooms will be looted, and the cellars as well . . .

Where shall I go? What shall I do?

"Babylonne!"

It's Gerard de la Motta, come down from the chapel.

Great.

"What's happened?" he croaks, pausing on the

stairs. His skirts are stiff with dried blood. "What was that noise?"

"The wall's down."

"What?"

"The wall's down. We're as good as taken."

As if to confirm this, a distant, swelling sound reaches our ears. It's like a thousand voices raised in triumph.

Gerard turns green.

"Then—then we must pray," he stammers. "Come. Let us pray together in the chapel and await God's pleasure."

You must be joking. "Not with my help, you won't."

He blinks.

"You can reap what you've sown, my friend, but I was never a Good Woman, nor ever will be." (So go and keep your own pestiferous company and leave me alone!) "You've always made that clear enough, you and all your friends—and my grandmother, too. Who am I but spittle on your boot sole? A failure in all things, according to you— well, maybe that means I should look to another path. Find another place."

"Babylonne—"

"And if I die, then so be it. But I won't die with you! God preserve me from that!"

It doesn't matter what I say, because we're facing the final hours now. We won't last long in this place. How are we to hold it in the summer heat? There's hardly any water. Even if we can repel them—huddled in our stone box, with the trebuchet pounding our walls—I'd give us three days at the most before we all die of thirst.

Bang-crack! THUD!

Activity behind me in the Great Hall. And Lord Pagan's voice, shouting orders. He must be smashing the outside stairs or preparing barricades or some such thing. I wonder if Olivier's made it back. Dear Christ our Lord, please let Olivier be all right. Because if anyone can save the rest of us, he can.

Meanwhile, what am I going to *do*?

If I stand against the French with a pair of scissors, they'll cut me down like oats. On the other hand, it would be a noble way to die. I don't want to be dragged out of here like vermin, clinging to the walls, pleading for my life. I don't want to be thrown down the well and stoned to death.

Oh, what am I going to do?

I can't think. I have to think! And now I can feel

tremors through the soles of my feet; are the French using a battering ram against the door, or is it the trebuchet again? There are noises, too: creaks and groans and shouts and long, drawn-out grunts and enormous *thuds* and a frantic hammering that makes my joints seize up and the spit dry on my tongue. I know what Lord Pagan is doing in the Great Hall. He's holding the door, and he has all his force and might wedged against it. Because if it gives way, then we're finished.

The French will slaughter us.

"To me! To me!" It's Pons yelling. He's pounding past me, up the stairs, waving his sword. With half a dozen blood-soaked archers scrambling along behind him. And a toothless old man. And who's that? Is that *Dim*? Dim the snot-ball? He's holding a *dagger*! (Where on earth did he get that?)

They must be heading for the roof. But they can't want *me*, surely?

"Come on! Quick!" Dim bleats, pausing to flap an unsteady hand. "Before they get here!"

Or perhaps they do want me. I'll be more use to them than that toothless old man. And here's a sweating, shaking cripple—all blood and bandages—emerging from the chapel. He's going to

359

join the fight, too. I can hear Pons, faintly, up ahead. Shouting orders.

I know what he's doing. He's trying to stop the French from smashing down the door of the keep. He's going to fire at them from above. Drop things on them.

It's not hard to drop things. I can do that. Here—let me past! Let me on the roof! I still have both arms. I still have all my teeth. I can fight as well as anyone.

"How can I help you? My lord?" The light's too bright out here. I'll have to shade my eyes. "Dim? Where are you?"

There he is. Cowering against a wall, his uplifted dagger trembling visibly. He shouldn't be here. He should be in hiding.

I wish I'd looked after him better. Isidore would have, I know. But I'm not Isidore.

I'm so scared. . . .

Tching!

"Fire!" shouts Pons. A couple of archers release their bowstrings, aiming high. They're shooting at the other archers. And look! The old man has found a plank of wood. He's dragging it toward this parapet.

Down there, straight underneath us, I can see

the French: a raging crowd of them, attacking the door of the keep. They break up suddenly as a bag of crossbow bolts hits its target.

"Ya-a-ah!" somebody screams. "Got 'em!"

The old man throws his plank, which spins as it falls. A Frenchman dodges it.

Quick! What else can we drop? We need fire. We need oil. We need boiling water. There aren't even any *rocks* up here!

"Bring sacks!" Pons cries. "Crocks! Stools! Anything!" And he's talking to me.

Yes. Ammunition. That's my job. Pons has turned back to his archers now; he's dividing them into two groups. Some are aiming high, some low. Dim has found an iron pot. His arms are so feeble that he can barely lift it—even though he's stuffed his dagger into his belt to free up both hands.

That boy needs help.

"Here! Dim!" He looks around when he hears his name, white-faced and wide-eyed. "Up on the merlon!" (Quick, quick!) "We can push it from there!"

Comprehension dawns in his terrified gaze. He grips the pot more firmly, bracing himself to lift it while I grab the other side. "On the count of three. Understand?" He nods. Good. "One, two, three . . . *heave!*"

Tching! (Curse those arrows!) I'm staggering beneath the weight of this thing, because it's so damn *heavy*. But it's up there at last. All we have to do now is push it.

"One more time! On the count of three!" My voice sounds odd. "One, two, three . . . *go!*"

Suddenly the pot has vanished. There's a crunch, and a scream, and—

"*Aah-aah* . . ." Dim groans. His face is pouring blood. He's been hit by a glancing arrow.

God. Oh, God.

"Babylonne!" It's Pons. Beside me. Using my name. "We need more! Now! Anything you can, quick!"

"But—"

"*Go!*"

Yes. Go. I'll go. But where? There'll be nothing heavy enough in the chapel. The Great Chamber's full of bolsters and blankets (too soft) and linen chests (too heavy)—

"Babylonne." This time it's Dim. He's down at my feet. There's blood in his mouth.

His dagger is shaking in his hand.

"Take it," he wheezes.

"What?"

"In case . . . they come . . ."

In case they come? God help us if they do. But I'll take it. Of course I will.

The buttery has knives, too. And stone mortars. And firewood. Maybe I'll try down there.

"I'm sorry, Dim."

What should I do? Pons needs me. He needs my help. But Dim . . . I hate to leave him. Would Isidore leave him? Pons is up here. Pons is better protection than *I* could ever be.

Maybe he'll look after Dim.

"Get going, you fool!" Pons bawls, and he's right. I have to go. I'm sorry. I'm so sorry. I'll be back as soon as I can. . . .

Whoops! Nearly slipped in that vomit. (Who's been puking on the staircase?) Those miserable, louse-ridden Perfects are busy praying aloud in the chapel, and I want to throw *them* off the roof, though they wouldn't make much of an impact. Too skinny. Unless you tied them together in a bunch.

CRA-A-ASH!

The trebuchet. Please, God, that it didn't hit anyone up on the roof—Pons especially. We need Pons. Pons needs me. Hell in a *harness*, what shall I bring him? I have to find something. I *have* to!

Buttery . . . buttery. Where is it? Over here. This

way. Just off the Great Hall, round the back, down a few steps . . . and a little farther down. But what's that? Is that . . . is that . . .

Don't tell me that's steel on steel.

A clashing sound. Unmistakable. There's nothing new about the shouts or the groans or the thumps, but the ringing of metal from the Great Hall—it means blade against blade. It means hand-to-hand fighting.

It means that they've broken through.

‡CHAPTER TWENTY-SIX‡

Oh, God. Oh, God, they must have broken through while I was passing the chapel. Now they're in the Great Hall, between me and Pons, and they're heading upstairs to stop him. And what can I do?

Nothing. I can't help now. I have to keep going. Quick, Babylonne, down to the cellar, *hurry*! You can do it. You can make it. Watch your step—don't trip up—fast, but not too fast.

They're coming. They're inside the keep. But here I am; I've reached the cellar; there's no one around and . . . Where shall I hide? I'll have to pick a good place, or there's no point hiding. They'll find me behind that coil of rope. They'll find me behind the barrels. There's not enough firewood left to conceal me. Those pots are useless.

BANG-CRASH!

Quick! Don't just stand there gawping—*move!*

Make a decision!

The sacks won't work. They're too small to hide in, and I couldn't tie them shut from the inside anyway. But those barrels . . .

What about those barrels?

They're big enough to climb inside. And they're empty, too. If I could wrench off one of their lids, I could pull it back afterward. I could stick this knife into the wood and pull the lid down on top of me.

This one, for example. Just stick the blade down that crack, and use it as a lever. (Come *on,* damn you, I can hear them coming!) And see how many barrels there are! Two score at least! How long will it take until they've tapped every one—a day or two? By which time I'll have slipped away, please, God, because the bloodlust will have eased, and the French will be sleeping off their crazed slaughter, and I'll have a better chance of surviving—or at least of killing Bishop Fulk.

If I have to die, I'd like to take him with me. In revenge for my mother. I'd have a better chance in this barrel; if they come to tap it before I escape, I'll burst out and stab one in the throat with my dagger. Take them all by surprise, before they throw me down the well. And then I'll dodge them, and find Fulk, and . . .

Hell's dung, my hands are shaking. I can hardly *hold* this damn knife, and now there's more shouting from upstairs.

Hooray! That's done it. The lid's off, and the smell of wine is overpowering. It's damp in here, too. Just a trace of dampness. No worse than Navarre's chest, not really. Where's my knife? Here. Stabbing and stabbing until the tip of the blade is stuck in the lid like an ax in a log, and I can pull the lid down on top of me. There's a thunder of feet on the stairs close by; is it Pons coming down, or the French going up? Both, perhaps. But I'm in my barrel. The lid slides into place as if it's been greased with honey. No trouble at all.

I even have a bunghole to breathe through. Not big enough for anyone to peer into (not in this light) but big enough to keep me from passing out. It's the ideal hiding place. I'll be safe now; I know I will. No one will look in here. No one will think that it's big enough to bother with.

Our Father, who art in Heaven, hallowed be Thy Name. Thy Kingdom come, Thy will be done, on earth as it is in Heaven. . . .

I'd better pull this dagger out of the lid in case I need it. I have to be ready. They won't find me—of course they won't—but just in case they do, I'll be armed. If I yank and jerk and twist and . . . there! The knife's free now. I'm all prepared. If only this smell didn't make me want to cough. If I cough, I'm dead. I have to swallow and swallow again. I have to think of something else.

Father Isidore, for example.

I never said good-bye. I never even said thank you. He was my good angel, and I served him with scorn. I wish that I could tell him how sorry I am. I wish he were here. And I wish I knew what was happening—it's hard to follow the fighting from inside this barrel. The noises aren't clear. I don't even know if someone's in the cellar or not.

Give us this day our daily bread, and forgive us our trespasses, as we forgive those who trespass against us.

Except that I don't. I *don't* forgive those who trespass against me; is that why I'm in this position? And now there are definitely sharp sounds nearby. They're even penetrating this barrel. God have mercy on a poor sinner—I'm so scared. I'm such a coward. But I can't cry or someone might hear me. I can't cough. I can't move. I must ignore my bladder, and the pains in my knees, and the suffocating smell.

What's happened to Pons? To Dim? To Lord Pagan? What's happened to Isidore? If I die today, what will happen to me? Have I lived a good life? Will I go to Heaven? Somehow, I don't think so. There's a weight like a stone in my gut, and I fear the worst. I don't even know what to believe anymore.

But I'll be safe here. As long as I don't make a noise, no one will find me. I'll just wait until . . .

Until what?

How will I know when to get out? How will I know whether it's day or night down here in the cellar? How will I know how much time has passed if I can't see the sun or hear a church bell?

Suppose the French billet their servants in this gloomy den, and I find myself surrounded by quarrelsome stable hands?

Perhaps if I put my ear to the bunghole instead of my mouth, I might have a better idea of what's going on. There. That's better. Not much better, but at least I can tell that someone's calling to someone else. I can't make out the words, though. I don't even know what language they belong to.

That's why I have to stay very still, like a little mouse. Because I'm pretty sure that whoever called out is in this cellar. Searching it, perhaps? Or looking for a hiding place? I don't know. Surely if it's a search, it would only be a cursory one. The French won't be tapping barrels yet—not while they're still fighting. Will they?

Oh, God, oh, God, please don't let them find me. If they throw me down the well, or . . . no, I won't think about that. Not here. Not now. After all, I might be lucky. Remember what Maura said? She said that the garrison always suffers but that people like her—like me—aren't worth bothering about. So the French might not bother about me. They might let me go (after emptying my purse and stealing my boots, naturally). And if they do that, then I won't go back to Toulouse. No, nor to the King of Aragon, either. I'll go to Compostela and find Father Isidore. That will be *my* pilgrimage. I'll walk all the way there, barefoot if I have to. And if I don't find Isidore at the end of my journey, I'll turn around and walk to Bologna.

Though perhaps I'll stop at Boulbonne first of all. Just to find out whether he arrived there.

If he didn't make it, I might as well . . . what? I

don't know. I can't see beyond that. It would be like a door slamming shut, and no other way out. Because if I have to crawl back to Gran, I might as well lie down and die. Right here, today, in this stinking barrel.

What else is there for me? For a girl like me? If I were a boy, it might be different, but if I were a boy, the French probably wouldn't let me go. There's nothing dangerous about a girl. Nothing useful. I'm like a piece of rubbish that they'd throw off the walls into a ditch. It's always been like that, hasn't it? Except with Father Isidore.

Wait a moment. What's that smell?

It's smoke. That's *smoke*. Someone must be carrying a torch out there—a blazing torch. And you wouldn't be carrying a torch if you were looking for somewhere to hide.

So the French must be searching this cellar. Very quietly, too, because I can't hear a thing. No voices. No footsteps. My cheek is itchy, but I'd better not move to scratch it. And what's that noise? Is somebody stamping on dry twigs?

Oh, no. There's a cough rising in my throat, and I *must* swallow it down. The smoke is making me cough. And the smell is getting worse; I know it is—the smoke is getting thicker. That's no torch burning. That's a fire, crackling and spitting and pouring smoke.

The French have lit a fire. They must have set fire to the sacks, or the wood, or the barrels.

What am I going to do?

I can't stay here. But if I leave, they'll be waiting. Why light a fire unless you're trying to smoke people out? Somebody coughs.

Clearly, I'm not alone in this cellar. Either the French are posted, waiting, just a few steps away, or I'm not the only one hiding among the stores. Or am I right on both counts? Because there's more coughing, and a bang, and shouts that tell me everything I need to know.

The French have been waiting at the nearest exit. They've smoked out one of my compatriots, and now they're busy with him.

Go, Babylonne! Take the back stairs!

The lid of my barrel makes a terrible noise, hitting the floor with a *crash*. Someone shouts—in French—but it's too late. I'm on my way. Move, Babylonne! Move, move, move! The smoke is so thick that it wrings a cough from my lungs; the fire is straight in front of me. There's still room to go around, though. The tow is burning, and some of the barrels as well. I would have been roasted alive.

"*Arrêtez!*" (They're French, all right.) "Stop!"

I hope they haven't found the back stairs. Please, God, please, God, please—ouch! My toe! It's so hard to see with all the smoke and the shadows, except that there's filtered light from the back stairs . . . and they're clear! It's a clear run!

"*Arrêtez!*"

No door to slam behind me, not at the foot of the stairs. I can hardly breathe—the Frenchman's closing in—there'll be French in the buttery— where shall I go?

"*Ooof!*"

It's a soft collision, but not soft enough. Suddenly I'm sitting down. Help! Don't touch me! "Get out of my way!" (Whoever you are.) "I have a knife, I . . ."

Isidore?

I know his boots. I'd know them anywhere. They're right in front of my nose.

"Babylonne?"

It's him. That's his mantle, and his girdle, and that's his face, way up there, hanging over me. All smudged with dirt.

It can't be. I'm seeing things. Am I dead? Am I dying?

"Babylonne."

He swoops down like an enormous crow— swoops down from the step above mine and enfolds me in layers of soot-black wool and velvet. Yes, I must be dead. *He* must be dead. The Frenchman must have killed me, and Isidore's welcoming me into Heaven.

Except that he seems very solid, for an angel. What's more, I can feel his heart beating. *Thump, thump, thump,* under my ear.

And when he pulls me up, his knees crack.

"Arrêtez!"

The Frenchman? No—Isidore. He's speaking. He's speaking in French to the Frenchman. The Frenchman protests sharply (I can understand the tone, though I can't understand the language very well), and Isidore responds with a volley of angry words that resonate through his rib cage.

He's not dead. I'm not dead, either. I'm still in La Bécède, alive, in the middle of a siege, and Isidore is here, too. He came for me.

He came.

"Are you hurt?" he says. His breath ruffles my hair. "Babylonne? Did they hurt you?"

"You came."

"Yes. I'm sorry it took so long."

"You came." I'm not going to let him go. Not ever. He is my good angel. "You came, you came. . . ."

"Shh. It's all right." His arms tighten around me. "I won't let them hurt you, Babylonne." And he says something else, in Latin—something that sounds like a prayer—as he rests his chin or his cheek against the top of my head.

I could stay like this forever. I've never felt so safe. But he shifts slightly, moving one arm.

"Give me that dagger," he says. "You don't need it anymore."

"Father."

"Yes. I'm listening."

"Take me away. Take me away from here."

"That's my intention, Babylonne. That was always my intention." He lays a hand on my head. "You'll have to move, though. Can you move now? Come. We'll take it step by step."

Step by step. Yes, we can't stay here. I don't want to let him go, but I have to. I must *force* myself.

His face is thinner than ever, and his eyes are rimmed with red. His skin has a sick, grayish tint to it, except where his cheeks are flushed.

"Are you ill, Father?"

"Ill? No, I'm just tired. I haven't been sleeping."

"How did you get here?" (How did you *know*?) "I don't understand. . . ."

"I'll tell you as we go. We can't linger, Babylonne."

"No. No, of course not."

There's fighting everywhere. Dust and smoke everywhere. We have to leave while we still can. But where are we? Ah—yes. I see. The Great Hall is just around that corner.

"We should go this way, Father. If the door isn't blocked." Which it might be. "It'll be dangerous, though."

"If I managed to get in," Isidore replies, "then I'm sure we can both get out."

"The French—"

"They know who I am, Babylonne. They'll not lay a hand on me."

"The French aren't the only ones with swords, Father."

"Maybe not. I'm afraid, however, that they are the only ones in the Great Hall. At least, they were when I passed through it."

He's right. The Great Hall is taken. There's no fighting in it anymore—just people rifling corpses and dragging them across the floor to a pile in one corner. (I won't look.) Armed men have been posted at every exit.

The rushes are soaked with blood. Isidore leads me across them, one arm draped around my shoulder. People stare, but do nothing. Say nothing. Perhaps they're too weary.

None of the corpses is Lord Pagan's, thank God. But where is he, in that case?

"What happened to Lord Pagan?"

"I don't know," Isidore replies.

"And Lord Olivier?"

"I don't know." Passing into the hard, bright sunshine, Isidore screws up his eyes. "Take care. The stairs are gone."

They certainly are. We're going to have to climb down into the bailey using the ladders that have been placed here. Isidore goes first. I'd better concentrate hard on not falling, because there's a tremor in my hands and my knees.

Steady . . . steady . . .

There.

"God is good, Babylonne," Isidore says, drawing me to him. "Every night, I prayed that I would find you safe, and I did. By His mercy."

"But how *did* you find me? I don't understand."

"It was difficult," Isidore admits. He seems to be scanning the bailey for something as we walk—for something in particular. I don't want to follow his example, because the bailey is a scene of utter devastation. I'd rather concentrate on Father Isidore instead.

"The knights who took you mentioned Humbert de Beaujeu," he continues. "They talked of reaching a destination before he did. So I decided to find Lord Humbert—after I'd purchased a horse from the Abbey of Boulbonne. It occurred to me that Lord Humbert might lead me to Olivier de Termes and thence to you. Even so, I couldn't be sure. It was a terrible uncertainty."

"Is your arm all right?" I can't see any bandages under all that flowing black. "Was it a bad cut?"

"Not at all. I was lucky. In every dealing, I was lucky. When I found Lord Humbert, I told my tale frankly and was kindly received. I told him that you had been taken from my care by the heretical knights and that I wanted you restored to me. He agreed to do so, though not before capturing the citadel. He would not let me into La Bécède under a flag of truce, despite my pleas." At last Isidore wrenches his gaze from our filthy, battered surroundings and fixes it on my face, hesitating slightly before he speaks. "You must understand," he adds, "that I was not . . . um . . . entirely truthful. That I had to lie concerning our friendship and your own beliefs, Babylonne."

"Yes." As if it matters! "What am I supposed to be? Your bastard daughter? I wish I *was* your bastard daughter."

His lips twitch. "At this point, you are my illegitimate niece," he explains. Oh, dear. Is that the best you could do?

"Your *niece*? Father, that's no good. Nobody's going to believe *that*. You might as well say I'm your concubine and have done with it."

"I think not."

"Because that's what they must assume, Father."

"Not at all."

"Yes, it's true. Most people don't have pure hearts, not like you."

"Babylonne—trust me. I am well acquainted now with Bishop Fulk, and he is a man of some penetration. He knows that I am innocent of any wrongdoing where you are concerned."

Bishop Fulk?

What are you saying to me?

"Babylonne." Isidore's voice drops. "Don't stop here, please. Keep moving. It's best if we get out of this place as quickly as possible."

"Did you—did you—"

"I know that you have no love for the Bishop," he continues, nudging me along and speaking very low. "You told me that he was present when your mother died. I can imagine what your feelings must be. But I had no choice. It was the Bishop who welcomed me, and who made a place for me in his escort. To reach you, Babylonne, I needed him. And it must be said that he has been very generous."

"Very *generous*?"

"Shh. Later. We can't talk now."

No. We can't talk now. Because heading toward us, picking their way through the jagged rocks and discarded helmets and bloody hunks of flesh, are half a dozen priests led by a tonsured monk. A tonsured monk wearing a stained white habit and a jeweled ring.

"Brother Isidore!" exclaims the monk, spreading his arms. "You have found her, then!"

"I have, my lord. Safe and well."

"Deo gratias," says the monk. Isidore releases me. He bows and kisses the monk's ring.

My lord?

This must be Fulk.

Fulk the Bishop. Fulk the Cistercian monk. He has round shoulders and a jutting Adam's apple. His eyes are as dark as mine. His teeth are crooked and yellow; there's a small scar on his chin.

I could kill him now.

I could grab my scissors, which are still in my purse, and drive their blades straight into Fulk's exposed neck. Now. Right now, as he leans toward me, tracing a cross in the air above my head. I could do it now and avenge my mother, and it wouldn't matter what happened to me afterward, because I would have rid the world of an evil force.

"*Ostende nobis, Domine, misericordiam tuam,*" says Fulk, whose voice is very loud and rough for such a small man.

I could kill him now, but I won't.

I can't.

I just can't do it.

"She is not herself," says Isidore, and lapses into the Latin tongue as my tears drip off the end of my nose. Fulk nods: once, twice, three times. When Isidore finishes, the evil Bishop responds with something that must be a prayer, because it ends in "Amen."

He shuffles off, at long last, and it's just as well because I'm shaking all over. Shaking with suppressed sobs.

"Oh, my dear," whispers Isidore. He presses me close and kisses the top of my head. "I'm so proud of you."

"I could—I couldn't—"

I couldn't do it. I couldn't open up another vein and watch the blood spurt. I couldn't bear the pain and the rage and the noise and the death— especially the death. I'm sick to my bones with all this death.

I don't want death anymore. I want life. I want to live.

"Come," says Isidore. And he leads me gently away from the bloody ruins, toward the open gate, out into the rolling green countryside beyond.

‡EPILOGUE‡

After the siege of La Bécède, Gerard de la Motta and the other Perfects were burned. Humbert de Beaujeu then turned his attention to Toulouse. For the fourth time in fifteen years, its suburbs were destroyed and its vines pulled up. By then, the people of Languedoc were tired of war, and in 1229 Lord Raymond of Toulouse made peace with the French King. In return, he was allowed to remain Count of Toulouse. His only child, Joan, was betrothed to the King's nine-year-old brother, and Raymond agreed that all his dominions were to pass to their children when he died.

Pons de Villeneuve, who survived the siege of La Bécède, was Count Raymond's first postwar Seneschal of Toulouse. Pagan de La Bécède, who also survived, became a *faidit* (or exile) and a leader of the remaining defiant heretics until he was captured and burned in 1233. In November 1228, Olivier de Termes and his brother made their submission to the King of France. At the same time,

Olivier converted to Catholicism, and he remained a Catholic for the rest of his life.

Bernard Oth also had a change of heart. When royal troops attacked Cabaret in 1228, he defended the fortress for a month and made sure that the two Perfects who had been living there were escorted to safety before he finally surrendered. In 1232, Bernard, his son, and two of Bernard's brothers attacked the lands of the Archbishop of Narbonne, burning buildings, driving off cattle, and wounding the Archbishop. Bernard and most of his family—including his mother—were finally condemned as heretics by the newly established Holy Inquisition.

The last Cathar fortress, Montségur, fell in 1244. Raymond of Toulouse died in 1249, leaving no male heir. His daughter and son-in-law both died, childless, in 1271.

And Languedoc became a permanent part of the French King's dominion.

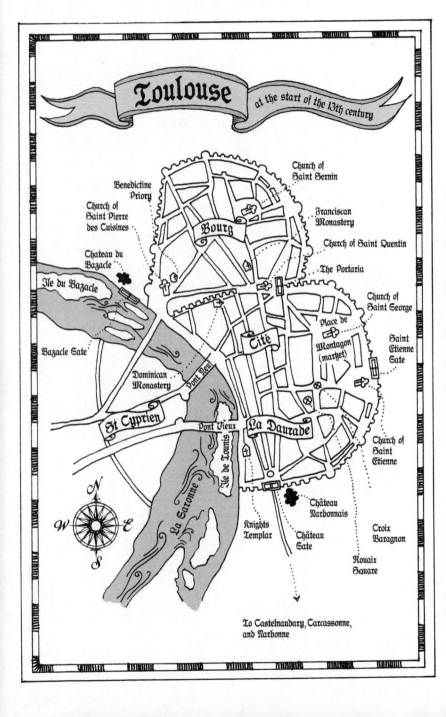

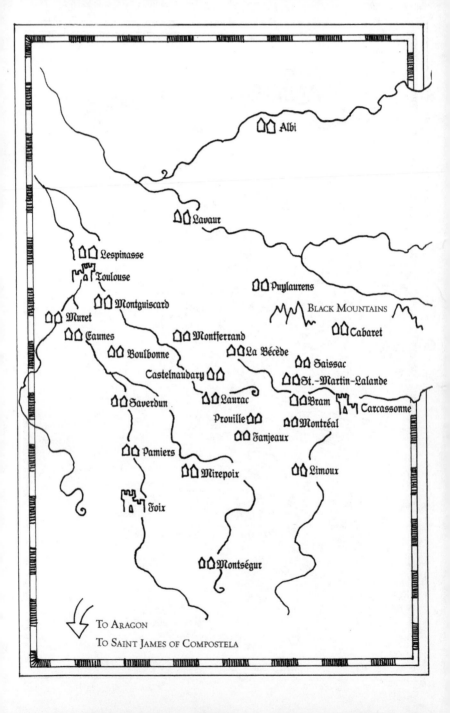

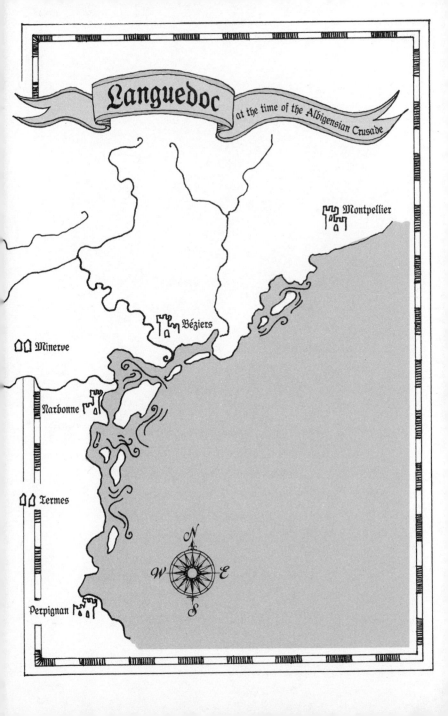